To Emily

Hope

What Happened to Coco

to Coco

V B Furlong

"This book will become your new obsession.
You'll struggle to put it down, and will crave to
find out what happened to Coco."
Georgina Bartlett, Author of *8*

"A juicy, accomplished debut."
Cecelia Ahern, International Bestselling Author of
PS I Love You* and *Love, Rosie

www.darkstroke.com

Discover us online:
www.darkstroke.com

Join us on instagram:
www.instagram.com/darkstrokebooks

Include **#darkstroke** in a photo of yourself
holding this book on Instagram and
something nice will happen.

For Mam and Dad,
sorry about the swearing, although
I did learn it all from you.

For Nan,
thank you for all the stories
you made up for me,
and for showing me
how to do it, too.

Acknowledgements

When I wrote What Happened to Coco, I was helping to care for my Grandfather with terminal cancer. It takes an army of people to get you through that, so from the bottom of my heart I thank Mam, Dad, Jonathan and Sarah, Nan and Gramps, and Emma and Hannah, for their unending support in everything that I do. Without them, the darkest days would be so much worse. And to you, Gransha, I'm sorry you were never able to brag about this one over a pint with your friends in the rugby club.

To my parents, thank you for putting up with me when I was the same age as Coco and her friends, and was just as lost.

To my Nan, your bedtime stories and our make believe games at your house cultivated my creativity and bolstered my confidence. You've always had such faith in me, and it's for your ongoing scrapbook of clippings that I do the things I do.

To Toby, who has loved me through all The Big Things, good and bad, I wouldn't want to do this with anyone else by my side. Still, I know that no matter what I do, the dog will still like you best.

To Nadia, who read this one first and told me to run with it, thank you. Without you, I'm sure no one would have ever read my words.

To the friends who had to read my very early writings when I was young – I'm sorry.

To Emma, and Ellie, Alex and Moose, Steph, Ben, Cadi and Basher, and Hannah, thank you for always cheering me on and being so ready to celebrate with me.

To the network of writers that support me every day, I'm sorry for all the rubbish tweets. Your advice, support and commiserations have made a gruelling process a fun one for me. Every agent, editor, fellow author and enthusiastic friend who gives their time to help others achieve their dreams, you're the angels of this community.

To George, Millie, and Archie, our walks always gave me my best ideas. A part of me is missing without our pack.

And to you, reader. Of all the books out there, thank you for taking the time to read this one.

About the Author

VB Furlong is a trainee lawyer and writer of young adult novels living in Berkshire, UK. She wrote her first "novel" at ten years old and has not stopped writing since then. As a teenager, VB Furlong wrote for her local paper and an online magazine whilst devouring any book she could find, and in writing for an older teen demographic hopes to instil the same love of books as she had, and still has to this day.

Through her writing she aims to explore many of the issues she faced herself growing up, in the hopes that others facing the same issues feel some solidarity. Her friendships are a huge part of her life and consequently is a major theme in her writing, exploring the way in which we interact with each other, especially in difficult times.

Originally from Mumbles, Swansea, VB Furlong enjoys the sun and the sea, and walking her three dogs across the cliffs. These walks have offered her inspiration for many pieces of writing, including What Happened to Coco.

What Happened to Coco

PART ONE
ELLA

Chapter One

In the misty darkness lit only by a blue streetlamp, Ella knew that she was not alone. She turned and saw the faceless figure far down the drizzly street. It came towards her at speed. It didn't seem to be moving, but she knew that it was gaining on her. She started to run, but her legs would not move. She was stuck, as though in quicksand.

When she dared check over her shoulder once again, the figure was only about five steps away, and she could see raspy breaths escape the black silhouette in a wispy white cloud. The scene whirred in front of Ella as she pulled on her legs, sobbing, begging them to move. But they would not. All she could hear was the breathing, slow and rattling, as though it was the figure's very last. Four. Three. Two.

It was the skeletal hand on her shoulder that woke her.

In the darkness of her room, she was alone. She turned her alarm off and felt uneasy in the silence. She was soaking wet, her back from sweat, her face from tears.

She washed her face, hardly daring to open her eyes and look into the mirror above the sink. She felt watched, hunted.

As she brushed her teeth, she turned on all her lights and opened the dreary brown curtains that Lainsbury Hall School had placed in all the dorms. But even in her bright vanity lamps that took over her dressing table, drowning her in bright white light as she did her make up, her eyes darted around the corners of her mirrors, checking all angles of the room in the reflection for the faceless spectre. She was not herself today. Then again, she hadn't been herself yesterday, either.

She knotted her school tie, adding the final touch to her uniform, and grabbed her bag. She checked her bag twice to make sure that she had remembered all the books. Not that it mattered. Her dorm was only across the path to the school, but she could not shake the feeling that she had forgotten something.

She knocked the door to Coco's room and crossed her arms, rubbing them in the cold of the dreary dorm corridor. It was always Ella who had to keep Coco on time, and she was not in the mood to miss breakfast this morning.

"Come on!" she yelled, but there was no answer.

"She hasn't slept in again, has she?" Bea asked, emerging from her own room. Bea's key clicked in the lock and she shrugged her rucksack over her shoulder.

"I don't know. She must have." Ella placed her hand on the cold metal door handle.

"Wait!" Bea grabbed Ella by her shoulder and she jumped.

"Sorry, but what if, you know, Harrison sneaked in last night? They might be…"

Ella shrugged. "I don't think so. I always hear them. She usually warns me."

Bea threw her a look of revulsion. "Oh, God. Ew."

Ella let out an exasperated sigh as she pressed down on the door handle. To her surprise, it was unlocked. Coco's room was dark, but they could see that her bed was unmade and empty.

"She must have gone to his last night," Bea said simply, shrugging and turning to leave. "Don't you think?"

But Ella stopped for a moment, peering into the darkness. Coco's room was usually ridiculously tidy. She rarely left her bed unmade, and whilst it wasn't unheard of for her to venture to Harrison's room at night, it was unusual. Ella stared at that bed, finding it difficult to look away, to shake the feeling reverberating through her bones, the build-up of something unfamiliar. It was almost a chill, but it seemed to stop as her back clenched in anticipation of the tingle down her spine.

There was something wrong with Ella this morning. She felt like a bird, or a deer, jumping at every small thing, not knowing which way was which. A mist covered the rolling grounds of the school as they made their way down the path to the dining hall and the air felt chilly and autumnal for the first time that year. They were flanked by the usual parade of weary-eyed students in expensive school uniforms, carrying bags and instruments, or wearing sports kits and carrying sticks or bats or balls.

They walked down the aisle in between the vast rows of benches and sat down next to the boys at their usual table in the furthest corner of the loud and warm dining hall. They had sat together at this table for all their meals for the past four school years, enjoying the sun which sometimes drenched them in the mornings as they ate breakfast. Coco loved the portrait of some ancient ugly headmaster from decades before, with *Twat* written on the glass in small letters in Sharpie that had as of yet gone unnoticed by staff.

Ella had hardly sat down before she and Harrison turned towards each other. "Where's Coco?" they asked at the same time, and a brief laugh passed over Harrison's face, his usual congenial smile flashing towards her before his frown of concern.

"She didn't answer her door. We even went inside and she wasn't there. We'd thought she stayed at yours."

"No, she didn't," Harrison said, looking over his shoulder, checking that teachers were not waiting nearby to confiscate his phone, and scrolled under the table.

"She didn't text me goodnight before she went to bed, and she was definitely awake at 1am because she was online. I thought she'd fallen asleep, but then she didn't text me this morning. I was waiting to see what I'd done wrong." He paused and turned toward Ella, who shrugged lamely. "But if you haven't seen her either, this is weird."

Ella's unusually pale face went unnoticed by Conrad. "Oh come on," he said with a mouth full of egg and toast. "She doesn't text you for a few hours and you're losing your minds! Are you sure she wasn't running late and hopped in the shower or the bathroom or something?"

"I guess so. If she was up late writing her blog or doing homework or… something, she could just be sleeping in and

7

skipping breakfast," Bea said casually, biting into a piece of buttery toast. But Ella couldn't eat and, it seemed, neither could Harrison. He towered over them all. He was built like a bear, and he ate like one, too. He had in front of him his usual enormous breakfast of eggs and beans, cereal, yoghurt, fruit, and a couple of racks of toast, which he and Conrad usually snuck into class to snack on.

Despite Conrad's confidence that they were all overreacting, Coco failed to turn up for registration. Mrs Turner raised her head when Coco's name was answered with a ringing silence.

Mrs Turner turned to their table, noticing Coco's empty stool next to Harrison. "Is she ill?"

"She wasn't in her room this morning. I knocked and peeked in," Ella said tentatively, her concern overcoming her fear of getting Coco in trouble for sneaking out.

Mrs Turner raised her eyebrows and looked towards Harrison. They had caused a scandal more than once after being caught in bed together, an offence that would have gained lesser-gifted students a hefty suspension, but they had never really been punished, only ever receiving a severe warning and a call home.

"Mr Fletcher…"

"I haven't seen her either. And she hasn't text me. I'm either in trouble…" the class laughed as he smiled guiltily, "…or something's up."

Mrs Turner stood and made her way over to her classroom door.

"I'm going to find Ms Hardy. You four ought to stay here until I get back. She may have some questions for you."

They sat staring at each other as the bell rang and the class raised from their seats and left the room around them.

"She really didn't say anything to you, Harrison? No family emergency, no big plans of escape?" Bea asked, trying to make light of the situation but failing through the tension in her voice. Turner's serious reaction had obviously changed Bea's mind.

"Absolutely nothing. Did any of you get a text, anything from her? Did you hear anything, El?"

Ella shook her head and delicately placed a piece of her shiny brown hair behind her ear. "I was tired last night," she said. "I didn't really sleep the night before. I was flat out at half ten." Harrison nodded, a contemplative frown on his forehead, the same look Ella had recognised from his expression during math class when he was working through a difficult problem set.

"She was texting me until eleven," he said, to himself more than to them. "But she wasn't saying much. She was being a little distant, I guess, but she said she had a lot of homework, which, to be fair, we do. I saw she was online, but she didn't respond to anything I sent her after eleven."

Conrad ran his hand through his copper curls, causing this hair to fall into a delicate mess, his nose wrinkling into a scowl as he tried to remember. "She sent me a picture at half ten asking what we needed to bring to history today. She was in bed then, and the picture was of her books laid out on her covers. It definitely didn't seem like she was heading off anywhere. She was in PJs when she sent me a picture of herself saying thanks,"

"Yeah, me too." Harrison waved him away.

"I mean, they're making a big deal out of this, though, right? She's only missed an hour of school," Conrad asked tentatively, running his hand through his hair again. It was a habit of his Ella had noticed that long ago, but today it felt like a nervous tick.

"A student isn't accounted for and the last time anyone can be sure she was around eleven last night. I don't think so," Ella said, and Harrison gulped, his Adam's apple rising and falling on his surprisingly delicate pale neck.

They sat in a contemplative silence for some time, listening to the stampede of their classmates' footsteps outside the room and in the classroom above them. Ella wondered which classroom it was, history, or maybe English, maybe even the library, when Ms Hardy, their headmistress, entered the room swiftly, pushing her outdated spectacles up her nose before stopping dead and folding her arms, staring at them sternly from the end of their table.

"So Miss Lyndham-Smith wasn't in her room this morning?"

"No, Miss Hardy," Bea stated, and Ella shook her head.

"She hasn't made you all aware of any plans to sneak out last night or truant today? Not to see a boyfriend?" Ms Hardy went on.

"That would be me. She hasn't messaged me since last night."

"Ah, Mr Fletcher. Now you mention it, I remember our last encounter very well. Sneaking around the girls' dorm at midnight like a scoundrel, I believe."

Harrison had the good grace to blush coyly at her before continuing. "But Coco hasn't told any of us where she went. It's odd."

She frowned and pulled Coco's iPhone out of her pocket.

"This is her mobile phone? It was on her bedside table."

"Yes, that's hers. She wouldn't go anywhere without it. If that was in her room, this looks really strange," Ella said. The others blanched, and even Conrad's usually handsome face now turned a pale green.

"This is her only phone? I know a lot of you have old ones that you use in class in case they get confiscated."

"It's her only phone," Harrison interjected, annoyed. "We're not stupid enough to cover for her when she should be here. She hasn't told any of us that she was going anywhere, and she really would have done. If her phone isn't with her, you need to start really looking into this. I know her. I know when something isn't right."

"He's right," Conrad said.

The many lines on Mrs Hardy's face now knitted together, and she looked concerned for the first time that morning, but she attempted to maintain a business-like tone.

"I asked around the staff room and no one has requested a meeting with her this morning. We checked the history class she's meant to be in right now, and she isn't accounted for. She isn't in her dorm, in the bathrooms, or the common room. If none of you have any idea of where she may have gone, I think it's beginning to look quite serious." She breathed heavily through her nose, reminding Ella of a wide-eyed rabbit smelling a fox. "I advise you all to go back to class, and if she has still not turned up at lunchtime, you might need to speak to the police. In the meantime, I will contact her parents. If she has deliberately missed school, she is in deep trouble. I trust you all understand this."

They all nodded and grabbed their bags, leaving the heavy door to close with a crash behind them.

"I don't like this. I don't like this at all," Harrison muttered, his jaw tight and twitching as they walked along the corridor.

"Let's just hope she's been an idiot and snuck out and lost track of time," Conrad resolved, and they nodded.

That morning seemed to last several long weeks. Ella constantly kept one eye on the door during chemistry, waiting for news of Coco's whereabouts. She checked her phone regularly, but as stealthily as she could. She could not afford for it to be confiscated, not today.

Coco had been in trouble plenty of times before and had been known to leave school early in the term, telling the teachers that it was due to yet another false family emergency, when she was really going on a trip to Paris or to her family's ski cabin in Val d'Isère with Harrison. But she had always been with one of the four of them, and always told the others exactly where she was. She always told the world exactly what she was doing. Her social media accounts were full of daily updates about her life. But today there was nothing.

Ella's lessons were a blur. She messed up her experiment, and didn't retain a single thing that Miss Jenkins had told her, and that was on the rare occasion this lesson that Jenkins was actually in the classroom and not the storage cupboard at the back of the room. Ella's notebook was empty when she stuffed it back in her bag as the bell rang.

It wasn't like her to be so distracted, especially not in chemistry, her new favourite subject. Maria Jenkins was Ella's favourite teacher, all because she had begged her to take her subject that Ella had decided to take it on as an A-Level.

Ella was flattered. She knew that the teachers made a bet

11

every year on whose students would get the best A-Level grades. It was big money, too, and the winner usually showed up to Lainsbury for the following term with a new car or set of designer handbags. This meant that right before the GCSE students picked their A-Level subjects, they would find their teachers either suddenly becoming salespeople and buttering them up so they would take their class, or doing their very best to persuade them to take another subject, usually the class of their least favourite co-worker.

Jenkins wasn't the only who that had cornered Ella, but she was the only one who had managed to persuade her. She knew she was going to take physics, which Jenkins also taught, as well as philosophy, history and maths, but she wanted to take an extra class. Jenkins had seemed so earnest, so sure that Ella could and would achieve great things, that she had taken chemistry.

Of the five of them, she had only approached Ella and Harrison. When Coco had voiced in one of their revision lessons, nearing their exams of Year 11, that she was considering chemistry or physics, Jenkins had enthusiastically told her how their art teacher, Mr Monroe, was saying, just that morning, how talented Coco was. She continued, saying that, in her opinion, to take a science instead would be a waste of Coco's creative gifts. Coco sat through her frantic lecture, her eyebrow raised and her arms crossed, not believing a word of it. When Jenkins had finished, Coco nodded once and didn't say a word in response.

Coco had stuck with English, which was a given, Latin, History, and Philosophy. They had all made a pact to take Philosophy together, after Hunter had pulled them in after one of their last GCSE lessons and spoke for half an hour, promising daily emails with memes in them and all the old-white-dead-guy related fun that he could squeeze into his lessons. They had liked him and he was true to his word, feeling as though he was one of them until yesterday's lesson, when instead he was serious, sullen.

Hunter had started their lesson like normal, berating them for making him walk the length of his classroom to return their homework assignments to them. "I don't know why you five always make me walk all the way to the back," he said, "You're all a pain in the arse, I tell you."

He slammed Conrad's essay on the desk, winking at him as he acknowledged his A* and his face lit up. Philosophy always was the only subject that Conrad excelled in, except PE, but they never let him count that. Conrad always loved an argument, and Philosophy offered him a medium to channel that instinct and actually seem quite insightful, when outside Hunter's classroom he was boorish, never being able to, nor wanting, to say the right thing.

Hunter had offered his condolences as he passed Bea her A.

"Almost there. Only a few changes." He swivelled in the aisle and placed Ella's essay on her desk.

"Brilliant as usual, Ella. I liked your take on Kierkegaard," he told her and she offered him a deliberate, fixed smile. She was used to A*s. She, like Harrison, expected them. It was only when they received anything less than that, did they take notice.

"I'm going to need more effort this week, Coco." He shook his head and turned on his heel as he placed the essay in front of her. Coco flushed red and stuffed the essay into her bag.

But as the essay left the pile, Ella and Coco noticed something red and lacy laying on the top of Harrison's essay. It was only there for a second, a flash of red, to be hastily stuffed into Hunter's trouser pocket. She and Coco shared a glance, wide-eyed, hysterical smiles on their faces.

"Yeah, great, Fletch. Uh, keep it up," he said, nearly sending Harrison's essay flying off the table in his haste to move back towards the front of the class.

Ella and Coco stifled giggles, turning red in the face. They had known, or at least he had given them the impression, that he could be a bit of a scoundrel, but to leave someone's underwear in the pile of homework was surely next level. Ella could hardly bear to think what it was that Hunter would be doing during the breaks he took from marking their essays.

"I didn't think you'd have time to gossip like that, Coco, based on your last assignment," Hunter said coldly when he turned around and reached his desk. His hand was white at the knuckles as it clutched the corner of his desk.

"Right, we're doing Utilitarianism today. Anyone have any ideas?" He tried to carry on as normal but was rigid with anger, and he paced the room as he lectured them when he would usually sit with a foot on his desk, leaning back in his chair. At any correct answers, Hunter only nodded, his lips thin, his brows knitted together. He snapped at any wrong answers and made them feel stupid for suggesting them. His usual jovial self was nowhere to be seen.

It was unnerving to them, like a cuddly pet suddenly turned savage. They were used to that harsh treatment from their other teachers, but they were always practically coddled by Hunter, and as a result of that change, they all left his lesson in a very bad mood.

"What the fuck?" Harrison had whispered viciously as they left, red in the face at just being berated because of his answer, to be told it was 'as deep as an episode of Keeping Up With the Kardashians'.

And then she had told him, Conrad and Bea about the underwear, and they had argued for the rest of the day about whose they could be. Jenkins herself was Conrad's top contender, although Ella doubted that. She was a lot different to Hunter; serious, sensible. It just so happened that she was the youngest female teacher in the school, so to the boys she seemed the obvious choice.

But that was yesterday. Today was quiet, stressful. She had a headache.

After chemistry, Ella and Bea walked to lunch to find Harrison and Conrad urgently conferring in the corner of their table, empty except for them. Conrad sat behind a barely touched plate of chicken and rice, and Harrison evidently had not even bothered to grab any food. The girls sat down, the scrape of the bench on the concrete floor causing them all to frown and groan.

"She wasn't in history. And she hasn't messaged, hasn't

14

contacted anyone. Her mum is going spare. I've just got off the phone with her." Harrison dropped his phone to the table with a thud of frustration, looking away from it in disgust as though it was somehow *Apple*'s fault. "How could she just do this?"

Bea raised her eyebrow and looked at her watch. "It's been over twelve hours since anyone has heard from her," she said.

At this, they noticed Hardy enter the dining hall, her head searching above the swarm of students lining up for lunch. She spotted them and approached their table. All pretence had been abandoned since registration, she looked downright panicked.

Chapter Two

"In my office, you four, please," she barked at them, ushering them through the dining hall. She motioned to younger students to hurry and to clear their plates, and they scowled and took them to the hatch into the kitchen with a huff.

Ella, Bea, and the two boys walked the five minutes to Mrs Hardy's office. Conrad put a comforting arm around Ella. Her face was ashen, and she was grateful for the support. He smelled good; of expensive cologne and hair products, and his arm was warm on her shoulder. She leaned into it slightly.

They entered the dated room. It always managed to signify trouble somehow, always commanding a tense atmosphere. Ella had only ever sat in the chairs in front of Hardy's desk a handful of times, always for her good grades, and even on those occasions she exhaled a sigh of relief when she was allowed to leave.

Sat in one of the chairs before Mrs Hardy's desk was a young policeman. He wore a solemn expression on his square-jawed face. His stubble was not the designer facial hair seen on actors or models. Instead, Ella felt it gave him an unkempt, dirty look. When she moved further into the room, Ella scrunched her nose at the aroma of coffee and stale cigarettes that clung to him.

"This is officer Hobbs," Hardy said quietly.

"I'll be having a short chat with you all today to find out anything that could help us. We need to hear an exact account of the last time you had any contact with Cordelia and any leads you think may give an indication of where she could be. Anything you think is relevant, please tell us now so we can find her as soon as we can. Do you understand?"

They all nodded. They were then told that they were to go into an adjoining meeting room separately. Ella was called first, and she felt her friends' eyes on her back as she shuffled into the office. She was afraid, of what she wasn't sure, maybe of being yelled at like they did on American cop shows, of slamming the desk and throwing curveballs at her, making her confused and messing up. She'd seen *Making a Murderer*.

She never really enjoyed true crime documentaries or conspiracy theories, but it was hard to be friends with Coco without being drawn into it and then listen to her ramble on for hours about how she always thought the brother seemed fishy, or maybe it was the maid, or about jet fuel and steel beams as though she was both a scientist and an engineer.

"Ella," Hobbs said, sending a warm and inviting smile in Ella's direction as he held the door open for her, but his yellowing teeth did nothing to ease her anxiety. She sat on an old wooden chair and Hobbs swept across the room in three swift strides. He slumped into the far comfier-looking chair across the table from Ella. This was the room that parents were called into, where expulsions and suspensions were issued as last resorts, thrown at students like cannonballs in a battle.

"So today I'm just going to ask you a couple of basic questions about... Coco you call her, yes? I understand you were close." He produced a notebook and pen from his jacket.

Ella nodded.

"How would you describe your relationship with her?"

"She's been my best friend since we were five."

"I see." He nodded. "And is she known for being a bit...reckless? Does she always follow rules?"

"She's careful. She wouldn't go out at night without her phone and tell no one where she was," Ella said, knowing to keep everything simple. *Only answer the question asked*, she thought, remembering again all those horrifying documentaries that followed people who were locked up for ten years for a crime they didn't commit.

"She's been found running around the school late at night with a Harrison Fletcher, though, hasn't she?"

"Yeah, in school, accompanied by her boyfriend. Never

outside, never alone. Never without her phone. We'd always known when she had done that too. She would tell us or post every second online like usual. She didn't do that last night though, did she?"

"Did she mention anywhere she would want to go? Any parties? Maybe a secret boyfriend nearby?"

Ella bit back an unwelcome desire to laugh. "She barely keeps her tongue out of Harrison's mouth for longer than two minutes as it is. She has no time to have a secret boyfriend. She goes to lessons, hangs out with us, or Harrison, and goes to bed. The five of us are nearly always together."

"Okay…" he said, somewhat distracted as he scribbled away into his official-looking notebook. Ella wondered what she could have said to spur so much movement.

"You sleep in the room next to her? Did you hear anything odd last night?"

"No. I mean, yes. I sleep next door, but I didn't hear anything." She bit her tongue, wanting to kick herself for losing her composure. She felt herself unravelling. "I went to bed early, about nine thirty. I didn't sleep well the night before, and I didn't wake up until this morning. I should have heard something. I should have. I could hear everything from that room."

Ella started crying, her face bowed, her tears dropped onto her crossed hands in her lap. It was as though the reality of the situation had suddenly hit her with such a blunt force, like a piano raining out of the sky and smacking her into the floor. Her best friend was missing, and even if she had left of her own accord, which was the best case scenario, that meant a different host of trouble.

Officer Hobbs offered her a tissue which she took and blew her nose with.

"I understand you're worried about her, but she hasn't been missing long. Not yet. And young girls can do things like this, can't they? So we just have to wait and see." He flashed her that revolting smile again, and Ella dabbed at her face.

"Maybe you can tell me about the day before. Did anything happen out of the ordinary?"

"No," she said too quickly, before elaborating. "I knocked her door like always, and we had breakfast together. The five of us, I mean."

Ella wondered how much of their boring daily routine Hobbs needed to know. There really didn't seem to be anything unusual worth mentioning. She was texting someone at breakfast and felt Coco's eyes on her the entire time. She knew that a teacher could confiscate her phone, that her friends would want to know who it was. Ella knew that she shouldn't be texting him in the first place, but her thumbs seemed to move without her thinking, and her hand seemed to reach for the phone as it pinged before she registered that she had even reached for it.

Ella decided Hobbs didn't need to know that. She knew idle gossip wouldn't find Coco.

"Who are you texting?" Coco had said, eying Ella with a shrewd, piercing look, considering her with her chin resting on her delicate hand.

"No one," Ella told her, because how could she even begin with this one? She could barely admit that this was now a thing to herself. *No*, Ella thought. *That can of worms was staying sealed shut.*

"We just talked like we normally did. School stuff, you know?" Hobbs didn't ask for more details. He only nodded. But his gaze made her shuffle in her chair. His silence meant that she wasn't dismissed.

After that there was little else left to say. They were busy at Lainsbury. Mondays were for lessons and sports in the evening. They had free lessons in sixth form, of course, but free lessons were spent trying to keep on top of their homework. Ella had barely seen Coco after that morning. Coco played netball after school when Ella ran cross country, and they had finished not long before bed.

"So nothing really unusual," Ella summed up, as she started to trail off and caught herself being vague. "Mr Hunter was in a bad mood which I guess was odd, but, I mean, everyone has one of those days. Coco didn't do so great in the essay he set, I think."

That was putting it mildly, Hunter had been in a raging temper throughout their philosophy lesson after the underwear incident. Still, her and Coco's theories distracted them from this for the whole two hours, ranging wildly from them debating what his secret drag identity would be to who he could be dating. "There wasn't anything weird about the rest of the day. Conrad and Bea argued some more about her girlfriend, India, he always pretends that he fancies her."

Hobbs sat up straight. "She's doing worse in school?"

"Only that one essay. As far as I know, she's doing about the same as usual in everything else. She's never been the top in the school, just, you know, normal." She didn't do as well as Ella, except, maybe, in English.

If the school was a society, a country, Ella and Harrison were the academics or scientists, breaking codes and finding solutions to everyday problems. They expected the highest marks, both staying afloat on the surface. In the same way that they wouldn't marvel at a boat for floating on water, they took their grades for granted, only taking notice when things turned south, when they started to sink.

In this society, Conrad was the sports star that late night talk shows begged to interview. Bea was the activist, a human rights lawyer perhaps, like an edgy Amal Clooney, only she was somehow also dating Amal Clooney. As the school's best tennis player, Coach Stephens hailed Bea the next Serena Williams, although she only rolled her eyes at that, and said it was just because they are both black.

But Coco was the socialite, a philanthropic and charming one, one that might have a TV show and a few books out. People, including teachers, liked her for being herself, for being an outspoken and eloquent person, but she never did shine because of her grades.

"You've been helpful, Ella. Thank you," Hobbs said, and she was sure he was lying. She said nothing, really. His eyes scanned her face as though she had written all the answers she hadn't given across her forehead. "You can leave now, unless there's something else you want to tell us, something that might have caused her to disappear like this. Anything out of the ordinary can help."

Ella dawdled in the doorway for a split second before speaking, racking her brains, memories of the last few days rushing by in a haze.

"No, I don't think so. It's really out of the blue."

"Very well."

Ella sat down in the waiting room with the others, and Harrison was called, and then Bea, and then Conrad. They each took only a few minutes, but Harrison was in there for longer than all of them, at least twenty minutes. He was clearly being grilled. Ella stared at the clock, watching the minute hand as it ticked by so agonisingly slowly that she could have sworn twice, or even three times, it had stopped working. Eventually, they were released and told that they would probably be asked for again sometime soon.

"They're not taking this seriously enough." Conrad glowered as they all walked along the corridor to the common room. They had a free period.

"You've changed your tune," Bea pointed out.

"Well they're banging on about her sneaking out somewhere, being young and dumb when we all know she hasn't done that. She was spontaneous, and raving mad, yeah, but to disappear like this... I think something is really wrong. Like, really."

Ella noticed Harrison's knuckles whiten as he clenched his hands, and his jaw tightened.

"We don't know that yet, Con," Ella said, pointedly, glaring at Conrad when he turned to her with a mutinous expression on his face, as though he were preparing to argue. Ella flicked her eyes towards Harrison, and when Conrad took in his expression, too, he relented.

"Oh, well, yeah... I'm just being dramatic. She'll turn up later with some long story about her shenanigans, and we'll be furious at her for putting us through this." But whilst he made a valiant effort, his bracing tone seemed to fool nobody.

Harrison had barely spoken all afternoon, and Ella felt as bad as Harrison looked, with a sickly white pallor on his usually pleasant face. She wondered what he had told the police in that room for such a long time.

They went to bed early that night, but none of them slept. Bea read a novel until she fell asleep around four. Conrad watched boring Netflix documentaries all night. Harrison lay in bed, straight as a board, and stared at the ceiling. He went over everything she had said to him, over everything that happened over the last week, to try and pinpoint a reason for her sudden disappearance, but he could think of nothing. By the time the sun began to fill his room, he was none the wiser as to any explanation for Coco's absence.

Ella cocooned herself in her covers, listening all night for sounds in the room next to hers, to signal Coco's arrival. But they never came. She kept her bedside lamp on all night, too anxious to confine herself to darkness. She spent her night trawling through Coco's social media, her latest Instagram posts, only from a day before. There were two pictures. One was of her alone, her newly-filled lips pursed, her bright blue eyes smiling, her glittery pink eyeshadow blended perfectly, her 'H' necklace, which she had received from Harrison for their anniversary over a year ago, was sat delicately on her neck. From the moment Harrison had presented the necklace to her, she had removed it only to shower, or at least that was what Coco had promised to Harrison any time it was mentioned.

"Why is it his initial and not yours?" Bea asked on the first occasion that Coco wore it.

"To show the world he's mine," Coco said.

Ella read her latest tweets. She read Coco's rant about respect in the online community. This was after a series of mean tweets sent to her by an online troll. For the last month, every post, every tweet, was followed by a sneering, personal attack on Coco. Most of them were pretty basic. They would call her stupid, some would contain sexist slurs. Harrison declared numerous times that he was going to kill the guy that wrote them. If Coco ever attempted to venture into political commentary, she was ordered to stick to handbags. She had reported accounts numerous times, most of them with no followers, and only ever tweeting her, but when each was shut down, a different one was made. It had started to become serious, and she was told to kill herself, spurring her rant.

Ella read Coco's tweets, about how excited she was to go to Munich at Christmas with Harrison, and about all the exciting things she was planning on doing whilst visiting, before then heading to Austria on a skiing holiday with her family, Harrison, naturally, in tow.

Ella then saw that Coco had shared the link to her new blog post. She didn't need to click it, she had already read it, and heard Coco's thoughts on the matter for the couple of weeks before.

The link went to the *Coco's World* website, where there were pictures of Coco lounging on a beach, facing a glorious sunset that sat on top of the still, clear sea, behind the curly-lettered title. Ella had taken that photo herself the summer before, when the five of them went to Coco's beach house in Miami, as her Mum filmed a holiday special of the Actual Housewives.

Coco's most recent blog article was titled *Vegetarianism, Halloween, and the Fendi AW Collection*. It was mainly about Coco's newfound vegetarianism, inspired by Ella's commitment when she announced she had been a vegetarian for two years at breakfast a couple of weeks ago. This caused a group debate around the merits of vegetarianism, after which Coco had been thoroughly convinced and wanted to give up meat.

Coco's vegetarianism lasted, Ella recalled, for one and a half days. The canteen served lasagne for dinner on the second day, and Coco felt that five meat-free meals were quite enough to make her point about the scandal of the conditions facing the meat industry that she had discovered days before. They laughed at her as she sat down to eat the sizeable, meat-filled lasagne on her tray.

"What? I'm not eating bloody tofu and peas for dinner. Besides, even just cutting down makes a difference." She glared at them, her nostrils flared, daring them to highlight her hypocrisy. Instead, they laughed into their plates of lasagne, well, 'bloody tofu and peas' for Ella.

Her blog was often more personal than this. Some expressed her love of her friends, some talked at length about the reasons she was lucky to be with Harrison. Some gave advice, like what you should expect as a bare minimum from a relationship, and some simply expressed Coco's thoughts. Sometimes they were deep thoughts (*'Is there a God?'*), some less so (*'Joey is the best character from Friends and this is why'*), and some more divisive, more controversial, (*'Did Bush Do 9/11 (Jet fuel can't melt steel beams')?)* This week's was shorter than usual, and less personal, less brave. It was one of the least interesting Ella had read, and Coco's blog was usually, she had to admit, an interesting read, even if she had heard Coco's thoughts already that week. She couldn't resist talking about her current chosen topic at every opportunity. As she read the post again, it felt to Ella like Coco had been guarded in her writing this week, that she seemed preoccupied, distant. This week's blog didn't feel like *her*.

Ella was the subject of Coco's blog more than once, and more than once, she found herself furious at the personal details Coco had disclosed without her permission. On one memorable occasion, during Valentine's Day of Year 11, Coco had posted, to Ella's dismay, possibly her most problematic post to date. It was entitled *Valentine's Day Lonely Hearts Club*. It contained a thinly-disguised column seeking dates for Ella, Conrad, and the then-single Bea. Ella could remember the standout phrases which haunted her still.

My longest and closest friend seeks a boy to bring her out of her shell, and take her on adventures while I'm busy.

Shy and reserved, she is still always surprising us with her quick witted sarcastic comments.

A tiny figure with an angelic face and soft brown eyes that could make your heart melt, and satiny brunette hair a boy could run his fingers through easily as he whispers pleasantries in her delicate little ears.

Ella shuddered at the mortifying memory. The thing about Coco was that she often had good intentions, but terrible ways of acting upon them. She had a huge heart, but sometimes failed to see things from a perspective other than her own. She saw the world through the wide blue eyes of a beautiful rich girl with opportunities at her feet, and thought her outlook was the same as everyone else's.

If someone had written that blog about Coco, Ella knew she would have fed off the attention, delighting in the complimentary tone. But that was because Coco was confident and gregarious and charming. To Ella and Bea, as they hid their red faces in class as the boys quoted lines from the article at them, it was a difficult few weeks.

Everything Coco posted, Ella knew the backstory behind, why she sent that cryptic tweet, where she had taken that photograph, where she had the idea for her blog. Ella was aware of every aspect of Coco's life, whether she chose to confide in her or not. Ella knew, for example, that Coco and Harrison had a huge argument the previous Thursday, because Coco was flirting with George Thomas after English class that afternoon. Ella knew that Coco wasn't happy her dad was not going skiing with the rest of her family at Christmas time, because he had to work. She could even hear Coco's snores (which she insisted did not exist, to Ella, Bea's and Harrison's loud objections, all of whom had had the unpleasant experience of spending a long night at Coco's nasally side). At that point she knew how long Harrison lasted in bed, for Christ's sake, all because she could hear through the thin walls that separated their lives, that hid, or were supposed to hide, their most protected secrets. Ella wondered, then, why she had no answers to probably the most important question about Coco's life so far: *where had she gone?*

It was strange that, thinking about Coco, she only considered the problematic parts. But she couldn't say, in all honesty, that Coco was a bad friend. *She could be obtuse and unthoughtful sometimes*, Ella reasoned. *But Coco was always there if she needed her, right next door*. It was true. Coco was always there for her, through the good and the terrible times, too.

Chapter Three

The worst day of Ella's life came when she was sixteen, although she didn't necessarily realise that at the time. It became what she would consider the worst day of her life, it affected her more and more as time went on. It was like a pimple, it was bad to start, but as she poked and squeezed and gouged at herself, it only got worse, until it was an unsightly, sizeable gash on her pretty face. You can't help picking at a spot; it's an instinct, something your fingers compel you to do, and Ella couldn't stop herself from drowning in her problem. Her insecurities crashed over her, pushing her under.

By the time Ella was sixteen, she still hadn't gotten her period, and her mum was worried. That was why, in the February half term of Year 11, Mrs Fitzpatrick ordered Ella to accompany her to the doctor. That week they had several tests sent to the lab. Ella was swabbed, inspected, and put under the microscope. Any shame she would have felt before that week was sure to be beaten out of her by the end of it through the endless blur of hospital gowns, of needles, of whirring machines, of intrusive exams. She was called back home two weeks later, and missed another day off school to visit the doctor once again, who told her that she had a rare hormonal condition.

Essentially, Ella had messed-up sex chromosomes, which meant she had never grown ovaries, so she had never had a period, and, in short, was all sorts of screwed up.

She was lucky, though, really. Some people with the condition were confined to a wheelchair, and faced severe difficulties. But Ella only had to suffer the knowledge that she had absolutely no chance of falling pregnant, ever.

Ella had sniffed at the word 'lucky' when her mother had tried to comfort her with it, between her own tears, in the car before they left the hospital. But no one seemed to understand, really, that it wasn't just Ella's chance of having a normal nuclear family that affected her. She never really cared about any of that.

What Ella *did* care about, however, was that any ounce of femininity she had ever felt was called into question since she had been told that she was no longer a whole woman. She was a part-woman hybrid, a hideous thought. And that's how it changed. Not straight away, not overnight, but slowly, Ella's self-confidence broke apart, piece by piece. It clawed away at her, that thought, especially after the hospital visits, when she had to stand half naked in front of some awkward doctor who had no idea how to deal with the teenage girl in front of him.

It was a thought that made her skin boil whenever it snuck up on her, made her cheeks pink with shame and horror. It was a feeling she couldn't shake, as she searched the internet for the physical side effects of her condition. She noticed them in herself: the wide neck, the thin lips, the swollen fingers, and the broad shoulders. If she could see them, then surely everyone else could, too. The thought made her paranoid, it made her terrified, it made her draw into herself. She never talked to her friends. She never told them how deep this self-examination cut her. And consequently, how would they know that she was feeling those things? They were all young, all attractive, all had everything that they could ever want. They wouldn't, they *couldn't* understand, and that wasn't their fault. But that did nothing to stop Ella feeling more alone than ever.

She spent her evenings in her room, staring at her blank wall, the malicious voice in her head telling her, no, *screaming* at her, that she was worthless for getting a lower grade than expected on her English test, and that if she couldn't be the best at English, would have no hope, because the only thing she could do was to write essays, and apparently, she couldn't even do that. The voice followed her, commenting on everything that she did, chastising her for every little thing she did wrong. When she told a joke at lunch time that no one laughed at, when she had a slight argument with Coco about her recent blog post, when Harrison whispered in Coco's ear, that voice did its best to convince her no one wanted her there, that they talked behind her back, that she was the least liked person in their group, that she brought the mood down, that she wasn't good enough.

The common theme was that she wasn't good enough, *never* good enough.

If she did something slightly dumb, like get a C on a random test in Chemistry that everyone else failed, she was stupid. But she wasn't just stupid, she was stupid, and then ugly, and then fat, and mean, and unpopular, and worthless. Round in vicious circles it went, day after day, she relived her worst moments, accompanied by slurs and insults screamed at her from inside her own brain.

When Ella told her friends, she was nervous. It was awkward. They asked a few times why she was taking time off on those days she was going to hospital appointments, and why she had pastoral meetings with Miss Turner, their then head of year.

She didn't have the energy to lie, so decided she would tell them. They went for a walk in the grounds. They found their favourite spot on the vast land owned by the school, a cluster of rocks near the back gate. They sat on one of the rocks and stared at Ella, waiting for her to speak. She told them she had news.

"So I've been off school a bit lately, and that's because I've been having hospital appointments with a specialist." She stared down, not able to look anyone in the eye. Her face burned angrily. The voice in her head told her they would laugh. It was so stupid, the shame she felt for something that she could do nothing about, but that shame was nevertheless there, forcing her to stare at her patent school shoes.

"Oh, my God. You're not really ill," Coco gasped and ran over to Ella's rock. She placed a delicate arm around her.

"No, I'm not ill. Not exactly, anyway."

"Then what?" Conrad began, and Ella mustered the

strength to look up at them all. Both boys were frowning, concern etched onto their faces. Harrison's forehead wrinkled as it did whenever he frowned. Conrad's big green eyes were wide, staring right at her. It seemed that Bea forgot to breathe for a moment. She had only been hanging out with them for a few months, but Ella didn't mind her knowing. She knew she wouldn't tell anyone.

"I've been diagnosed with something. It's a bit weird, but…" She took a deep breath and started talking fast. "Ok, so, it's this hormonal condition. It basically means that I don't get all the hormones I should, and it's the reason I'm short I guess, and basically it means I can't have children. That's, like, the main bit. Never."

Their mouths hung open. Coco's arm left Ella's shoulders abruptly as she swung around to stare her in the face.

"How do you feel? Are you okay?" Coco said, and searched Ella's face for the answer, her hands gripping her arms tightly. Her gaze was so intense that Ella looked away.

"Yeah, I guess. I mean, it's a lot to take in but, yeah, I'm fine." Ella had no idea how big a lie this would turn out to be, and how more and more obvious a lie it would become as time went on. The others rushed over to the rock she sat on. Conrad squeezed her tightly around the waist, and moved her head so that it rested on his shoulder as he sat next to her.

"We're here for you, El. If you need help, please ask us for it," he whispered so that the others couldn't hear.

"Thanks, Con," she replied, ashamed to find tears brewing in her eyes.

Harrison squeezed her shoulders from behind. "You sure you're good, El?" he asked softly, and she nodded, unable to turn and look him in the eye.

He thinks I'm different now. Conrad, too, Ella thought. *I bet they see me as some strange being, tainted by this bullshit.* She gulped, suppressing an unwelcome sob. *And every guy I meet from now on will feel the same.* In the world of love, she felt wretched. Doomed for eternity.

Bea sat opposite her and squeezed Ella's legs.

"I can't imagine what you are going through, but it's *got* to

29

be hard, and you're tough as nails for dealing with this so bravely. But you can't do this alone. You have four people here that want to be here for you. We want you to let us help you through this, so please talk to us, please let us help you, please make us understand how you feel."

Ella nodded, her voice stuck in her tightened throat as the others agreed enthusiastically with Bea. They sat for a while, comforting Ella in their own ways, giving her far more attention than she wanted at that moment, when she just wanted the ground to swallow her.

"Things won't be that different for you, you know, El. Loads of people have problems like this, but there are ways, you know… adoption, IVF, all sorts," Harrison said.

He thought he was helping, but instead, he did that classic boy thing, thinking that a solution to the problem helps more than words of encouragement or love. But sometimes there isn't an answer, sometimes all a person needs is someone to say, *Yeah, that's shit. I'm sorry you're so goddamn unlucky, and that life seems to enjoy smacking you across the face with a shovel.*

Ella offered a small smile. It was easier than explaining that wasn't the point. She didn't care about the babies she wouldn't have. What she hated most was that she was *different*, weird, an exception. She just wanted to be normal, like anyone else, with the same options, the same opportunities, unimpeded by some stupid random problem with her DNA that altered everything about her. It was strange. A few weeks ago she had been normal. Now she was the furthest thing from it.

"Hey," Conrad began, a wicked smile forming on his mouth. "At least for a while it just means that you don't have to worry about pregnancy scares, right?"

"*Conrad*!" Bea yelled.

"Really? *Really*, Con? That's got to be the last thing Ella's thinking about!" Harrison began, his thick eyebrows demonstrating his distaste at his best friend's lack of tact, even though he had actually been even more tactless. Conrad looked ashamed and started to fumble an apology.

"El, I'm-"

"I have been thinking about that actually," Ella said, smiling now. If there was one thing she could count on in all situations, it was Conrad's inappropriate comments. The normality helped. Conrad smiled again as Harrison looked shocked.

"See," Conrad said.

"Well, he's right. I mean, at the moment, a baby's not something I want, is it?" Ella shuddered at the thought. "I guess when I'm thirty it'll be a bigger problem, or not. I might not even bother. Who knows what I'll want?"

"But for now, carefree shagging, right?" Conrad butted in, and everyone rolled their eyes and groaned in unison.

"Not exactly." Ella offered a weak laugh. "But it does take off a bit of pressure, yeah."

Harrison pointed somewhere to the left. "One more outburst and you'll be getting a time out on that rock over there. I don't know why we allow you to be included in serious conversations in the first place. Honestly." He shook his head in disbelief.

"You don't think you'll ever have a family, El?" Bea asked.

"I don't see why I'd bother. I don't actually *like* kids. I don't see why it's expected that I do. It's not that that's the issue."

"So what *is* the issue?" Conrad's eyes were shrewd and his face earnest. Ella knew he was keen listen to her, to learn from her. That look, that face, filled her heart. He didn't offer her a pair of sad eyes and a 'poor you' expression, or avoid her gaze, not knowing how to react, asking stiff questions like everyone else. He was just being Conrad, and she liked that.

"It's, like… It's hard to explain."

He frowned. "So try." He said it so authoritatively and upon realising how forceful it sounded, added, gently, "please."

She looked around. The trees behind them basked in the setting sunlight. It would be getting dark soon, and Ella and the others didn't have long before they had to go back to the dorms. She had been answering questions and listening to commiserations for what felt like hours. She was exhausted.

"Well, how would you feel right now if you found out... I don't know, that your sperm had low motility?"

"Crap. I guess...like I wasn't a 'real man'."

"Exactly. You see how our identity is so seeped into all this stuff? We're told we're useless if we can't reproduce. It's that old survival instinct. It's apparently part of who you are. It's a part of being human, being told you can't. It makes you feel... lesser, maybe?"

Conrad suddenly looked stricken, as if the true magnitude of the situation had hit him. It was as if he truly understood, not like the others, who looked with sympathy. That look could see into Ella, and she knew he felt what she felt. "Fuck, El," he said.

Ella nodded, a tight smile to her lips.

"It'll feel better eventually, though. It doesn't change who you are," Coco said quickly. "You were magnificent before you knew all this, and you'll be magnificent afterwards. Don't forget, this has *always* been a part of you. You were Ella when you didn't know you had it, and you're Ella now. You look no different, sound no different." She turned her head into Ella's armpit and sniffed. "You *smell* no different." She giggled, and Ella joined her. "You're you. And that'll only change if you let this thing change you, which you can't. It's a part of you that will take some getting used to, but you will."

"Coco's right, you know. We loved you before, and we love you now," Bea said, checking her watch and standing up. "We should get going, anyway."

"El, I'll donate whatever you need if you do decide you want kids in the future, a womb, an egg, you name it, you got it. That is, if mine are okay. I mean, it leaves you thinking, doesn't it? Fertility really is a minefield," Coco said as they all walked towards the school.

Ella laughed before scrunching up her nose.

"I think that would be weird as hell, but thank you, Coco. Oh, how gross is that word 'fertility'? It feels weird... ugly." Coco raised her eyebrows.

"Makes it feel real?" Conrad asked.

Ella ignored that.

They reached the boys dorms when Harriso. touched her arm.

"Take it easy, El. We're here." It was simple, few words but an important sentiment. For that moment, for that day, her friends were there to get her through it all. And that was comforting. If only it had stayed that way.

"I'm sorry you have to go through this, El. But you'll make it through. Even the most awful things look better with time, trust me." Conrad said, with bracing certainty. Of everyone, he knew what it was like for the rug to be swept under his feet, for life to be imbalanced in just a day, how it felt for there to be a *you* before, and a *you* after The Bad Thing. What Conrad went through made Ella feel that her issue was trivial. It offered a perspective that she would eventually lose sight of. Because that's how depression works, Ella supposed. It's tunnel vision, being unable to see the world as it is, only from the bleak outlook from which you are forced to look. It's so introspective, that it makes every problem magnified tenfold, a hundredfold even. But at that moment, at least, everything was okay.

Coco's arm was around Ella's shoulders the entire time, even when they reached their own dorms and punched in the keycode. Bea turned into bed straight away, and Ella was keen to do the same.

"I'm staying in here with you tonight. We're going to lie in your bed and talk. It'll be like a sleepover. And don't say you don't want me to, because I am," Coco said as she unlocked her door and ran inside. Five minutes later Coco was curled up, in her little nightdress, in Ella's bed, watching Ella brush her teeth.

"Are you worried, El?"

Ella shook her head before spitting toothpaste into her sink.

"No, not really. I mean, it's pretty set in stone. There's not much to panic about, like, what else could happen?" she said as she wiped her face with a towel.

Ella pulled open the duvet and joined Coco in bed.

"It just sucks, you know?" Ella said, staring at her grey ceiling. Coco sat up straight, watching her face. "At the hospital, it's horrible. All I can think of is the physical stuff they're looking for and see in me. It's like I'm under the microscope, and my short legs and tiny boobs are there being stared at, being examined, and they're determining that there must be something wrong with me. It's like, picture your biggest insecurity. You hope it's worse in your head, that it's only really you who sees it. But it's as if you're going to a doctor who takes one look at that part of you and says, 'yeah, there's obviously something really wrong here. We need to sort this out.' And it feels as though the whole world is looking at your ugly nose, or cankles, or whatever. And you're the world's biggest freak. That's the worst part. It's so *embarrassing*."

Only, it wasn't just embarrassing, Ella thought. It was that sort of mortification that left her hot and itchy, wishing to be somewhere else, anywhere else. It was that nightmare where you turn up to school naked but real, and a hundred times worse. Coco stayed silent for a while, until Ella could hear how loud her own breathing had become.

"El, I'm going to say this, and believe me when I say that I'm not just trying to make you feel better, I'm speaking the truth, and you should listen. The whole world isn't going to take one look at you and think 'oh, shit, there's something wrong with her.' You would never know to look at you that you have anything out of the ordinary affecting you. You are beautiful, and you have everything going for you.

And even if you weren't beautiful, so what? There are so many things you should be, and you *are* before your looks, like kind, like witty and funny, like loyal and confident, like eloquent and empathetic. Honestly, being beautiful is, like, number one-hundred on the list of things you should worry about not being. It's unimportant. You scoff, but it's true. Being pretty isn't something you should strive for, because it can be all you have, and it wears thin. Think about it. Everyone can see your face. It's not something that tends to

34

change, and it doesn't develop, it doesn't evolve. And that's just so *uninteresting*, a novelty that fades so quickly. Why do you think celebrity marriages never last? Maybe it's because two beautiful people fall in love with an outstanding face and realise they don't like what's hiding underneath, and what is under your skin is the most important. *That* is who we are, not our faces.

And don't let some insensitive prick of a doctor let you think you're different from anyone in a bad way. You *are* different, and you do stand out, but in the same way the moon stands out from the stars. You shine before everyone else. For me you do, anyway, as I'm sure you do for everyone else that meets you."

She paused for breath and stared at Ella, her blue eyes meeting the beautiful, expressive dark ones that she had looked into throughout her whole childhood. "I didn't realise how intrusive this would have been for you, but it sounds horrendous. But the good thing is, you've coped, you're working through it, day by day."

Coco grabbed Ella's hand and squeezed it. "I'm so proud of you," she told her. "I'm so proud that I have such a brave, such a strong, best friend. You're incredible, El. I mean it, and don't forget that. You truly are amazing."

Tears ran down Ella's face in the darkness that had surrounded them. They slept well that night, in each other's arms. It comforted Ella more than Coco would ever know. It made a difference that Coco cared so much.

But the trouble with situations such as those was that, when The Big Thing is announced, your friends are there, happy to help. They don't always realise that sometimes the most random things are a product of a mental illness that develops as a result of our problems.

Ella's crippling insecurity manifested itself not through her staring at the mirror crying, but through her bitterness, through anger, resentment, and perhaps jealousy.

It wasn't always so easy for her friends to pinpoint that Ella was having a down day, so it wasn't always easy to excuse her behaviour. Coco could do something that wasn't too out of the ordinary, like tell Ella she was going to Harrison's room one night instead of watching a movie with her. But, when Ella was at her worst, it made her angrier than she had ever been when Coco casually mentioned that change of plans, which she often did in the past to no consequence. It made Ella call Coco a terrible friend. It made her paint Coco as a selfish brat, and herself as a victim.

But it was never the fact that Coco blew her off that was the issue, it was that Coco, as Ella well knew, was putting on her best underwear, taking her silkiest pyjamas, and sleeping with her handsome boyfriend, and Ella was consequently alone in her room. Ella's anger was not as a result of Coco's absence, but as a result of the evil voice inside her head telling her that it was unfair Coco was allowed to be normal, and pretty, and fancied, and smart, and funny. And all Ella was allowed to be was *Ella*. She was incensed with the injustice placed upon her, with the burden she was forced to bear, simply because science said so, because she was unlucky.

It hurt her. It hurt Ella to see how good things could be, how wonderful and happy and fun life could be if she was just someone else, how there was a whole pool of potential, of opportunities for pure happiness out there, if she only found a way to shed her own skin and become someone else.

She should be a better friend to Coco, she knew that. But she couldn't see straight in those moments. She couldn't see sense. She saw only part of the situation, her mind blocking out the rest, blocking the parts that would lead her to act rationally. It is no hyperbole to stress that she was *ill*, not with snotty tissues or vomiting or a broken arm or leg. She was ill in another way, in a way that only let her see the badness in people, the badness in the world. The things that made her appreciate the world, the people and the things around her, were now dulled, diluted, grey, when they were once golden and shone over the bad aspects of life, an awful symptom of an awful illness.

Her perspective changed, and she couldn't change it back. A light switch in her brain was turned off, and she had no means of switching it back on.

Chapter Four

By the time Ella knocked on Coco's door that morning and discovered she wasn't there, their friendship had become frayed. It felt to Ella as if the only way they could communicate was through bickering. What Ella once accepted about Coco now drove her nuts, like a marriage that had run its course.

It was little things that Coco did, never anything very malicious or badly intentioned, but pushy and interfering, meddlings Ella could have lived without like what happened at the end of Year 12 party. It wasn't a big deal, but they had ended up shouting in the middle of the dancefloor, rounding on each other. It was all over nothing, really, but to Ella it felt so significant at the time.

They finished their Year 12 AS exams, so Coco, Ella, and the others persuaded Miss Turner and Mrs Hardy to let them have a party in the common room. The glass doors were open onto the lawn, allowing the warm summer breeze to inject some life into their dated and worn common room. The party was loud, full of excitable girls in floral jumpsuits with big hair, and boys who smelled too strongly of cologne and all seemed to wear exactly the same beige chinos. All except for Conrad, that is. His green trousers meant he was obliged to stand in the middle of the photo Coco was taking of the boys stood together, for symmetry's sake.

Ella used to love the boarders parties. She used to love dancing, used to love the possibility of romance, of kissing boys in dark corners and feeling reckless. But when she found herself in the middle of the common room, with two couples swaying either side of her, sucking each other's faces in the grossest way, she didn't feel a part of it. She felt like an outsider looking in, like someone who would never fit in there, no matter how hard she tried. She felt lost, little red riding hood in a room full of wolves.

Coco, however, was having the time of her life. As always, the room seemed to stop whenever she entered it. Boys nudged each other, and girls whispered enviously. Her flowy, summery fuchsia dress and gold gladiator sandals, her hair partially pinned back with golden clips, meant that you couldn't miss her, and that was how she liked it.

Bea held hands with India, the couple the school couldn't stop talking about. Bea's short yellow dress and this week's turquoise hair were obviously conspicuous. Conrad had told her that she looked like a sexy Flounder from The Little Mermaid. India had laughed for five minutes straight at Bea's face, and then changed into a floral green crop top and purple skirt to make her feel better. They were in an abstract couple's costume.

India grabbed Ella's hand and twirled her towards the circle in which they were dancing. Ella smiled and moved self-consciously, laughing as Coco wrapped her arms around her, and they swayed together, stumbling clumsily. They broke apart when they had to catch their balance, and when she looked again, Coco was entwined around Harrison. Bea and India were standing close, uttering private words into each other's ears, and then India started kissing Bea's neck as Bea giggled uncontrollably, a sound escaping her that was high-pitched, flirtatious, and extremely un-Bea.

Ella saw a pair of familiar green chinos in the corner of the room, and she made her way over to her only other eternally single friend, to find that Erica Lovelace, the school's netball star, had already reached Conrad. Touching his arm, and leaning in close, her blonde hair offering a curtain to hide the ugly site of her mouth meeting his. Everyone seemed to be in that relaxed summertime spirit where nothing had consequences. But Ella couldn't get into it. Somehow she couldn't relax, she couldn't *un*tense, she was constantly on edge, even when there was nothing really to worry about. Every time she found herself in a social setting, she ran conversations back through her head. She worried so much about how she came across, it was exhausting.

She put down her drink, a disappointingly virgin, un-spiked punch, and resolved to go to bed, when she walked into Harrison and Coco.

"El, we've been looking for you!" Harrison said, eagerly.

"You have?" she said, and he nodded, about to speak, when Coco grabbed her elbow.

"You know Harrison's friend, Adam? He likes you."

"What do you mean? What's he said?"

"I wanted to tell her!" Harrison told Coco off, and she rolled her eyes. He gently nudged her out the way and crouched to Ella's level so she could hear him over the music, and she and Coco both looked at him as he talked excitedly. From the smell of his breath, Ella suspected his enthusiasm was due to a substantial amount of beer drank by him and the rest of the football team before the party.

"He asked if you were seeing anyone before, a few weeks ago now, but with exams and everything, I'd forgotten to tell you, and tonight when we were getting a few in before the party, he had a couple and asked me to put a word in." His brow furrowed as he tried to remember the words exactly right. "He said you were intimidatingly pretty, so I told him how nice you were and he asked me if I'd talk to you about him. What do you reckon?"

"Do you think I should give him a chance?" Ella asked, her eyes meeting his.

He shrugged. "Yeah, why not, right? I think he's a little boring, but you might not."

"Maybe. I don't know. This is all a bit sudden. I've barely had a conversation with him…"

"Oh, come on, El, don't be silly. It'll be good for you to talk to a couple of boys, have a bit of fun," Coco said, already seemingly losing patience in the matter. Her eyes scanned the room, and she made out Adam. She took Harrison and Ella by the hands as they glanced at each other wearily, and marched over to the corner where a couple of the boys stood.

"Hey guys!" she shouted over the music, starting to dance with Harrison.

"Adam, you've met Ella, right?" Harrison asked over Coco's head. He winked at Ella and left space for Adam to approach. By the time that Ella offered an alarmed look in return, Harrison was already kissing Coco against the wall.

"Hi!" Adam said, rubbing his neck. Ella glanced once more at Harrison and Coco, getting steamier by the second, before admitting defeat.

"Do you want to go outside for a minute? It's so loud in here."

He nodded and placed her hand in his, leading her through the room. *Wow, forward,* she thought. They left the stuffy common room and sat on the stone steps separating the patio from the green lawn.

"I'm so glad we got out of there. I'm not really into parties," he said.

"Yeah, me neither," Ella sighed.

"Hey, I hope Fletcher didn't say anything too weird, I just said…"

"I don't think you're a stalker or anything, Adam. He was cool about it." Ella laughed and he smiled at her.

They heard the squealing giggle of an unseen girl and the *Sssh* of her unseen Romeo in the distance. There were a lot of people outside; girls sat around a patio table, comforting their crying friend, the loners, people who weren't really enjoying being stuffed into a tiny room with a bunch of sweaty and probably drunk dickheads, and a few couples. Ella hadn't realised until that moment how incestuous sixth form had really become. It seemed that almost everyone was paired off.

Adam noticed her looking around, and they both sat for a minute, watching a couple exchange saliva, hearing as much as they could see.

"You are really pretty, you know," he said, a shy grin on his face.

"Thanks, that's sweet of you." Ella turned her head towards him. He was quite good looking, she supposed, in perhaps the most lukewarm way possible. There was nothing wrong with his short brown hair, and his intelligent brown eyes, or with his slightly wonky, broken nose, but there wasn't anything life changing about him either. He didn't make her gasp when his arm brushed hers gently, she didn't feel that electricity, that devastating feeling that rises inside you, crashing through everything in its wake, through sense, through morals. Ella knew what it was to fancy someone, to really want them, to be infatuated, maybe in love, and poor Adam didn't do that to her.

"It's a nice night," she said, looking up.

"I love it when you can see the stars like this." He looked up too, and his expression changed. He was so enthusiastic, so dizzyingly content. He gently pulled her arm so that it pointed to the sky. "You see those stars there? The one that kind of looks like a wheelbarrow? That's Ursa Minor, and that next to it, just down there, that's Ursa Major. The big bear and the little bear."

"Do you know a lot about astronomy?"

"Not as much as I'd like to but the sky's so massive, it's nice to be able to make sense of it. I have this app, look." He took his phone out of the pocket of his beige chinos, and launched an app, holding it to the sky. "It uses your location to show exactly what's above you, like Google Maps for the sky. Oh, look, there's Gemini."

"What's that one?" Ella asked, excitedly pointing at an interesting cluster of stars.

"Well, that's Jupiter right there, the really bright one, so that must be Leo, and that's Virgo."

"Ooh, I'm a Virgo!" she said, and he gave her a withering look.

"You believe in star signs?"

Ella shook her head, her cheeks pink under her make up. "No, but it's still exciting to see *my* constellation. Unless you can tell me there's the Ella Fitzpatrick constellation up there, Virgo's the closest thing I've got."

"Why don't you name a star after yourself?"

"You can do that? Ok, how about that one? The twinkling one."

"That's an aeroplane." Adam chuckled, his eyes, slightly droopy from the beer, boring into her face. "Although I doubt there's a star out there bright enough to be an Ella Fitzpatrick."

She grinned at him, suppressing a giggle.

"That's one hell of a line, Adam."

He was close to her now, his nose nearly touching hers. She would have moved away, should have perhaps, but she was curious.

"I'm sorry," he murmured, but he didn't look it as he tilted his head and kissed her, and she kissed him back.

It was… nice, she supposed. The butterflies, the fireworks, the heat wasn't there. It was like binge watching a show on Netflix that she had seen a million times because there was nothing else that she wanted to watch, it was fine, nothing new, nothing to sweep her away. They started slowly, his lips gently moving against hers, but then his hands started to wander around her little golden playsuit and she stood up instinctively.

"You want to go somewhere?" he asked, and stood up. He was completely unaware of the lashings of her pink lipstick around his mouth. Ella carefully wiped around her own with the back her hand.

"I- uh- not tonight, Adam. I'm sorry, I just- I'm not in the right mindset for this now and it wouldn't be right. I am sorry, honestly."

He seemed to deflate before her, his shoulders sinking, his eyes wide like a puppy who just had their paw trodden on.

"Oh, okay… I'll see you around next year then. Have a nice summer, Ella."

She touched his arm. "This was lovely, Adam, really," she said. "You're lovely. This is about me, not you. I hope you have a good summer, too." She turned and ventured back into the party to find Coco, Bea and India drunk, swinging around the room, giggling like maniacs.

"Ella!" Bea squealed, pulling her under her arm. "Where've you been?"

"And why is your lipstick smudged? Oh my God, you

kissed him!" Coco squealed, jumping excitedly, taking Ella's hands in hers.

"Who did you kiss?" India asked.

"Adam Foster-Wakeley," Ella said without enthusiasm. "I dunno, Coco. I kissed him, and he's *so nice*, but just... I'm not into him, and now I feel shitty for acting like I was."

"Hey, you can kiss someone and decide you don't like them, Ella, that's allowed," Bea said sharply, earnestly. "It really doesn't matter."

"Wait, *who* again?" India asked, scanning the room.

Coco nodded to a corner across the room, where Adam was stood alone, morosely drinking punch. India offered an unenthused sound.

"Yeah, I see what you mean. He's okay, nothing exciting."

"Exactly."

"Oh well, maybe next time." Coco grinned at her, looking around. "Who next?"

"No, Coco. He's pretty upset because you had to get involved, and you just don't care? You want me to go and mess around some other guy? I'm not a fucking Barbie that you smush together with a Ken doll, making kissy noises. People get hurt when you get involved like this."

Coco was taken aback, shocked at Ella's anger. Bea and India shared a significant look and hastily walked outside, and Coco and Ella faced each other in the middle of the room, Coco's face crumpled into an angry grimace.

"Look, I'm sorry you didn't fancy him, El, but you can't pin that on me. He's a decent guy, and got a little sad when you rejected him, so what? I hate to say it but, he'll get over it, it's not exactly going to be an event that changes his life, is it?"

"You really don't care, like, *at all*, that someone is upset because of something you did?"

"I didn't do anything! I walked over to where he was and danced a little. Where is the link there between my actions and him being sad? Sometimes things just happen, and we get over them, it's *life*, Ella!"

"But he's sad because of me, because of us!"

"Yes, so get over it! He's not exactly going to be throwing darts at a photo of your face, is he? You're allowed to try things, and they might not work out. It's a *risk*. Jesus Christ, El, what is this?" Her arms flapped at her side in exasperation, hair flying around her.

Suddenly Ella saw Coco clearly, indignant at the ridiculousness at what she was saying, and Ella felt silly. She saw behind Coco's shoulder Adam talking to a girl in their English class, who was giggling loudly at something he said. Ella strongly suspected that he wasn't a *funny* guy, not that funny anyway. He caught her eye and smiled, before returning to his conversation. Their little escapade wasn't that big a deal, after all.

"I don't know, I'm sorry. I guess things got a little out of my control and I couldn't deal with him looking at me all sad..."

"Hey, it's okay. I'm sorry that happened, alright? Are we good?"

"Yeah."

"Good! Now come with me and have a fucking vodka and lemonade, God knows we need one, or three." Coco grabbed Ella's hand and pulled her with surprising strength to the drinks table, pouring two strong drinks. Ella drank it quickly, stood with Coco, grabbing another before watching the crowd before them.

"Adam's chirped up. Is that your lipstick or Georgiana's on his face?" Coco nudged Ella's waist, shining a cheeky smile at her.

"I'm glad. Hey, where are the boys? *Our* boys?"

"Harrison's around somewhere with the lads, and Conrad, get this, wandered off with Erica Lovelace. They're probably doing it as we speak!"

"Wow."

"I know, big night, right? Everything is alright right now, you know? It's warm outside, everyone is happy, Bea and India are enjoying their last night together before she goes off travelling, Harrison's being lovely, Conrad's getting it on, you're here next to me. Life is alright, really, Ella. Things are going to be okay." She nudged her plastic cup against Ella's.

"I suspect this almost empty bottle of schnapps has something to do with that too, right?"

Coco grinned at her mischievously, picking up a bowl from behind her and thrusting it into Ella's face. "Have a vodka gummy bear and shut up," she said.

Ella laughed as she swallowed the awful, stinging, slimy sweet. Harrison and George Thomas, a reasonably hot guy from the football team, clocked her and Coco and stumbled through the crowd.

"Ladies…" George slurred, grabbing a rather sinister looking bottle from the table and pouring a far too generous measure into four clean cups. "What we need right now is a shot."

He handed a cup to each of them, who scrunched their faces in turn as the Ouzo burned their throats.

"Oh, God," Coco squealed, shaking her head and jumping up and down dramatically. "That is *awful.*"

"You're right," George said, wiping his mouth with the back of his hand and grabbing the bottle again. "Let's have another."

"Absolutely not," Coco said.

"Me neither," Harrison said, his face green, his jaw tight.

"Oh, come on, guys, the night is young. We need to celebrate!"

"I'll have one." Ella noted the stumbling people around her, the wasted Harrison gripping the table for support, and realised she was the only relatively sober person for a solid twenty metre radius. Coco and Harrison cheered as George poured the bottle straight into her mouth.

"Fitzpatrick, I never had you down as a wild one." He sized her up, looking her up and down, ogling even, before pouring even more of the disgusting drink into her mouth.

Before she had a chance to respond, Coco's favourite song blasted from the speakers and Ella's arm nearly escaped the confines of its socket as she yanked it onto the dancefloor. Bea and India also suddenly appeared and they danced together, laughing madly.

"We're all friends again, then?" Bea asked, pulling Coco and Ella under an arm each.

"Of course!" Coco yelled over the music. "We can never be mad at each other for too long, right, El?"

"Right!"

"Good! If you two stopped talking, I'd have to talk to Conrad, and I couldn't bear that."

She grinned at them both, and they ended up in a group hug. India tagged on the outskirts, producing her phone and telling them all to smile. When she turned it around for them all to inspect, they marvelled at how good they all looked. They didn't consider that they wouldn't be saying that in the morning. As they broke apart, Ella felt a hand gently touch her arm. George and Harrison joined them.

"Dance with me," George said as he ran his hand down to her dainty fingers and twirled her under his remarkably solid arm, before pulling her close and dancing, like, real dancing. His hand on her waist, hers on his shoulder.

"You're a good dancer," Ella said.

"This is nothing." He smirked and picked up the pace, whirling her around and leading her into a low dip. Ella giggled loudly the entire time.

"I like your laugh," he whispered into her ear, sending a tingle down her spine. His hand moved to her lower back, pulling her closer.

She grinned. "I like you making me laugh."

"You're a lot of fun, Miss Fitzpatrick."

"As are you, Mr Thomas."

They stopped dancing for a moment. His hand that was held out, holding hers a moment ago, was now caressing her side and he stared into her eyes deeply, intently. Ella placed a hand on his chest and rose to her tiptoes, and at that very moment Harrison decided to try spinning out of an enthusiastic and very silly dance with Coco, and stumbled into George, who went flying.

"Fletcher!" he shouted as Harrison clapped him on the back.

"I'm sorry. I just tried to do a dance and you were *there*, you know?"

Coco, Bea and India looked on in hysterics as George smiled at him.

"Well I'm sorry that me and Ella were in your way, but you need to watch out, you could've bumped into her." He grinned in Ella's direction and Harrison's gaze followed his. "And I hear she has one hell of a right hook so I wouldn't piss her off."

"Sorry El!" Harrison hugged her and beckoned George nearer, putting an arm around them both. "Look, I just want to say... George is the best guy, El, he's a good lad. And George, Ella is amazing, one of my best friends. If you hooked up it would be, like, *magic*."

George rolled his eyes.

"It's hard to believe that this is apparently the cleverest nerd in school," he said to Ella, across Harrison's vast chest. "Alright, mate. Time for some water, I think."

Coco scurried over, on cue.

"No, no, I'll look after him, he's my mess to clean up." She held out her hand and stared at him expectantly. He took it, of course, and they went over to the drinks table for what Ella prayed was an orange juice.

"You hear that? It would be *magical* if we hooked up." George grinned at her.

"He's off his tits." Ella giggled, finding herself edging closer to him.

"Well, a drunk mind speaks sober truth," George said, running his hand down her back.

"And you're a good lad, apparently."

"Not all the time." He smirked as he pushed her against the wall and kissed her, hard. It was hot, hot enough that she was glad the party had very much depleted in the last half hour, narrowing down the witnesses. He tasted like beer, but it didn't make a difference. His lips still caused her hands to grip the back of his shirt. She felt attractive, for the first time in months. George was handsome, posh, and as she kissed him, she imagined them together, being the gross couple in the group for once, Harrison overjoyed at her being with his friend, Ella being able to whisper about their sexual

47

escapades with Bea and Coco. He kissed her neck and she smiled as her breath caught in her chest.

"HARRISON!" Coco screamed. George leaped off her and they rushed across the room, weaving through the small remaining crowd, to find Harrison bending over an already substantial pool of vomit.

"Ella, go get the sand from the cupboard down the hall."

She and George looked at each other.

"The *sand*?"

"Yes, Ella, the sand. That's what you do for sick, isn't it? Chuck sand on it."

Ella hurried down the hall as George followed. He grabbed her hand as she went to open the cupboard.

"Want to make our excuses and get away?"

"What? No, Coco needs…" He stopped her talking by kissing her again, pulling her tight against him. She pushed him away, having to use more force than she really should.

"Come *on*," he urged, teasingly shaking her arm a little, and pulling her in again.

"*No,* we have to help clean up. Your friend is off his face in there and you just want to run off? We should help."

"You want me to spend the night cleaning up after Harrison?" His eyes narrowed. Ella opened the cupboard and grabbed the sand bucket and a roll of bin bags for good measure.

"Well, someone has to."

George sighed and rolled his eyes. "I thought…" He shook his head and turned on his heel. "You know what? Never mind. See you around, Ella."

"But…" she said as he turned around the corner, out of sight. Frowning, she shut the cupboard door with a crash and walked back to the party, tipping the contents of the sand bucket over the extraordinary mess Harrison somehow managed to create from just his stomach. She walked outside to find him bent over a bush, Coco rubbing his back.

"Oh, good!" She sighed as she grabbed a bin bag and directed Harrison over to the bench where they all sat down, Harrison in the middle, his head bowed, heaving into the bag.

"Where's Bea and India?" Ella asked.

"Ran off to make the most of their last night together. Where's George?"

"Apparently his idea of fun *isn't* nursing a vomiting idiot. Who knew?"

Coco laughed. "I'm sorry, El."

"No I- I'm sorry. It's my fault," Harrison said, once he managed to stop gagging for a moment.

"It's fine. I'm pretty sure he didn't have love on the mind anyway."

"I ruined it, though. He really fancied you."

"For about a minute, yeah," Ella said, suddenly finding the whole situation a little less amusing now she was sat outside, once again surrounded by couples. "I guess that's the best I can hope for now, isn't it?" Ella wasn't exactly sure why, but she started crying. Tears fell down her cheeks and she couldn't stop a sorry little gasp from escaping her. Her eye makeup ran down her face as she rubbed her cheeks dry.

Coco and Harrison exchanged a concerned look. Harrison put an arm around her.

"I'm sorry, El. You're great. It's me that ruined it, and he's a bloody imbecile if he can't see that you're amazing."

"You probably had a lucky escape. This is all him, not you," Coco said softly, ruffling Ella's hair, her arm extended across Harrison's shoulders.

"I can't believe I was such an idiot that I ruined your night like this," Harrison groaned woefully.

"Yep, yes you did, you absolute vom explosion." She giggled and nudged him gently. "And in Miami, you are buying me cocktails until I look like you do right now."

He laughed into the bin bag, spitting.

"You don't want to look like this, kid."

His eyes met Ella's as he lifted his head, his face serious.

"I'm so sorry."

"It's *fine*. I'm being drunk and silly. It's the alcohol."

He squeezed her shoulders again, before urgently rushing to stick his head into the plastic bag once more.

Coco wrinkled her nose. "Can we think about me for a

moment, please? I have to go to bed with *this*."

Harrison placed an arm around Coco and squeezed her tight.

"I'll make it up to you tomorrow, when I'm substantially less sicky, I promise."

"And that's my cue to leave." Ella slapped her legs bracingly and stood up, stumbling as she did so.

"No, we should probably get to bed, too." Coco stifled a yawn and grabbed the roll of bin bags. She held a hand out to Harrison. "Come on, loser," she said. "Let's get you out of here. You've embarrassed yourself enough for one night."

"Aw, I *have* haven't I?" he groaned again, rolling his neck. He stood, and Coco steadied him by wrapping her arm around his waist. The three of them walked across the dewy grass to the dorms.

"Are you ashamed of me, Coco?" Harrison asked as Ella punched in the keycode for the girls' block.

"Yes, very," Coco said with a wan smile.

"You're still here though, and so is Ella. Are you still my friend, El?"

"Until my dying day. But at the rate you're going, you two are going to have to build me a granny flat in your house where I can grow old in spinsterhood. I hope you like cats."

Coco cackled, but Harrison still looked concerned.

"I can talk to George. I'll say…"

"Don't bother, he's not worth the fuss," Ella cut him off, not meeting his eye.

"I feel personally ob-obl- *obliged* to set you up with someone now, though. Who do you like? I'll make sure he'll be proposing by the end of the week. You're brilliant, it'll be easy. Just name your boy."

Ella stopped at her door, turning to face Harrison, who stood expectantly, looking lopsided in the awkward crouch he was maintaining to keep his arm around Coco. Ella forgot just how tall he was. Coco looked up at him, her eyes twinkling, a dazzling smile shining at his face. Even in their drunken, messy state, they were a beautiful couple.

"*No one,* Harrison. You're fine. Goodnight guys."

"Night, El," Coco said as she fumbled with her keys, finally finding the right one and opening her door. She stood aside and considered Harrison, who was leaning against the wall for support. Her face set as she realised she was in for a long night.

"Get to bed, and for the love of God, brush your teeth." Coco grabbed his arm and steered him past Ella's door, towards her own.

He patted Ella on the shoulder.

"Night, night, El. Sorry about the cockblocking, or the *vom*blocking." He giggled at his own bad joke.

She laughed and shook her head, and then closed her door.

Ella woke up the next morning feeling a little better than she expected, and decided that she could manage some breakfast. She meandered over to the dining hall, feeling warm in the early morning sun. Bea and India were sat at their table, Bea leaning against her, her eyes closed, sunglasses covering most of her face. Conrad sat in the end seat, his head in his hands.

"Don't we all look chirpy?" Ella grinned at them, before yawning herself. India chuckled.

"Do you have to *scream*?" Conrad pleaded, raising his evidently sore head, his greyish pallor telling tales on him of the night before.

"Not feeling too clever?" Ella teased, and he glared.

"Obviously."

"Where's Erica?" Ella asked, and to her surprise, his face crumpled even more.

"Not with me, that's for sure," he mumbled, a shade of pink injected some life into his complexion.

Ella could only offer an inquisitive glance at him before she saw Harrison enter the room, his arm around an extremely dishevelled Coco. He was grinning as he clapped Conrad on the back.

"Hey, Casanova. How's Erica?"

Everyone stared at him expectantly, Coco squinting in the daylight. Bea even opened one eye under her glasses. He paused for a moment, squirming under the attention.

"Oh, come on. Don't get coy on us now," Harrison said, marvelling at Conrad not wanting to be the centre of attention for once.

"Alright, *alright*. It's like bloody Summer Nights from Grease all of a sudden."

"Well, did you get very far?" Ella asked, and Harrison laughed.

"Does she have a car?" he added, grinning, before they sang in unison. "*Shoo pa pa, shoo pa pa.*"

"I am actually going to kill you both. I'm going to literally *murder* you." Conrad's glare was so severe that if looks could kill, Ella and Harrison's heads would have exploded.

"So tell us then, come on," Harrison urged him, unrelenting.

"Nothing happened…"

"Pull the other one."

"For the love of God, alright. So we get back to hers…" They all leaned in, Conrad too, relishing in his story now, he was back to his normal self. "And we're kissing, and she's like, grinding on me, still with clothes on, but…"

"I am *way* too hungover for this. See you all later." India laughed, as she kissed Bea on the cheek and sauntered off to pack.

"So yeah, it's heating up and we take off some of our clothes, I'm just in my trousers and she's in her underwear-black and lacy, really sexy. Anyway, so she's, like, kissing my abs, giving it all the *Oooh you're so muscular.*" He gestured to his torso.

"Get to the point," Bea snapped, her head in her hands.

"So she's kissing my abs and she starts undoing my trousers…."

"Jesus, I think I'm too young to hear this," Coco said, pinching the bridge of her nose, sipping Bea's water.

"Anyway, it *just* starts getting good, and she seems completely fine, but then she suddenly stands up and runs out of the room, covering her mouth."

"Wait, what?" Harrison asked, wide eyed.

"So I wait for a while, but then it's been, like, fifteen

minutes and I'm thinking *this is getting ridiculous*. I walk out of her room, and there's splatters on the corridor floor, leading to the bathroom. And I hear this terrible retching sound and I knock the door, like *Erica, you alright?* And she shouts back *Yes, I'm fine, just let me...*" He demonstrated a gagging sound and they all recoiled, Bea gagged a little herself. "But she obviously wasn't fine, so I opened the door and she's sat on the floor, where's there's definitely some escaped sick surrounding her, vomming her guts out into the toilet."

"So what did you do? Did you leave?" Harrison asked, offering a sympathetic look. Conrad's eyes widened.

"What? No! She was ill, I couldn't just leave just because I realised she wasn't going to have sex with me, could I? I ran out and got a big glass of water and covered her up with her dressing gown, and I held her hair back for a while until she stopped being sick. Then, like, *days* later she stopped exploding from the mouth enough to go to bed, so I took her to her room and put her bin next to her bed, and talked to her till she fell asleep, then I felt weird sat there just watching some girl sleep so I left... I hope she's still alive."

"What a night, eh?" Harrison said through guffaws.

"That sounds like my night," Coco said, her narrowed eyes flashing at Harrison.

"You were sick?"

"No, Harrison was. All over the common room, in front of everyone. And then he just fell asleep, snoring like a fucking train as soon as he hit my bed. I've had like two hours sleep."

"You were sick in the *common room?*" Conrad laughed jovially. "Poor you."

"Thank you for your sympathy. It's only something that'll probably scar me for my entire adult life. It's cool."

"Not you, fool. Coco."

"To be fair, I think it's Ella that's the worst off," Harrison said, a cautionary glance towards her.

"What, why?"

"Well, she was *on fire* last night." Bea smirked. "Snogging Adam Foster-Wakeley-"

53

"Ugh, grim." Conrad cringed. "What was that like?"

"Hey! He's a nice boy," Ella said, indignantly. "It was *fine*."

"Uh-oh. That doesn't sound promising."

"That's why she chucked him for George Thomas," Harrison interjected.

"Oh!" Conrad said in surprise.

"…And then *he* chucked *her* when she tried helping Harrison instead of running off to his room to get it on," Coco added.

Conrad's head moved between them as though he was watching tennis.

"The scumbag!" he said, before scanning Ella's face with a searching look. "Honestly though, El, neither of these guys are really *you*."

"Well, who is *me*?"

"I dunno, do I? Just not some wet blanket or some guy that's had as many bangs as birthdays."

"Says the lad being grinded on by Erica Lovelace!"

"I'm just saying, it's a bit out of character for you…"

"Well, Adam was our idea, to be fair," Harrison reasoned.

"George was all Ella, though. He was all over her," Coco said, with a menacing smile. "I have photos."

"You what?" Ella and Conrad asked in unison, except he was grinning, and she was mortified.

"Show me, *right now*," Ella demanded through gritted teeth.

"I was drunk, El, and it was so shocking, you getting all up on him," Coco said, passing her phone to show a dark picture. You could make out the silhouettes of two figures against the wall, the girl with her leg wrapped around him, his hands all over her. It was an undeniably grim picture.

"Wow, El…" Con snickered. "You really got stuck in, didn't you?"

"Fuck off," she seethed, deleting the photo.

"I didn't get a good look!" Harrison wailed.

"Why do you *want* a good look?" Coco asked him, her voice sharp.

"Because it's *funny*, Ella getting down and dirty."

They fell about laughing, all except Ella.

"Oh, come on, crack a smile. You had a wild night, good for you. I mean, I wouldn't choose those lads, but still," Conrad said.

"Oh really? What lads *would* you choose?" Harrison smirked.

"Oh, you any day, gorgeous." He grinned, running over to lock Harrison in his arms, peppering his cheek with kisses, to giggles and shouts of *gerrrooff*!

"Can you stop *snogging* him, please?" Coco laughed, pushing him away.

"Sorry, Coco. I'll keep my hands to myself from now on. Unlike Ella last night." He winked at Ella's scowl. "Really though, El, if you start causing fights on the football pitch I'll have to stage an intervention."

"Don't worry. I think my days of snogging multiple boys at parties are on standby for the time being."

"Isn't it funny how the sluttiest two last night went home alone?" Harrison jibed.

"The *sluttiest*?" Ella gasped.

"I will not be slut shamed during our night-out-debriefing brunch, thank you, Fletch," Conrad said. "Just 'cos you're basically *married*, it doesn't mean we have to behave."

"It doesn't always mean you have to behave," Bea intervened, a sly smile upon her lips.

"Well, at least one of us had a successful night," Conrad said.

"Uh…" Harrison blushed.

"You didn't! How?!" Conrad asked, astonished.

"I just sobered up a lot after all the sicking, and Coco did most the work. And it'll be a week or so before I visit her. I brushed my teeth, don't worry."

Coco's head was in her hands, somewhere between a fit of giggles and mortification.

"What?" he whispered to her, gently pulling her arm away to see her face.

"Speaking of vomit…" Conrad whispered to Ella, and

they chuckled together.

"What an absolute shitshow of a night. Well done, everyone. I'm immensely proud at all we've achieved," Bea said, shaking her head and smirking despite the raging hangover.

That afternoon they were forced to attend a spontaneous assembly where they were told that the state of the school that morning had been outrageous, that the school had never seen a more irresponsible sixth form class and that they were under no circumstances allowed to have any sort of social event as long as they remained in Lainsbury Hall School. Their hungover fellow students did their best not to fall asleep, or else vomit, during the assembly, and there seemed to be a school wide nap before they were all scheduled to leave that evening for the summer holidays, which, Ella was completely unaware would cause more than enough drama and excitement for the rest of her sixth form life. She didn't quite expect such a saga of love, loss, a few emotional arguments, and a hate crime.

But she didn't want to think about that as she lay alone in her bed, thinking about the missing Coco, about what could have happened, trailing through her mind for ideas about anything she may have said that would hint at where she could be.

PART TWO
BEA

Chapter Five

The next day, the four of them met on the chilly lawn in front of the girls dorm and wandered into the great hall together, which was full when they arrived.

The whole school was summoned to an assembly held by Mrs Hardy, but this meeting had an ominous feeling unlike the routine ones they attended every week. For one, the police stood at the back of the hall were conspicuous in their uniforms, drawing concerned eyes from innocent year sevens and stoner sixth formers. It was a serious occasion, everyone could feel it, and it stirred a sort of warped intensity to the atmosphere, where the groups of children all around the hall were exchanging wide eyed, excitable mutterings, only feeling the magnitude of the situation in a disconnected, hollow way.

As Bea, Conrad, Ella, and Harrison made their way down the aisle, to the sixth form seats at the front of the hall, a gentle whisper from the huddles of fellow students washed over them. It was a wave, starting as a ripple, rising to a significant crash.

"People are so bloody tactless. Are they *enjoying* this?" Conrad seethed, his face red with fury as he slid along the pew. He always loved to be the centre of attention, but this sombre celebrity status they all found themselves holding was not sitting well. It was ironic that, at a time when all four of them would rather stay out of the limelight and worry in peace, they were thrust so unfortunately into the school's public eye.

"They probably think she's going to turn up in a day or two, which she will." Bea urged. She wished her voice didn't sound quite so hopeful. She wasn't reassuring anyone.

Mrs Hardy took to the podium and began explaining the situation, when Coco had left, and mentioning that the police had started sharing her photo online, and that it would help if everyone shared the photo, although Bea doubted that Hardy had any real idea about such things as an Instagram story or a retweet.

"And I urge you all, if you have any information regarding the night before last, if you saw or heard anything around B Block that could remotely assist in us finding Coco safe and well, please let a member of staff know. It is vital that we have as much information as we can. I thank you all for your cooperation during this difficult time."

As they shuffled out of the hall, Bea noted the concerned looks on the faces of the teachers, stood at the back, waiting for the students to leave before they could attend a crisis meeting with the police. Hardy herself looked greyer than ever and even the usually easy-going Hunter looked positively ashen, even ill, talking intently with officer Hobbs. Miss Jenkins was stood next to him, her eyes enormous, sunken into dark circles. Mr Graham, the history teacher, even looked close to tears. It was unnerving to see them all so concerned, when she and her friends were just trying to keep their heads clear, and barely succeeding at that. If the adults, the authority figures were panicked, she was doomed.

Hunter made his way over to the group as they were about to leave for breakfast.

"Guys, I hope to God that Coco's okay. You know you guys are my favourites. It's going to be weird as hell tomorrow if she isn't there." He looked between them all, his eyes flitting fast between them. "Do you have any idea where she might have gone? Because, I mean, she must have just run off somewhere, right, after an experience to blog about?"

"We're pretty worried. She didn't tell us anything, we have no clue where she might be," Ella said.

"Well, she's always been spontaneous. Let's just hope she comes back with an exciting adventure, right?"

They all mumbled nondescript acknowledgements of his positivity, the fear on their faces obvious.

"She'll be fine guys, obviously. Try not to panic. Focus on chemistry or physics, or whatever boring subjects you have when you're not larking about in my class."

Bea offered a small smile as she muttered her thanks, but she could tell he was putting it on. He was doing that adult thing where they pretend everything is okay for the sake of the children, but he was barely an adult himself. Sure, he was twenty-eight, but in reality, he had the mental age of around nineteen. Hunter was no more responsible than they were, although he made a valiant effort at comforting them.

They reluctantly ate their breakfast in a strained silence. For Bea, it made it so much worse. Without Conrad's jokes and Harrison hanging on Coco's every dramatic story, everything was different. There were no distractions, nothing to berate Conrad for, no teacher affairs to discuss. It was hard to believe how *normal* things were just two days ago, and now they were stuck in a solemn trance, a sobering panic that made them all quiet, not themselves.

She noticed Ella swirling her porridge around distractedly, staring off into some spot between Conrad's and Harrisons' heads.

"Eat," Bea told her. "You'll only feel worse if you don't"

"I feel sick," Ella said quietly.

"I'll hold your hair back if you bring it all back up again, but try, El, please."

She sighed and took one mouthful, staring Bea in the eyes defiantly as she did so. When she tasted it a couple of seconds later, she frowned and spit it into a napkin, gulping down water to cleanse her offended mouth.

"That's *awful*," Ella said, breathless, as her glass thudded on the wooden table. "I tried."

The boys didn't bother to comment. Conrad was absentmindedly eating toast, and Harrison was compulsively flicking between the police social media sites.

"Just wait until Coco finds out they used this picture. She'll go mental," Bea said, as she saw the post on his phone. He offered only a brief, small smile in response.

It seemed that every time they went online they were faced

with Coco's pout, the same one that was present in every single photograph taken of her, her full lips outshone only by her protuberant icy blue eyes which stared out at them all, surveying every action, every dark deed. It was as if Coco was daring them to spill their own, or her secrets, if only they knew of them. Her photograph was being shared all over the country, she had gone viral overnight, it seemed that the whole country was willing her to return.

As Bea stared at these posts, she saw Coco's face, and noted how, for the first time ever, Coco seemed young in that photo. It was as though Bea was seeing her face for the first time. She saw the slight chubbiness to her cheeks, the playfulness in her eyes. She was just a kid, a lost child, and now, they all were.

In the absence of any real present conversation, Bea remembered how she liked Coco from the first proper conversation they ever had together, two years ago, in the very room in which she was sat now. They were both staying at school over the half term break, when most people had gone home for the week. Coco's parents were busy somewhere in America, Bea's were on a cruise.

Bea's mum and papa were retired, they were older than most parents. Her mum was forty-two when she was born, her dad fifty. Her dad sold his printing business for a huge profit when Bea was nine, and they both lived in a relaxed, slow-paced luxury since.

Bea and Coco were the only two girls in their year to stay at that time, a fact they discovered when they went down to the dining hall and Coco saw Bea sitting alone, and joined her.

"Hey, Beatrice. How are you?"

"Call me Bea." Bea grinned. Coco was the resident 'it' girl in school, and whilst Bea did her best to actively protest such concepts, she couldn't help but feel excited that Coco was talking to her.

"How come you're staying here this week? Why aren't you going home?" Coco asked her with genuine interest, and she explained about her parents being away.

"Is your girlfriend not staying?" Coco asked her abruptly. Bea choked on the chicken pie she had tried to swallow at that moment. She hadn't come out to anyone yet.

"My girlfriend?"

Coco blinked at her. "Genevieve. Your girlfriend, right?"

"She's not my girlfriend," Bea said, shaking her head and faking a laugh.

"Oh, I'm sorry. When did you break up?"

"Break up? We were never…" But there was something about Coco that made Bea want to confide in her. She was the first person she was comfortable having this conversation with, and she barely knew her. Somehow, she knew she could trust her. She looked around to check that no one was looking, and sighed.

"Alright. In August."

"Why?"

"I realised I didn't see her in that way. I realised I didn't like girls."

Coco narrowed her eyes in that shrewd way that Bea would discover she always did when she was about to say an uncomfortable truth. "You mean you tried being straight."

Bea looked as though Coco had slapped her. She had never met someone that could see through her the way Coco could. "I- uh- yeah," she said, staring at her plate, her face burning.

"Bea, have you come out to anyone yet? I mean, officially," Coco asked her softly, placing her delicate hand on Bea's wrist.

"No, not 'officially'. What does that even mean?"

"Well, don't take this the wrong way or anything, but, to me, at least, you're so obviously gay. Even without that moment where you have to say it, it's obvious, you're totally gay."

Bea stared at her in shock. "How?" she said. "Because I don't go out with the dumbass boys in this school? Because I won't subject myself to finding a companion in an immature prick of a boy? Maybe I'm waiting for someone better?"

Coco rolled her eyes. "Alright. Firstly, drop the defensive

act, it's totally uncalled for, you're gay, we both know it. Secondly, some of the boys in this school are wonders to behold, it's not their fault you don't fancy them."

It was Bea's turn to scoff.

"And thirdly..." Coco ignored her. "You so obviously fancied Genevieve for ages. The way you looked at her as she read in class, the way you laughed too loudly at her jokes, the way you stared when she wasn't looking. I noticed. I knew you were gay like two years ago."

Bea sniffed.

"No, really, you were both at a boarders dance and you were *gasping* to dance with her. You got her a drink and everything you said to your little group of friends you directed at her, every joke you made was for her to laugh. I'm sorry if I'm being a little imperious, but you're honestly not very subtle. I always thought it was a fact, a well-known one at that."

Coco sat back, inspecting her nails, and then surveyed her. Bea was shaken. She remembered that dance, and everything Coco said was true. And now Bea felt under scrutiny under her gaze which seemed to x-ray, to expose the naked truth.

"When did you actually get together?" Coco asked. Bea knew it was useless to be anything but honest.

"Last March. We went on a school trip to Paris with art. We shared a room and we bought some wine and snuck it back one night. We drank it, the whole bottle, and she told me she thought she might be gay. So I kissed her, and then she told me that she knew she was gay." Bea smirked. "We didn't think people would take it well in school, though, so we kept it low key and tiptoed around until summer."

"I bet it's dead easy sneaking into each other's rooms at night when you're in the same dorm," Coco said with a mischievous smile.

"Oh, yeah." Bea grinned and Coco frowned.

"But you ended it? Why? You love her, even still. Get her back!"

Bea shook her head. She went on to learn that Coco had a habit of making extremely grey situations seem black and white. In a world of maybes, Coco thought everything was and should be *yes or no, this or that.* Coco was never concerned with such mundane things as dating, because being straight, smart, and unbelievably beautiful, there were no worries or concerns for her in the dating category.

"It was pressure, hiding it, introducing her as my friend. It got to us, it got to me. I freaked out and ended it on a whim. Went out with some boy at home for a while, maybe a couple of weeks, which was completely and utterly gross. I mean, he was nice, but, you know…" Bea's voice trailed off.

"A boy, yeah, exactly," Coco added excitedly. "So, what, Genevieve doesn't want you back?"

"It would be so difficult to get back on track. And I don't think she's forgiven me, really. She's told Georgiana and Maggie that I did something, I think, probably something horrible. I guess they think I'm the worst person in the world, and they've all sort of buggered off."

"So you're pretty lonely," Coco said baldly.

Bea nodded. "This term has been proper crap," she said.

Coco grinned at her.

"Not anymore. You're my friend now. Let me tell Ella."

And with that, Coco took a picture of Bea and sent it to Ella with the caption *Bea's our friend starting today.* Ella replied with a thumbs-up, grateful for someone other than Conrad to talk to when Coco and Harrison were kissing in public.

"Coco, don't tell people though, please."

"Tell them what?" Coco asked, now distracted, staring at her phone.

Bea lowered her voice and looked around again, just to be sure. "About Genevieve."

Coco placed her phone face down on the table and glared at her. "I won't. But I can't unsay what your eyes have already screamed from the rooftops."

Bea chortled. "Alright, but just don't say anything with your mouth, yeah? I haven't told anyone and my parents are going to be weird about it and people will talk and-"

Coco squeezed her hand and looked her in the eyes. "I'll

help you out. It's all in your own time, of course, but when you're ready to tell people I am absolutely here for you. We're friends now, remember?"

Bea nodded, at a loss at what to say. She never faced such immediate kindness from a person she was properly acquainted with for mere minutes.

"You have to tell me exactly what happened with Genevieve though, because it sounds heart-breaking," Coco said.

Bea sighed and relayed the story to Coco. She didn't have a single person to confide in about it before today, and over a very long dinner she gave Coco every detail, to her gasps and wide eyes. She and Gen had been friends since Bea's very first day at Lainsbury Hall School when they were fourteen. It was one of those friendships that had started very quickly, and it took only one long conversation for them both to realise how much they had in common.

As they became almost inseparable, Bea found that she didn't just want to be Gen's best friend. Every time Gen hugged her, every time she smelled Gen's strawberry shampoo on her hair, something rose within Bea. She would never have considered herself gay back then, but she knew that she wanted a lot more from Gen than what she was being offered as friends.

When Bea turned fifteen, she allowed herself to admit that she fancied Gen. She could find no other explanation for the stupid laugh that escaped her whenever Gen made a joke, far too loud and for far too long, or the way Bea gasped whenever Gen's hand brushed her own. And then they went to Paris.

As they took in the sights, giggling at the busty ladies painted or sculpted in the Louvre and the d'Orsay, taking pictures of each other around the city, at the Notre Dame, at the Eiffel Tower, Bea found herself admitting to herself that she was undeniably, uncomplicatedly in love with Gen.

Then it was the night before they were to leave, and as they scoured a little gift shop for a magnet for Bea's Papa, Gen looked at her with huge, bespectacled brown eyes, and said to her, "Bea, we could probably get away with buying wine here in France, right? You could pass for sixteen." Bea giggled and nodded, and Gen looked around to check that no one was listening. "Then maybe we should buy some and get drunk together, tonight. It's our last chance," she said.

"Christ, Gen, you're acting like we're the Cray twins." She couldn't help laughing at Gen's soft, innocent face. To her, buying wine underage was akin to robbing a bank or snorting coke. It was cute. "You're right, though. It'll be fun to get a little tipsy. Maybe I should buy it though."

Gen stood outside the small, shabby shop when Bea bought two bottles of merlot, wrapping one in her jumper so they didn't clink together in her backpack and cause suspicion among the teachers. They waited until lights out and sat on their little balcony, overlooking parts of the city, whispering and giggling more and more as they drank quickly from their glasses.

It did not take long for Gen's cheeks to flush with mirth as she clumsily leaned ever closer in her chair, her hand resting on the armrest, just an inch from Bea's.

"I'm obviously rather drunk right now, but I just have to say…" She whispered, her intense, wide eyes offering a conspiratorial edge to the conversation which sent a tingle down Bea's spine. "I'm so glad I met you. I've never enjoyed spending this much time with anyone before. I think you're incredible, so funny and smart and…I like you a lot," Gen slurred and hiccoughed as she talked, but she spoke with such earnestness. She stared into Bea's eyes in that way that made her face burn and smiled.

Bea smiled back. "You're drunk," she teased, poking her arm.

Gen shook her head slowly, serenely. She was contemplating something, buying time.

It seemed to Bea that she was working hard to form coherent, sensible thoughts. She shook her head as though to place the words and letters into a better order.

"You know, I really do love you. Possibly in a way that I didn't think I would ever love girls." Gen tentatively placed a hand on Bea's shoulder, who sat bolt upright, leaning in towards her.

"Really?"

Gen recoiled, hiding her face in her sleeve. "I know I shouldn't have said anything. Please don't let this be awkward. I just thought that, maybe…"

"No- Alright. I have to say it now, but if you don't feel the same way we need to just gloss over this and mark it down as a weird night, okay? But I'm-" She cleared her throat as Gen sat close to her, her eyes shining, eagerly listening to every word Bea was saying.

"I'm in love with you. Like *in love*, totally mad about you, and I always thought you liked guys because it's as if we're supposed to like boys but I've never looked at a single boy and felt the same way that I do when I look at you. You're wonderful, like *no one* else is."

Gen leaned over in her precariously balancing wicker chair and kissed her. Bea's hands ran through her strawberry scented hair, her thumb tracing her porcelain cheek. Her lips tasted like the Carmex she had borrowed so many times, and it was perfect, a Gen taste.

They broke apart and Bea stared into her flushed face. Gen's chest was rising and falling rapidly beneath her cardigan.

"Without a point of reference I'm not sure how good kisses can be but I have a feeling that was pretty spectacular, yes?" Gen was beaming. Bea nodded.

"So… you maybe like girls then?"

"Well, you're 'girls', and I definitely like you."

Bea chuckled as she leaned in once again. "Good."

They never truly knew if Georgiana and Maggie, the other girls they hung around with, had noticed a change when they returned after Paris, but everything did change, of course.

She and Gen became obsessed with each other, spending every night sneaking between their bedrooms and every weekend in town, going on dates in inconspicuous places, to tea houses and eating fish and chips on the beach that was close to their school. Their favourite place was the old cinema. They could have plastered their walls with the terrible movies they watched just so they could kiss in the back seats. Bea still had those tickets in shoebox under her bed, although she tried not to think about that as she told Coco the story of her and Gen, because every time she thought about that box, it reminded her that it was the only relic she still had of her time with her, that and a reel of pictures she considered deleting so many times, but found herself unable to do so.

"It's all so perfect! But..." Coco began excitedly, her tone changing as the reality of the situation dawned on her.

"But you know that it ended, yeah. We were great together, but then she came to stay with me for a few days over the summer."

They were apart for a month once school had ended, and Bea nervously asked her parents if 'a friend from school' could come and stay for a week. They agreed, and Bea was so excited, but when Gen had arrived, things were weird. Every time they were in the presence of Bea's parents, they second guessed themselves, questioning constantly if they were being obvious, if it wasn't already obvious that they were together. They were paranoid. And it didn't get better as the days passed.

They were sat sunbathing next to the brook at the end of Bea's garden. The sun glittered on the water as it bubbled and glugged along. Bea was admiring the goosebumps rising on Gen's skin in the English breeze. She ran her hand along her tanned arm, when Gen pulled it away and looked around for signs of Bea's parents, before frowning.

"How are we going to work if we always have to hide it, Bea?" Gen asked, her voice low.

"Of course we can work, we'll wait until we're older, until we're off to Uni, when it doesn't matter anymore."

"But what if it didn't matter *now*? What if we came out, like, now?"

"It would be so much drama. Everyone would have an opinion. It would be stifling, and I don't think I'm ready for that."

Gen closed her eyes and sighed. "Isn't that the price you pay, though? You tell people, you face it because you love

69

someone so much you want everyone to know about it," she said.

"It's not that simple. You said yourself that your parents would freak out."

"They can go to hell if they have a problem with us. I'm ready to do it, Bea. Are you?"

In the lingering silence the brook rushed and the birds sang in the trees. To Bea it sounded aggressive. It wasn't a mating call, it was a warning song. "I can't, Gen. I can't handle it right now. I don't want to be the girl everyone's talking about," she said.

"It would be weeks at the most, and then people would forget and things will be normal, the sooner we do it, the sooner people get used to it, used to us."

"I said I can't, Gen. Why are you pushing this?"

"Because I can't hide this any longer. This week has been so weird, I need to know that our whole relationship isn't going to be like this. I just realised that I can't do this forever." Tears filled Gen's eyes as she looked into Bea's.

"Once we leave school…"

"That's *three years*, Bea." She stood abruptly, casting a long shadow over Bea's squinting face.

"I can't be your secret any longer. I need a time frame, a promise that we'll tell people soon."

"Don't do this," Bea said, her voice curter than she intended.

"No, I need to know that I mean something to you."

"You mean *so much* to me. You know that."

"I don't. Not as long as we're hiding in cinemas and creeping around corridors. This has to change or…" Gen's voice trailed off and she closed her eyes momentarily, steeling herself.

"Or what? You'll leave?"

Bea stared at her, the harshness in her voice made her wince. Gen frowned and nodded.

"Jesus, Gen!"

"Promise me, promise that you'll tell people. That I'll go home and we'll pick a day and we tell our parents and we change our Facebook statuses and we become a normal couple." Gen's voice shook with emotion, her words garbled as they left her mouth.

"I- I can't do that. I- I need more time," Bea stuttered in her panic.

"But *how long*? I can't wait for this forever, I'm not being a secret forever."

"I can't."

"Then neither can I."

"Gen..."

"No, Bea. I want to be with you, but not like this. I want to shout about you to everyone I know, I don't want to be ashamed about it. I hope you figure yourself out. If you do, let me know. But for now, I'm..." She gulped back a sob, as she mustered up the strength to finish her sentence. "I'm going to have to go."

"Don't leave. Please, stay. *Please*."

Gen shook her head. "Tell your parents I started to feel ill. I can walk to the train station from here."

"Please."

Gen couldn't respond. Tears running down her face, she could only shake her head and walk away.

Bea was stunned, rooted to the spot, blinking into the sunlight in disbelief. She wandered, dazed, into her house only minutes later, once she regained her composure, ready to talk some sense into Gen. She called her name as she ran through the house, slamming open every door, hoping to find her sulking in a room somewhere. She was gone. Bea had curled up on her bed as the sun set around her, as her room changed so fast from being seeped in molten gold, to covered in an inky blackness. The night enveloped her like a great duvet, suffocating and heavy.

She tried getting in touch, but Gen had blocked her from all social media, and ignored her calls. She cut Bea off, Bea thought perhaps for her own sake rather than out of spite. When they returned to school, a month later, Gen ignored her to her face. She avoided her in corridors, sat apart from her in class. Bea was heartbroken, desolate.

But then she met Coco and became a part of their loud and glamorous group. She was getting used to people looking at her, and she was getting used to being around people who accepted her for her. Coco heard Bea's story, and didn't push her to come out.

Coco didn't even mention it until weeks later, as they wandered to the dining hall from maths class, both of them admiring the rainbow that had appeared over the school, the bittersweet result of the weak sun meeting the all-too-common English drizzle.

"So have you thought more about coming out? Are you ready to do it any time soon? Or are you content to stay inside the safe and warm little closet, or is it a wardrobe in England?"

"But it's such bullshit. Why do I even have to come out? Why do I have to sit down every person I know and tell them my sexual preferences? Straight people don't have to do it." Bea said, then made a growl of anger and ran her hands through her blue curly hair.

"Bea. I have something to say, and it's not altogether easy and it may surprise you but... I like men. I am a heterosexual, and damn it I'm proud."

"Oh ha-ha."

"Well, maybe don't. Maybe just drop it in. You know, *oh my celebrity crush is Margot Robbie.*"

"I'm more of a Scarlett Johansson kind of girl."

"Good to know, but that's not the point. Just sort of say it casually, work it into the conversation. I doubt anyone would even bat an eyelid."

Bea thought for a moment, her forehead creasing with concentration, and then spoke. "Maybe you're onto something there."

"I could help, if you like."

Bea laughed. "*How?*"

"By linguistic subtlety. Although, if you ask for my help, the others will know by the end of the day. Maybe even the end of dinner."

"Christ."

"Are you ready?" Coco asked. Bea gulped. She rubbed Bea's arm, her eyes softening. "They'll be fine and, even if they're not, I definitely will be. It doesn't have to be now, but why not now? It's as good a time as any."

"Thanks, yeah..." Bea stopped mid-stride, deep in thought. Coco, a step or two ahead of her, turned on the spot and watched patiently as Bea contemplated the biggest decision of her life, as she considered revealing the truth she had tried for years to hide.

Finally, a few long moments later, she frowned and blinked hard as she exhaled, before shaking out her hands and jumping on the balls of her feet, psyching herself up, her heart in genuine danger of beating too hard and breaking through her skin and whacking Coco in the face, cartoon style.

"Okay, let's do this. If not now, when?"

Coco squealed with excitement and hugged her. They walked to dinner with purpose and sat down next to the others, Bea's new group of friends. They sat, with weary faces, listening to Conrad jabber on.

"So then I smashed the last goal right into the top right corner and won the match. It was like the end of a movie, you know? My hair flowing in the breeze, everyone calling my name *Conrad, Conrad, Conrad...*"

"Hey." Harrison smiled as he kissed Coco's cheek. "Hi, Bea."

"Thank God you've arrived. I thought I was going to die of boredom listening to Mr Hockey King here." Ella yawned as she spooned some peas and gestured her elbow towards Conrad's beaming face.

Conrad raised his knife and fork in the air in a nostalgic re-enactment. "That's what they were chanting! *Conrad is our King!*" he said.

"Oh, will you give it a rest?" Harrison grinned. "It was a great goal. I *saw* it, but they're not going to buy the film rights for it, and Domnhall Gleeson is not going to play you," Harrison jibed, grinning even more broadly at Conrad's affronted expression.

"He would be honoured to play me. I'm way better looking than him."

"Oh but he's so sweet in that film we watched the other day… what's it called?" Coco asked, stepping on Bea's foot under the table.

"Uh- About Time?" Bea replied.

"Oh, yeah. Isn't he the *perfect* guy in that? Super sweet, eloquent, just *delightful*, right?"

She offered some wide eyes in Bea's direction, who sighed. *This is such a lame idea,* Bea thought, already wondering why she ever agreed to this. She gritted her teeth, ready for the onslaught of stupidity.

"Yeah, but so is Rachel McAdams. She's beautiful, so cute in it," Bea added, rather honestly, her face feeling flush, her heart racing so fast it was about to cause a stir at Ascot.

"Yeah, I have such a girl crush on her!" Ella said.

Coco rolled her eyes. "I hate that. It's like the ultimate 'no homo'. It's like you're saying, *'Oh my gosh they're so attractive but like, I'm not a lesbian, god forbid*!'. You either fancy someone, or you don't."

"Well, it was alright when Bea said she liked her!" Ella was indignant, shocked at Coco's berating. Bea took a deep breath and prepared herself. *Time to rip off the plaster.*

"I didn't say I had a 'girl crush'. It's more that I have a crush, just, like, an ordinary crush."

"Oh, right." Ella's cheeks pinked, and Coco winked at her meaningfully, as she simultaneously squeezed Bea's hand under the table.

"Can you pass the mustard?" Conrad asked, unfazed. Bea frowned and placed it in front of him heavily.

"I have a crush on her because I like girls," Bea said, glaring at him, her irritation making her forget her nerves.

"Yeah, I got that. But that doesn't add any mustard to my chicken, does it?"

"Yeah, but guys, I like girls because I'm gay, like, a lesbian. *Gay.*"

"Do you want to say 'gay' one more time, Bea? I'm not sure you were clear enough," Harrison chuckled.

"Maybe you should spell it with your carrots, just to be sure," Conrad added, his white teeth shining through his grin.

"So, what, you all just don't care?"

"Sure, it's great that you told us but... weren't you already out? I already thought you were gay," Conrad said, frowning.

"No, I wasn't- I'm- This is a *big* moment, guys. I've been panicking about it for years and this payoff is definitely not worth it."

Conrad gave an exasperated groan before composing himself and sitting upright. "Okay, we're sorry. Tell us again, Bea. We'll rewind," he said.

Trying not to laugh, Bea said again, "Guys... I'm gay."

On cue, Conrad shouted loudly, "WHAT?" and his empty plate fell to the floor with a crash as he jumped up in mock hysteria. Bea hid her face.

"S*it down*," she whispered. The whole hall turned to stare. The remaining three were in hysterics, almost falling on the floor with laughter.

"Sorry, everybody. Just had some *very* surprising news. Continue," Conrad announced as he sat down, grinning again.

"You are such a piece of shit."

"You wanted drama, sweetheart, you got it."

"Well," Coco began between giggles. "I'm still proud of you. It took guts, even if they, you know, don't exactly *care* at all. It still took a lot of courage to say that. It's a big step. We all love you and respect you for doing that."

"Yeah, of course. I didn't think it needed to be said, but nothing has changed. You're still the coolest one out of all of us." Harrison offered a genuine smile in her direction.

Conrad stood up and moved towards Bea, wrapping his arms around her shoulders and squeezing her tight.

"You're our super-hot lesbian princess, and we'd probably kick you out of our club if you were anything less," he said.

Before she knew it, all four of them had huddled around her in a group hug that there was nowhere near enough space for. "Thanks guys," said Bea. "Now, can you stop being so nice to me? I don't think I could handle any more affection today."

"Yeah, I think that's the kindest we've ever been to each other, like, *ever*," Conrad added and they laughed.

"So what's next? Are you going out with anyone? Are you looking to? Are there any other gay girls in Lainsbury?" Ella asked.

"Ooh, now maybe you can talk to Genevieve and…" Coco began, before Conrad interrupted her, stricken at this piece of information.

"Wait a second! This is *real* news! You like Genevieve? *Really?* Of all the girls you could pick you choose *Genevieve?"* His eyes scanned the dining hall to find her face.

"Jesus, Conrad, don't stare at her. She's my ex. She ended things this summer when I didn't want to tell everyone about us, and Coco wants us to get back together. But she won't even talk to me, and now this is out and I'm really thinking about it I don't really want to open old wounds. I feel like pining after her again isn't going to make things easier."

"Good for you. I mean, *Genevieve?* Ugh. You could do a lot better. Bea, you're a real nine and two thirds," Conrad went on.

"Hey, now!" Bea scolded.

"She's right, you're being rude. Although… I mean, he does sort of have a point, you weren't exactly an even match," Coco reasoned.

"She's fun, and kind, and one of the smartest people in our year. It was me that was reaching."

Conrad snorted in derision as Harrison offered a disbelieving, pitying grimace.

"Yeah, but that *fringe*," Ella gasped, and the others cackled, four witches sat around a cauldron.

"Oh, screw you all," Bea sulked as they all continued to bash Genevieve, pretending that she actually disliked the normality of her group of friends talking shit about her ex.

"Wait, is this why you stopped talking to Georgiana and Maggie too?" Ella asked.

Bea nodded. "Gen must have told them I'd done something bad to her," she said. "They didn't know we were together."

"That was shit of her." Conrad shook his head, glaring unashamedly at the table Bea's three ex-friends were sat at.

Coco's eyes widened. "If Harrison and I broke up, would you guys run off with him?" she asked.

"Course not," Bea said immediately. Ella and Conrad both avoided her gaze. Coco folded her arms and stared at them both.

"Obviously I'd take your side," Ella laughed, offering an apologetic glance at Harrison, who smiled down at his plate.

"Uh…" Conrad said, panicked, looking between them both.

"It's okay," Coco said. "Harrison can have you. He needs *someone,* I suppose." She grinned at Harrison.

"Alright. I get custody of Conrad but I'm *not* giving up the timeshare or the air miles," Harrison said, and nudged Coco's ribs gently.

Coco's eyes narrowed. "Give me the Bentley and I'll allow it."

"Deal." He laughed, shaking her hand before kissing her.

***

Bea Skyped her parents a couple of weeks later, after she prepared a speech, and had enough time to practice it for a few hours in front of the mirror. She told them. It was awkward, she had to text them the classic line, the *I have something to tell you.* But logging in and listening to the annoying call tone, it felt almost freeing. No matter what happened, she wasn't alone. Knowing that Coco and Ella were across the hall, ready to hear her summary of the conversation she was about to have, it made things slightly easier for her. She drew in a breath as both her parents appeared on screen, well, her Mum and half of her Dad, just his shoulder, cheek and eyebrow.

"Hey, guys."

"Bea, tell us your news! Have you had an award?" Her mum was beaming.

"Uh, no. I haven't."

Her papa's eyes narrowed. "You're not in trouble are you, Beatrice? Because we didn't raise you to go around giving teachers a hard time and…"

"I'm gay." She blurted it out, the words escaped her, as though they jumped from her throat themselves and slapped her parents across the face. That was how mum and papa looked, too, as though they had been slapped.

Silence.

More silence.

"Mum? Papa?"

"*Wow,*" her mum said, open-mouthed.

"Are you angry? Upset?"

"I'm *so* mad you told us when we couldn't hug you in person, but I'm glad you've said it. Congratulations, Bea. It must have been tough waiting all this time to finally tell us."

"Thanks, I- wait, you *knew*?"

"Something told me that Genevieve was more than a close friend." Her mum's eyes glittered with pride and tears.

Papa still looked shocked. "I- well, I didn't know *that*. If I had, she definitely wouldn't have stayed in your room, you sneak! But I…" He exhaled slowly, pulling off his steamed glasses and cleaning them on the hem of his shirt before daring to look back into the computer screen at Bea's face, frowning with anxiety. "I'm so proud of you, Beatrice, and that is not dependant on whether you fall in love with a man or a woman, that is absolutely inconsequential to how much I adore you. I love you today as I did yesterday, and as I will tomorrow."

"I love you guys." Bea wiped her tears with her sleeves as her mum touched her face on the computer screen, stifling a sob herself.

"Don't you *dare* cry, Beatrice Amari Evans. You'll make me…" Her shoulders shook as the tears flowed onto her dress.

Papa placed his arms around her, turning to the camera seriously. "I still expect you to find a respectable partner though, a doctor or a lawyer," he said. "And you have enough colour in your hair for one person, I don't want to see another blue or bloody pink head in this house, yours is bad enough."

Bea's mum gently hit his arm as he smiled, and Bea rolled her eyes, failing to hide her grin.

"Alright then," Bea said.

"We'll visit this weekend. I need to see you in person, make sure you're free on Saturday."

"I will, Mum. I can't wait to see you."

"So, have you been punished this week because of that dreadful piercing in your nose?" her papa asked, spurring a completely normal conversation, as though she hadn't just opened up her heart to them. She spoke to them for a while, talking about school and the town gossip she was missing out on, the same conversation she had most weeks with her parents. She was proud of them, they were old-fashioned, but surprised her with how open minded they had been.

Ella and Coco grinned when she told them about it, as the three of them sat, cross-legged, on Coco's bed.

"So, that's it! You've told everyone you need to tell," Ella said excitedly. "It must feel like such a weight off your shoulders."

"It does." Bea checked the time on her phone. "But I've been out for three hours. I'm sure not everyone is going to be as cool as my family and you guys."

"I bet some people will be shit. But you have everyone that matters on your side, right?"

"That's the most important part, yeah…" She shook out her blue ponytail before running her hand over her cheek and adding, thoughtfully. "Jesus, I can't believe I've done it."

"I'm so proud of you." Coco placed her hand on Bea's. Her eyes gleamed in the dim glow from the fairy lights, and because of the pride shining from Coco's face, Bea felt it in herself.

Chapter Six

Before she knew her, Bea always saw Coco as a typical Queen Bee, and she and Gen laughed about her. They laughed at the way she flounced around, the long words she used but seemed childish in her mouth, like she didn't know what they meant.

Although, of course, Coco did. Bea blamed herself for that assumption. Beautiful girls are always underestimated. Gen laughed at the way Ella followed Coco around like a silkily groomed spaniel, like a loyal pet, and as did Harrison for that matter, her two lapdogs. And then there was *Conrad fucking Huntingdon-Peakes*, forever the joker, always something to say, even when he shouldn't say it, especially when he shouldn't say it. Gen always made clear that she hated him with a passion. He was everything Gen detested: vapid, all bravado and pomp. Bea suspected there was more hidden beneath the surface, that his jokes masked some insecurity, or maybe even some good-naturedness, but then again most days he made her doubt this, leaving her sure he was just an ass, nothing more.

She learned quickly that there was more than met the eye to the most enviable kids in school. There was more to them than flashy Instagram posts and loud laughs. They posted the good times they had together, because they did have good times, they laughed loudly because they were all funny. They were smart, Bea already knew that. She was in their classes after all, and Conrad especially never shut up in them. But the thing was, it was hard to deny that he knew his stuff, that he talked sense. He was wild at times, coming at points from strange angles, but he had those points, he understood things. And Harrison and Ella were the two best pupils in the school, and that was a fact, not an assumption. They were the shining lights.

And Coco was, well, Coco. She excelled at what she wanted to, and she had a way with words, everyone knew that. Her stupid, superficial blog was essential reading for anyone at Lainsbury, her tweets iconic. She was going far, and it was so painfully obvious that it was difficult to *not* be jealous of her.

But she was more than carefully crafted words on a screen, or maybe not so carefully after all, they always seemed to come so easy to her. She was a person, and a remarkable one at that. In a sea of teens who were clueless about ideas such as empathy and compassion, Coco was an expert in these fields. Coco was kind, in a meddlesome, sometimes obnoxious way, but with a good heart, and she was, on occasion, surprisingly grounded. But above all she was, no matter what, always surprising.

Coco quickly became the quirkiest person Bea had ever met, from her extraordinary mind, and her comical parents, to her never-ending stories. She was truly unique. She was unique in the way she always mispronounced words deliberately because they 'sound better that way', and in the way she simultaneously obsessed over the Kardashians and Russian literature.

For months, Bea was surprised by similar admissions, everything had to be a particular way for Coco to be happy, like the way she always had to sit on the inside desk during lessons for some reason, or how she refused to wear heels, no matter how pretty they were or how tall they made her. She deemed them *oppressive devices made to cripple women into submission*, after which, Ella had added, "She's never been able to walk in them, not even two-inchers."

"I'm not injuring myself because of some arbitrary ideal of tallness. It's ridiculous," Coco argued.

"They were actually invented to correct your posture, to make your legs look thinner and arse more shapely," Bea added.

"My legs are fine, and my arse is already shapely." Coco

said, and shrugged.

"If you say so yourself." Ella was taken aback at Coco's self-praise.

"Well, I don't see any harm in enjoying the way I look, but there *is* harm in me twisting my ankle in ridiculous devices that claim to be shoes but don't actually allow you to walk anywhere."

"It must be so nice being you," Ella said, laughing at her.

Coco's confidence was infectious, her compliments reserved not only for herself but for everyone she held dear.

Before long, Bea felt a protection surrounding her from being around people who actually cared. It really started the day she came out, but she felt it again on the day she was invited to Miami, when Coco had come to the common room at the end of Year 12 all excited.

"Guys! I have some wonderful, fantastic news!" Without waiting for any response, and without even taking a breath, she flopped on the sofa and went on. "So the Actual Housewives are doing a Miami special. I know that show is stupid, but Mum feels guilty about spending so much time filming, so I managed to get her to agree to us all staying at our house in Miami, all five of us!"

"What, so we're all going to Miami for the summer?" Conrad asked, as the others whooped.

"For like, a month, I was thinking. The house is right on the beach too. It's going to be perfect."

The casual inclusion of Bea meant more than Coco could ever know. It was the perfect way to celebrate finishing their exams. Coco was constantly yelling about how many days they had left to go, like an obnoxious talking calendar.

There was a palpable excitement in the air that hung over them even as they revised. They were geared up to have the holiday of their lives. They arrived at Miami just three days after they finished their last AS exam.

Harrison was at home at once, having visited twice before and being comfortable with Coco's family.

"Harrison!" Coco's mother shrieked as he opened the door, and he hugged her.

Coco rolled her eyes. "You'd think I was the pool boy. Mum, this is Conrad, and this is Bea," she told her as her mum shrieked.

"Come in, come in! Call me Harriet!"

Harriet hugged Ella, and then took a step back to admire her from a distance. "Ella," she said. "You grow more beautiful every time I see you, you're positively *radiant.*"

Harriet then moved onto Bea and extended her arms, scrutinising her closely.

Bea felt awkward. She cleared her throat.

"My word, dear. You are gorgeous!" Harriet said.

Bea laughed and muttered '*thanks*'.

"As are you!" Harriet pushed Conrad next to Bea. They exchanged quizzical glances.

Conrad raised a thick eyebrow as Harriet stood back to examine the effect.

"Kids," she said to Coco, Ella, and Harrison. "Aren't they gorgeous together? Honestly you two, if you're not a couple, it's a crime."

They caught each other's eyes and laughed hard.

"What did I say? They would, honestly, I can't think of any reason why."

"Save your breath, Mum. Bea's not into boys, and even if she was, she'd avoid Conrad like the plague."

Harriet was now laughing too. "Well, I can't imagine why, he's such a handsome young man," she said.

"*I'm* aware of that, but because of my good looks Coco seems to have gotten it into her head that I'm a bit of a scoundrel, actually," Conrad said, a crooked smile commanding his face.

"That's because you are," Harrison interjected.

Harriet laughed a familiar cackle that reminded Bea of Coco's. "Oh, you're all so bad. It's so fabulous to have you here, let me take you to your rooms." She grabbed Bea's massive suitcase and wandered up the stairs with it in her hand as though it was nothing more than a handbag. "Follow me!"

Coco's house was a six bedroom palace with outstanding

ocean views, and all their rooms were beautiful, crisp, white paradises. Coco's was decorated to her taste, with old posters for movies she loved as a kid surveying her from the wall, alongside pictures of old teen heartthrobs from films a few years old now, their chiselled faces watching them inquisitively. It was a haven of scented candles and fairy lights, of fussy pillows, soon to be covered in heaps of designer clothes thrown unceremoniously onto the floor and her desk chair. It was strange to see such a messy, personal space, in a house that otherwise felt like a hotel; so clean, so welcoming, yet so generic.

"Now, Ella, dear, this can be your room, with an en-suite just for you," Harriet said. "There's a towel and toiletries on the bed." She extended an arm and presented the room with a flourish.

"Oh, this is wonderful!" Ella exclaimed as she dropped her bags on the bed.

"Okay, so, Bea, you'll be next door. The bathroom is right next to you, you'll have to share it with the boys, I'm afraid. Although, I suppose you could share with Ella if you'd prefer."

"That's not a problem! This is lovely, thank you," Bea assured her, keen to make no trouble.

"Now, boys, you'll be in the twin room opposite. Although, Conrad, I'm expecting you'll have it all to yourself knowing these two." She gestured towards Coco and Harrison and raised her eyebrows.

"Honestly, if he wasn't so lovely I'd have banished him from the house by now, the amount of times I've caught them sneaking around. I gave up in the end, they're uncontrollable."

She put her arms around Harrison's shoulders, standing on her tiptoes to do so, and shook her head in a mock chastising. He squeezed her with one arm in response, smiling cheekily.

"So that's that, and I'm sure you want some time to explore!" She turned to Coco. "I'm off for the day filming, there's lots of food in the fridge, just heat it up later on, and *behave,* okay?" She kissed Coco on the cheek and flounced down the stairs, out of sight.

"Yeah, so, Conrad, you can just push those beds together now, he's not sleeping there. Other than that, she's right, let's head to the beach!" She squealed the last word excitedly, running off, followed impatiently by Harrison into her bedroom so that they could get changed.

The first two weeks went by in a daze of sunny days and drunken nights. Their evenings seeped into a routine of drinking on the beach, too often resulting in the four of them stood outside locked bathroom doors telling Coco to let them in as she was sicking-up rum based cocktails into a toilet after an argument with Harrison, usually over him making an inappropriate and far too detailed comment to the others after a few beers.

"If Harrison's being an arsehole, just let us in, we'll lock him outside instead!" Ella shouted before whispering her apologies to Harrison, who smiled and call her a dick before rolling his eyes and pleading with Coco to stop with the dramatics. They occasionally went along with Harriet, and even once or twice with Harvey, Coco's pompous and usually absent father, to meals out at fancy restaurants or on trips to the theatre. Harriet loved spending time getting to know them, and Bea couldn't help but like her.

They watched a few episodes of the Actual Housewives at school before the summer to get them in the spirit for their holiday. Coco had vehemently protested, and spent most of the evening hid behind a pillow or kissing Harrison, but Conrad, Ella and Bea watched, wide-eyed as the drama unfurled over the series, shocked at Harriet's brutal nature, at the arguments she found herself having, at the catty remarks that seemed so at home on her full, usually red, lips. Ella had told them that Harriet was nothing like this character she played on the TV, but Bea was still shocked at how different she was. In person, Harriet was unfathomably happy and bubbly, had such a genuine interest in all their lives, that Coco's apathy towards her seemed almost cruel.

But then they were invited to be a part of the show and

Bea had a glimpse at the business minded Harriet, one which was substantially different from the woman they had encountered up to that day. It was during the second week of their holiday, after they were all sufficiently bronzed and achieved that relaxed, holiday glow, Harriet approached them tentatively at breakfast one morning.

"What are you guys up to on Saturday? If you're free, we're holding a garden party here, for the show, and the other girls' children will be here. They're all around your age, and we need some of the kids there, so it'd help us out a lot of you could get involved."

"Why do you need us there?" Coco asked, her eyes narrow and suspicious.

"Because it's meant to be a celebration of Rosie's birthday, and our kids are supposed to know each other."

"Rosie is awful, and I'm pretty sure her birthday is in March," Coco huffed and crossed her arms.

"It won't air until then. Come on, Coco, help me out. You won't have anything to say, you just have to wander around in the background. Fans know what my daughter looks like, you've been in it before, please, just do this for me."

"I told you, Mum, I didn't want to be on that show! What if I want to be a lawyer? Or an accountant? It might be held against me that I'm involved in something like this."

"I remind you that this is my *job* you're disrespecting. Anyway, you wouldn't be in the shot for longer than a couple of seconds. It'll be fun, there'll be food and drinks and games, it'll be a fabulous day." Harriet said. Her eyes narrowed, and her lips thinned as she considered her daughter with a look of such severity that even Coco relented, although she spent the few days leading up to it in a fearsome temper, and she and Harriet barely exchanged four words to each other before the day of the party was upon them.

They all put on their best outfits, which were approved by Harriet before they left, but things were still tense between her and Coco.

Coco walked into her kitchen in her long skirt, with a leg slit, and lacy floral pattern bodysuit, looking like some sort of overgrown flower fairy queen in a fantasy film, and Harriet eyed her thoughtfully.

"What?" Coco asked.

"It's just- oh, it doesn't matter."

"Well, come on. Spit it out."

"Alright, it's a bit *tight*, darling."

"Oh really?" Coco said through gritted teeth. "And *where* is it a bit tight?"

"Well on your stomach, and your bum." At this, Conrad leaned backwards in an exaggerated attempt at sneaking a peak at Coco's voluptuous assets, and Harrison slapped his arm, giving him an exasperated warning look.

"So?" Coco asked abruptly, and Harriet looked panicked.

"What do you mean?" she asked slowly, tentatively. She was walking through a minefield, tiptoeing to avoid the explosions that were waiting to be set off.

"Well, so what? So you can see that I actually have a belly, I do have one, I'm not ashamed of it. I'm asking *so what*?"

Bea and Ella glanced at each other worriedly, as Coco and Harriet stood amongst them. Coco was red in the face, matching her outfit.

"Well, I mean, girls of your shape don't usually…"

That was it. Coco took a deep breath, and launched into a speech she was obviously planning for some time, cutting Harriet off at her last few words.

"Wear clothes? I look fantastic, mother, and I don't need your go-ahead to feel that way. *You* might have felt the need to starve yourself in consistently creative ways over the years, offering a brilliant example to your young daughter, by the way, but that cycle stops with me. I'm wearing this, and I'm going to feel great in it and I won't apologise for that. Maybe you should focus on the numbers next to my A-Level grades more than my clothes labels. I don't recall you ever taking much of an interest in them."

Coco was breathing heavy, staring her mother down, who shook her head and frowned.

"You're right. I'm sorry."

"I know," Coco said, her arms folded, but Harriet launched

upon her and hugged her tight.

"I'm sorry, okay?" Harriet said, staring intently into Coco's face. "Have a fun night, you guys. Don't get into too much mischief."

Coco nodded once and led them all into the garden. They found a corner on the far end of the lawn with wicker sofas adorned with pretty, intricate pillows that weren't there the day before, and a new colourful rug that felt soft under their bare feet once they took off their sandals and sat down. There was a good view of the patio from those seats, and were occasionally in the camera shot, but were far enough away to be out of focus most the time.

"Avoid everyone, basically," Coco warned them, sipping her flavoured cider and eying the women sat around the long table with malice.

"Yeah, these people are terrible," Ella joined in, laughing. "The amount of times I've been recommended a plastic surgeon is unreal."

"Tell me about it. They all love telling me their favourite diets and handing out their personal trainer's details, telling me I'd make a great model if I lost a couple of pounds, only a couple, mind," Coco said, snorting with laughter. "I tell them I'm happy being more a Marilyn than a Kate Moss, and that if Kate thought nothing tasted as good as skinny feels, she's obviously never had a KFC. I'm sorry to subject you guys to this. Not all of the kids are terrible, though," She offered an apologetic grimace as she looked up at Harrison from under his protective arm.

Bea was always astounded by Coco when she was like this. They were teenagers, they were *meant* to be insecure, but Coco just missed that memo. She didn't buy into it, she was happy, in her dubious size twelve clothes that clung to her body, her curves that were definitely there, she owned it, and it didn't stop her from being effortlessly gorgeous, in fact, it enhanced it. Some people are meant to be skinny, but Coco wouldn't be the same, she would lose some of her glamour if she lost weight. It was almost like her curves, her 'extra few pounds', the softness to her edges, were what made her so striking, so unmissable. Her clothes clung to her in a way that they wouldn't otherwise. Even in the kind of environment created and built upon insecurity, she managed to exclude herself from that narrative, and to stand up to everyone in such a way was admirable, Bea knew that she wouldn't have been able to do that.

The sun dimmed in the sky as the Actual Housewives ladies grew louder and more obnoxious with every sip of wine, as did Bea and her friends, on the alcohol Harriet allowed them to drink as long as they promised not to tell their parents, and Bea was sure to leave out this part of the story when she told her Mum and Papa about her holiday. They managed to have a decent time, being silly and talking for a while as the then familiar sensation of haziness in the evening heat overcame them. And a little while into the festivities, a group of teenagers made their way towards the corner in which they found themselves so at home.

"Coco!" the tallest boy shouted in glee as she stood up and hugged him. "Gorgeous as ever, I see," he said as he picked her up and spun her around. Harrison raised his eyebrows.

"Guys," Coco began, giggling, her mood suddenly lifted. "This is Brad. He's Marsha's son, and he isn't too terrible, at least not all the time."

Brad grinned at them, his smile fading as his face found Harrison's less-than-impressed expression.

"Oh, and here's Rosie, Brad's cousin. Happy fake birthday, Rosie!" She offered a chuckle that a tall, slender girl with dark hair and a deadpan expression didn't return. "Uh, this is James, boy Charlie, and girl Charlie." Coco indicated towards the others, a short guy with curly, mousy hair and a dimpled chin, a bulky guy who obviously played some sort of sport, Bea suspected American football or possibly rugby, and a girl with long blonde hair and soft doe-eyes that radiated something resembling innocence, or maybe it was just stupidity. Bea tried to reserve her judgement for later.

"Guys, these are my school friends! You've met Ella."

"Jeez, you've changed!" James exclaimed, eyeing Ella shrewdly, and she blushed whilst waving from behind Conrad.

"This is my Harrison," Coco exclaimed in a dreamy voice, leaning over to place a long, slender arm around Harrison's broad shoulders. The boys nodded their acknowledgement to Harrison's sarcastic smile, whilst girl Charlie twirled her hair and Rosie looked bored, as though no one here was worth her time.

"This is Conrad," Coco went on, and Rosie looked up and smiled at him, before going back to examining her manicure.

"And this is Bea," Rosie sniffed whilst the boys expressed overly friendly greetings. Girl Charlie said a quick 'Hi' before whispering to Rosie behind her hand. Bea wondered how long she would have to hang out with them, and decided that if it was longer than an hour or two, she was going to suddenly come down with some imaginary illness.

"I think the drink throwing is due any minute. You're going to want to get out of the splash zone. Why don't we go to the beach? We'll get a bonfire going," Brad suggested, eyeing a woman sat at the table who had the same strong jaw and blue eyes as he did. She was shouting in a loud roar that carried across the vast garden.

"Sure. I'll raid the liquor cabinet and we'll head down."

"Sounds like a plan, diva," Brad grinned.

"I'll go with you," Harrison demanded, and Bea, Ella and Conrad exchanged significant looks, smirking.

"One hell of a girl, isn't she?" Brad said, watching Coco walking back into the house, enjoying the view.

"Harrison thinks so," Conrad said coolly.

"Well, I hope he does," Brad said, smiling, unabashed.

"Ella, how've you been?" James asked, sitting down in Coco's spot, opposite Ella.

"I'm good. Still getting caught up in these shenanigans."

"Tell me about it. I just wanted a quiet holiday at the beach." James rolled his eyes but still smiled, staring back at Ella, as though he never saw anything quite like her. "I was wishing I was back in Maine when I heard you were here with Coco again."

"How are you doing, Bea, is it?" Boy Charlie asked.

"Yeah, *Bea*, really? As in, like, the bug?" Rosie chimed in, avoiding Girl Charlie's gaze.

"As in, like, Beatrice," Bea grinned. The others chuckled, except Rosie and girl Charlie. "And I'm fine, thank you," she added, answering Charlie, but still staring Rosie down.

Coco then returned with Harrison. Both of them red in the face and breathing heavily, and holding hands a little too tight. They each carried a bag of bottles and snacks.

They headed to the beach and before long there was a roaring fire to toast marshmallows in.

They laughed and chatted, James especially to Ella, Brad to Coco and Harrison, Rosie and Girl Charlie to each other, and only to each other.

Boy Charlie feebly attempted to talk to Bea and Conrad, with little luck. "So, Bea, where are you from?" he began. Bad start.

"Bristol. And you?"

"Oh, I've been a valley boy all my life."

"Nice."

"I mean, where are you originally from, though?" Boy Charlie went on, blissfully unaware of how close he was to facing a full Bea Evans lecture.

Bea pretended to misunderstand him, frowning in fake confusion. "Uh- Bristol? Oh, well my Dad is from Cardiff, so I guess I might have a slight Welsh twang."

"Oh, right. So your mom is from…"

"Bristol, yeah. All her life."

Conrad grinned at him, sensing the potential danger Charlie was oblivious to.

"But I mean, where do they originally come from?" Charlie asked.

"Oh, well *their* parents obviously came from warring African tribes, who wore nothing but animal skins, and spoke in a dialect that wasn't heard in the western world until 1972."

When his eyes widened, she laughed maliciously. "My parents are British," Bea said. "Always have been. *Their* parents were Zimbabwean, that's why I'm black, if that's what you're wondering."

They were silent with each other after that, both sipping their beer quickly.

An hour in, they had drunk a fair amount, enough for the now familiar sensation of drunkenness to cloud their better judgement

"Why don't we play spin the bottle?" James said, pulling out an empty wine bottle.

"Sure, and then we can braid each other's hair and tell all our secrets," Girl Charlie protested.

"Sounds ideal," Conrad said as Charlie rolled her eyes and Rosie actually giggled. They sat in a circle, and James placed the bottle on top of a box of cheese crackers, spinning it. It landed on Girl Charlie.

"Come on Charl, give me a snog," he said in a terrible imitation of an English accent, crawling over to the spot in which she sat, and she kissed him on the cheek, then spun the bottle herself. It landed on Rosie, who she kissed hard on the mouth.

Ella, Bea and Conrad raised their eyebrows.

They could hear snippets of Coco, Harrison and Brad's conversation through the pauses in the game.

"The last time I saw you, you had brown hair. It looks good blonde."

"Oh I've been blonde for years, I had no idea it's been so long."

"Yeah, I noticed from your selfies, it's definitely been a long time."

"Oh so you're the guy who always comments on Coco's posts! I thought you were a cousin."

Rosie spun the bottle. It landed on Brad.

"Oh hell no," they said at the same time.

"Hey, I'm catching up with Coco. You guys carry on."

"We can't really play anyway," Coco added, pointing between her and Harrison, and they shuffled outside the circle a little, James closed the gap, edging closer to Conrad.

"While we're negotiating, I'm not kissing any guys," Bea said.

"Why?" Rosie asked.

"Because I don't kiss guys." Bea answered bluntly.

Conrad chuckled as Rosie's face showed comprehension a few seconds later and said, "Oh."

"Plus, I have a girlfriend, so I really shouldn't kiss anyone."

"But you could just get kissed on the cheek, right?" Ella asked, her eyes pleading Bea not to leave her.

"Well, uh," Bea sighed. "Yeah, I guess." She offered Ella a significant look that said plainly, *you owe me for this*.

"So you guys are pretty serious then?"

"Yeah I can't believe it's been two and a half years *we've been together, Coco, right?"*

"I know. It feels like we've been together forever and also for no time at all. It's strange, right?"

"Alright then. I go again," Rosie announced. The bottle landed on Conrad. She smiled as his eyes widened. Crawling towards him, she straddled his lap, kissing him fiercely. When Conrad emerged a little while later, his face was bright red.

"You're blushing!" Girl Charlie announced to the party.

"It's just sunburn," he said and grinned, and winked at Rosie.

"It's that ginger skin!" Harrison shouted into the circle, clearly uninterested in the conversation being had by Coco and Brad, and they laughed.

Conrad spun the bottle. It landed on Ella.

He approached her slowly, allowing the panic to rise within her as he crawled across the circle, his eyes locked with hers.

As he placed a hand to Ella's cheek and leaned in, she stood up.

"No, nope. Too weird," Ella said.

Rosie rolled her eyes, but Conrad just stared up at her, in a comical position, leaning facing, her knees, his lips pursed. He then stood too, placing a hand on Ella's arm.

"It's just a game, El. You don't have to." The hurt he felt, in Bea's opinion, was pretty ill-disguised. The colour rose in his cheeks again, an angrier, patchier red this time. He smiled at her. His face was close to hers. "Don't worry, it's a stupid game," he whispered.

"I- I know. Sorry."

He gave her one last supportive smile, before sitting back down, still keeping an eye on her weary face. She watched Conrad stare at Ella, and wondered if she missed something going on between them. Then again, she suspected that neither of them were in the headspace for anything serious, not after everything they had both been through.

"You can kiss me again, Conrad," Rosie said.

Conrad shrugged and made his way over to Rosie. He kissed her intently.

"I guess that game's over then," James said, laughing and leaning in close to Ella. "You alright, gorgeous? I'm sorry if it made things weird."

Ella shook her head. "No, it's cool. Me and Conrad, we're just…. friends, you know? It's awkward," she said. She eyed Conrad as he snogged Rosie with an almost indecent enthusiasm. Girl Charlie sat next to them, staring at her phone, determined to look anywhere else.

"Hey, Coco, remember when we were young and played this with all the others? We did a lot of making out that summer…"

"Oh my gosh, yeah. We were, what, thirteen?"

"I was fifteen, I think. You said I was a great kisser, if I remember correctly."

"Has something happened between you guys?" James asked Ella.

Ella turned her head. Bea thought she might be wondering if Conrad was listening, and Bea was sure he was. He kissed Rosie but was facing Ella's direction. "No, nothing's happened, I just…" Ella began.

And then the circle was broken. Harrison stood up and started shouting, causing everyone to either turn or stand instinctively. "Alright, mate. You've been trying it on all night, that's enough, leave it, now."

"Hey, she's a friend!" Brad yelled a little too quickly, his scowl doing little to disguise the lie he was telling.

"Oh, she's not though, is she?" Conrad added. *"One hell of a girl, isn't she*? You know exactly what you're doing."

Coco stood by, saying nothing, apparently rooted to the spot in shock at how quickly the situation escalated. But her silence was a significant one. Harrison, with Conrad at his side, his fists clenched, and Brad stood squared up to another, waiting for Coco to pick a side.

When it was obvious that Coco was not going to intervene, Brad held up his hands. "Alright, we'll go, he said. "I'll see you again, Coco, maybe…"

Coco did not meet his gaze as he walked off in the dusk, towards Coco's garden. It wasn't very far, and he walked fast in his anger and embarrassment. It wasn't long before he reached Coco's garden gate.

"It wasn't really a party anyway," James muttered as he gathered his things.

"What was that?" Conrad asked, his voice loud. He smiled a horrible, cocky, mirthless smile that Bea hoped she would never be on the receiving end of.

"I said it wasn't exactly a rager, was it? I had better plans for tonight than entertaining the unhappy couple, this asshole, the frigid bitch, and the dyke," James said, pointing at each one of them, to emphasise each insult. With each word, Bea felt the anger rise from the pit of her stomach until it reached her throat, bitter and harsh.

"The fuck did you call me?" Bea shouted. Conrad held her back with one pasty, muscular arm, his face set, his jaw twitching in fury.

"I called you a miserable, fucking, dyke," James said, edging closer to her.

"Apologise," Conrad said baldly, his voice raised.

"Or what?" James now stood face to face with Conrad, geared up to fight.

"Or you're a snivelling shitstain. Apologise, now."

James stared him in the eye, stubbornly, resolutely. He wasn't budging.

"Fuck it," Conrad said, ensuring he spat as he enunciated, and released Bea. He punched James in the face, as Bea kneed him in the crotch, causing him to hit the floor. Rosie and girl Charlie screamed as the remaining two boys, Charlie and Harrison, squared up, hurling insults at each other.

James stood, holding his nose, which was spurting blood, and walked away swearing viciously, the others in his wake, concern on their faces as they staggered behind him.

Shaking out his fist, Conrad walked towards the side entrance of the house, as his four friends hurried in his direction.

"Sorry about ruining your night, mate. That Rosie was well into you," Harrison said, embarrassed, as he gained speed to catch up with Conrad.

"They were douchebags, the lot of them. I mean, really, Coco, I've never met a more fucked up group of people." Conrad was still breathing heavily as he whirled around to stare angrily into Coco's mortified expression.

"I know," Coco wailed. "I've known Brad for ages. We've been friends since we were kids, his friends are weird, but I used to get on well with him."

"Yeah, because he fancied you. He always has," Ella said.

"Thank you!" Harrison said loudly.

"No, because he's really easy to talk to," Coco said coldly, eyeing Ella with displeasure.

"Uh- *because* he fancies you," Ella scoffed and rolled he eyes. "I remember that summer he was on about, all those years ago. I remember you being quick to play spin the bottle then." The boys laughed but neither of the girls did. Bea could sense something big happening under the surface, ripples showing that were about to become a whirlpool.

"Go on, boys," Coco said to Conrad and Harrison before whispering waspishly to Ella "What has gotten into you?"

Bea stood by, shuffling her feet. She wasn't dismissed like the boys, but she still felt that this was too private for her to hear. Nevertheless, neither of them mentioned her presence, so she stayed, staring at a spot a couple of metres away from them to the ocean, all the while hearing their muted argument. It felt strange to Bea that such an ugly occurrence should happen in such a beautiful setting. The low sun was golden in the pink sky, reflected in the clear, calm waves of the ocean, still barely visible to them through the flowers at the end of Coco's garden. Between this and their pretty dresses and the boys' smart, colourful shirts, the night should have been more of a fairy-tale than the nightmare it became.

"Those guys were complete arseholes, Coco. You just liked them because they liked you. If they worship the ground you walk on, they're okay according to you, right? You heard the things they said about us, about Bea, you must have known they were like that, but you still got them to hang out with us, for your ego boost. Now Bea's had to deal with that, Conrad's been in a fight and Harrison's upset and you're saying what great mates you are with the guy responsible for all of it. I mean, for Christ sake."

"Don't. Don't you dare. Not tonight."

"Don't what?" Ella asked defensively, her chin in the air.

"Don't get mad at me for no real reason again, please. I can't take it, not today."

"For no real reason? Coco-"

"Just stop!" Coco screamed. It was as though her voice had been carried away by the breeze, as when she spoke again, she was quiet. "Can you please stop projecting, just for tonight? I can't take it right now, I can't take *you* right now."

"I'm sorry. I can't just switch 'me' off. And stop pretending this is all in my head! Do you have any idea what it's like to be your friend, to wander in your shadow as you walk around oblivious to everyone in your life, oblivious to shit caused by the stunts you pull, to be the prude, the ugly friend everyone puts up with so they can hang out with you? It's *hard*, Coco." Tears swam in Ella's eyes as her hair blew wildly around her in the breeze.

Coco pulled her into a fierce hug, sniffling herself. "No-one thinks that. No one would look at you and think those things. And the way people think about you shouldn't indicate how you feel about yourself. It starts with you," she said.

"No, I'm not you, Coco. I'm not going to have boys falling at my feet. It's going to be a lifetime of awkward conversations with *awful* guys like that loser just now. I'm left with the James' of the world and always will be. You have no idea how it feels to be me, when you're so...you. You can't tell me not to base my confidence on what boys think of me when that's your entire life."

Coco's face was red, an unattractive mix of alcohol, sunburn, and raw emotion. Her curly hair flew around her as her body seemed to explode in pure frustration at what Ella was saying.

"You have no idea what you're talking about! You *need* to snap out of this, I hate to say it, but you're acting crazy. Really fucking crazy. You push away those who like you, and only see those who don't. You're focusing on the negatives, on all these bad thoughts on all this... horrible bullshit. It's going to drive you nuts,. Please."

She grabbed Ella by the shoulders and stared into her eyes. They were stood close, it was an intimate moment, the kind of moment that doesn't happen between two people without a history. With a pang, it reminded Bea that the only person she ever felt that bond with was Gen. But India's face appeared in Bea's subconscious vision, and she blinked Gen away. That was over. A different era, a different time.

"I'm saying this because it would be for your own good, no judgement, no embarrassment, but... you need help. You do. You need to discuss this with someone who knows how to deal with it, because I'm trying, El, I'm trying, but I can't deal with you when you're like this. Please, talk to someone, someone qualified, because this is scaring me. You're not doing so well. You're not." Coco said softly, her voice quaking, matching her body. She seemed to tremble with emotion, as though Ella's issues were an earthquake to Coco's equilibrium, that seeing Ella in this way spiralled all of Coco's senses. That even though Ella was a separate person, her health affected Coco too, and in that moment, they were almost one entity, albeit one at war with itself.

When Ella spoke again, it was in the muted, dignified voice of someone desperately trying to seem calm.

"I'm fine. I'm just trying to come to terms with being the

friend that always has to follow you. It's just hard."

"What you're seeing isn't about me, it's not my fault. I'm doing nothing wrong, and I won't let you tell me that I am. I'm here for you, but you're- you're sick. You're just so different, even in just a few months, you're- I used to look up to you so much, you were always so confident in yourself, but I'm seeing you now and I don't recognise you. You can't even talk to a boy you like. Earlier, with Conrad…"

"I don't like Conrad."

"You do. I can see it. Bea can see it. You like him, and he knows it. And he likes you too. You'd be good together. But you can't even talk to him to take it to another level."

"Have you stopped to think," Ella snarled, "that this isn't about me being a pathetic little girl?"

"That's not what I'm saying."

"I just don't want to make a dick of myself again, okay? I'm getting sick of that."

"You won't make a dick of yourself."

"How could you know? Just because he'd drop everything for a night with you doesn't mean the same for me, okay?"

"He wouldn't drop everything for me, Ella. He doesn't like me, he likes you," Coco said, her voice thick with emotion. Ella scoffed, and Coco ignored her. "He might have, once, a long time ago, but I *know* for a fact that he doesn't like me now, actually."

Ella blinked at her, curiosity taking over the anger. They were standing close, facing each other, Ella took an aggressive step towards Coco, and her foot was threateningly pointing in Coco's direction. Coco was leaning away from her. It was ironic that Ella was feeling attacked but Coco was the one who truly felt in danger. Ella was an animal, backed into a corner and ready to fight her way out, and she had the upper hand, especially after what Coco had just said.

Did that mean what I think it means? Bea thought.

They were silent for a couple of seconds when Coco spoke again. "And at any rate, you wouldn't look a fool," she began quickly, skating past what she said. She continued, in a strange, business-like tone that was unlike her usual dreamy, sentimental voice. She sounded detached, but in an all-too-deliberate manner. "We both know he's sensitive. You wouldn't like him if you didn't know he had that side to him. If he didn't feel that you would be right together, he wouldn't leave it feeling awkward, and he definitely wouldn't joke about it. He's better than that, give him credit."

Ella nodded. "He's a good guy," she said. "But I- God, I don't even think I fancy him. He's my friend, a close friend. It was just weird earlier, that's all. We can drop it now."

Coco sighed and shook her head. "Okay, El, whatever. I'm going to bed. But I think we need to talk a little more soon, when we're not drunk and when you're feeling better, okay?"

Ella walked away fast, shaking her head, muttering, "I'm fine."

"She's really not well," Coco said quietly, a deep frown wrinkling her forehead, her lips tight with concern.

"There's a lot going on in her head, and none of it is coming out of her mouth," Bea agreed.

Coco shivered in the cold breeze. Bea put an arm around her. "Are you okay?" she asked.

Coco nodded as they began walking towards the house again. She nuzzled her head to below Bea's chin, and Bea felt the flyaway hairs tickle her face.

"Nothing bad happened to me. I'm sorry they were so awful to you. The last time I saw them, they weren't like this…at least, I don't think they were…" Coco's voice was tired and sad.

"You're not responsible for them. It's cool, I'm fine. I don't think James' balls are though, or his nose."

Coco giggled. "My God," she said. "He deserved it, didn't he?"

"Oh, yeah."

Coco paused before stepping away slightly and tentatively looking Bea in the eyes. "Wasn't Conrad so…*gallant*, though? Standing up for you like that? He's about the only decent boy left that I know."

"Hey!" Bea said. "You told me that there were plenty of wonderful boys at Lainsbury!"

"Yeah, well, maybe my perspective has changed." She looked down at her feet at that, frowning at them as though her sandals themselves were offending her. "But still, it was brave of him."

"Yeah... Hey, Coco?"

"Yeah?" she responded airily, only half-listening.

"Are you alright, you and Harrison?"

"Hmm?" Coco asked, apparently distracted and feigning temporary deafness.

They reached the house and she sped up the steps, making a show of yawning. Conrad was lounging on the giant sofa in the open plan living space, his hand covered with a bag of frozen peas.

"Harrison's gone to your room. Think he wants to talk," he told Coco, and she nodded and left to find him, undoubtedly to face yet another argument tonight. Bea felt a pang for her, for trying to bring everyone on holiday so they could have a good time, and having to answer to everyone.

Ella sat on the opposite side of the sofa to Conrad, they were both watching crappy TV.

"I'm going to head up, too," Bea said. "It's been a long day."

"Alright, night Bea." Ella waved.

"Night, dear," Conrad called, winking.

"Hey, Con, thanks. For earlier, you know."

"Any time." He grinned at her. Bea turned into the hallway and climbed the stairs, wondering if they would ever work it out between them.

Chapter Seven

The view was so different, three months later, as Bea sat in the cafeteria that seemed so grey in comparison to the memories she had, where life was golden, rose tinted. It felt odd to Bea, to think that there was a time when her life was made up of sunsets on the beach, of larks in the school grounds, of sneaking around with India and of running around secretly with Gen, when today was so tense.

Ella, Harrison and Conrad sat before her, all paler than usual with dark eyes, the strain of worry and lack of sleep taking its toll. No one looked at each other, no one saying a word. Since Coco had vanished, it seemed that talking should be a priority, but that was exactly what they all seemed to be avoiding.

They constantly asked each other about Coco's secrets, and racked their brains about her, but failed to cast a light onto their own, onto their own things that they should say, but won't. Bea stared at Ella, who was staring off into the distance once again, zoned out, frightened.

It was weird not having Coco sat opposite her. It felt like they were having a normal meal which Coco was late to, as though she would flounce in and dramatically announce her arrival at any minute. A part of Bea also knew that wasn't going to happen and that, even if she did, things wouldn't be the same.

The surface under which they held all hidden things was fragile, and was about to break, Bea could feel it. It was like watching the sea quickly pull back before the tsunami, it was only a matter of time before things were ruined, whether Coco returned or not, and not even she could predict the extent to which this was true, and how bad things might get.

She stared at Coco's seat, imagining her sitting in it as she did three times a day, and Bea remembered the most startling greeting Coco had ever offered her. The day Coco had set her and India up, another huge occasion which had happened because of Coco's meddling. But Bea didn't mind so much about that in the end, since Coco's meddling always seemed to end in something good.

One day at lunch, in early March of Year 11, Coco flung her tray upon the table with enthusiasm, and sat opposite Bea. "So, India Parker-Holmes," she said, without a *hello*.

"Yeah?" Bea recognised the name, an extremely pretty girl from a couple of years above. Coco blinked at her in confusion, as though disbelieving that Bea could take so long to catch on.

"Well, she's really hot, right?"

"I'll say!" Conrad chimed in, but Coco raised a manicured hand to silence him.

"Yeah, I guess… but I don't know her," Bea said.

Coco batted this comment away with her hand. "Oh, she knows you. I was chatting to her just now, after netball, and she was saying how she was so ready to go on a date again after her girlfriend didn't work out, and her rebound boyfriend, Christopher Granger, cheated on her like three months ago. So I told her that my friend Bea is wanting to go out with someone new, and she asked me if that's the girl with the great hair and a nose ring that I hang around with. So I said yeah, and she said she was keen! I set up a coffee date for you both during the trip to town on Saturday. 11:30, the coffee shop on High Street. I'll text you her number, don't be late."

Bea and the others sat with their mouths open. It was a bold move of Coco, to do that without Bea's go ahead.

Bea went through a lot of emotions in a very short timeframe, from anger, at her sheer cheek of asking someone out on her behalf, to a resolve that Coco did it for her best interests, that she wanted her to be happy and that was really kind of sweet. Also, India was, undoubtedly, objectively, ridiculously, hot, and her fancying Bea was a massive deal, but then there was the panic. Oh, God, the panic. A date with India, with legs that never ended and the cheekbones of a Grecian statue. Bea would have to impress her, would have to keep her interested, and how the hell could she do that when she was so devastatingly goddamn normal?

"What if I said I didn't fancy her?"

"Oh, come on, it's India Parker-Holmes. Everyone fancies her."

"She's got a point there," Conrad said, grinning.

"You really are a force of nature," Harrison told Coco, staring at her dreamily.

"But what do I do? How the hell am I going to talk to her? I've never spoken to her! And isn't she a lot older?"

Coco reluctantly removed her lips from Harrison's and rolled her eyes at Bea. "She is in the year above, yes, but let's not get hysterical. I mean *really*," she said, and glared at Bea reproachfully. "And don't give me those big, scared eyes. You aren't exactly innocence personified. India is hardly going to corrupt you. Plus listen to this. You both love reading, she wants to go to Uni to study English Lit, she loves all the same music, that weird alternative stuff…" She swatted Bea's question away with her hand. "You've got a lot in common, trust me."

Bea frowned. "But what if I make a massive tit of myself?"

"You won't make a massive tit of yourself. Just try and be an actual human being, unlike Ella when I set her up with Angus Stanstead last year and she was dreadfully hard work."

"He was an arsehole!" Ella protested. "You only set me up with him because he was Harrison's friend, and it's a good thing nothing happened because they had that massive falling out."

"He is a dick, to be fair," Harrison reasoned.

"Well, whatever, you could have tried harder," Coco scolded her.

As Ella opened her mouth to argue, Conrad spoke "Hey, why don't you ever set me up with people?"

Coco stared at him for a moment, considering him. "Because I wouldn't want to put anybody through that," she said.

"I'm a catch, Coco, help find me a girl!"

"Yes, but you're difficult too. I'm yet to figure you out like that…" She paused, considering him and smirking before adding, "Go out with Ella. She won't speak. You won't stop. It could work." Her eyes gleamed with laughter.

"Oh, please," Ella squealed as Conrad put his arms around her shoulders.

They began arguing, Ella about how it would be a terrible idea, Conrad saying the positives of them getting together ('You'll enjoy constant laughs', 'you get to show that you're involved with this face, to the world', 'I have a Netflix account', 'I've been told I'm an excellent kisser'), whilst Harrison and Coco resumed kissing.

Bea sat in between them, staring from one pair to the other, and finally shouted, "Can we get back to my problem?!"

But Bea didn't need to worry. She and India hit it off straight away, spending the whole day together on their first date, with no awkward silences. They were immediately drawn to each other, and it was all down to Coco.

Chapter Eight

Without the presence of any real, active company, Bea
ventured onto her social media. As she stared at the
numerous posts of Coco's face on her newsfeed, she felt for
the first time, the huge void that was made by Coco's
absence, the change in the dynamic, the quietness. Bea had
so much to be thankful for, thanks to Coco, and in that
moment Bea prayed she was okay, begged the universe to
bring her home, since any alternative was too awful to even
consider.

She made her way through the Instagram clothing shops,
the ads and the travel blogs, until she scrolled past a picture
that she almost missed. India and her friends were walking
along a vast beach, a golden sunset causing her to be only a
silhouette, and one of five at that, but Bea would recognise
her anywhere.

IndiaPH *These are the days I'll remember forever.*
GraingerChrissy_ *Photo cred to yours truly <3*
IndiaPH *Of course, my dear ;)*

Bea frowned. She checked her messages, the last time
India messaged her was two days ago. This wasn't the first
time this had happened, either. India was away travelling
since the start of the summer, before Bea went to Miami, and
she had always been terrible at texting. Bea treasured the
short conversations they were able to have, but it was getting
ridiculous. She sent a message on the day Coco had gone
missing, and India responded within minutes, for once.

*OMG!! I hope she turns up soon, bet she will. Miss you
lots, Beabea*

*Me too. It's probably nothing, but something doesn't sit
right. Miss you too*

It'll be fine! Hope you're okay?
I'm okay, I guess, just worried. How is Peru?!

India didn't reply. Bea was panicked, she needed India's support, but she was evidently too busy walking along beaches with her friends and being cute online with her ex-boyfriend to call her. Bea sat, staring at the picture, her face hot, thinking that perhaps it was time things were to end, or maybe not, was she in a bad mental state at that moment? Would she change her mind when Coco returned and they could all relax? Her stomach churned. She could use Coco's help right now. She would know what to do, she always did.

"I'm going to the library, I've got homework," Conrad said out of the blue, causing Bea to jump. His voice was hoarse from lack of use, perhaps the first time he could ever say that.

"I'll come with you. We could do philosophy?" Ella piped up.

"Sure." He shrugged, and they picked up their bags and left Bea and Harrison alone, looking at each other.

"I'm going to visit Hardy, see if they've found anything."

"Harrison, I'm sure she would have found us if…"

"I need to check," he said, a finality to his tone that meant there was no point in arguing. Bea shrugged at him and waved as he left.

She sat alone, cradling a cup of tea, listening to the rain that had just began hitting the windows. She thought about Coco, about where she could possibly be, about the endless bad possibilities, and what would happen if she returned to the mess that had been created in her absence. She felt a tear roll down her cheek, when Genevieve sidled onto the bench and sat next to her.

"Hi," Gen said sheepishly. Her voice sounded the same. Not that she hadn't heard her speak in the corridors or in class, only it was never directly to her, of course. Now that she spoke to her once again, it was with the same warmth that Bea always felt she reserved just for her.

"Uh- Hi." Bea turned her head towards her, feeling the blood hammering its way through her body, her heart banging on the wall of her chest.

"I know this is weird, but I was watching you, and then I saw- I thought I'd come over and check on you. How are you doing?" When Bea didn't answer immediately, she added, "I'm here for you, Bea, alright? I'm so, so sorry about your friend, that you're going through this." The earnestness of Gen's expression was surreal, as if she really cared.

"Really?"

"I know you're devastated about her. You must be, I've never seen you cry before now."

"Of course you have, when we finished..."

"Not a tear from you. I resented that. I was there, sobbing, and you looked... bored." Bea was surprised to find that Gen was smiling.

"I cried about it for months! You must have known that, tell me you knew that."

"I knew you must have been pretty upset, but I also sort of thought you would have changed your mind, you know? I waited for a while, waited fantasising that you would come running up one day and kiss me in this cafeteria and we'd give everyone who was staring the middle finger. Then you came out so I thought you actually might... but then India..."

"Yeah. India." Bea heard the lack of enthusiasm in her voice and wanted to kick herself for it. Gen, of all people, didn't need to know about her and India's problems.

It was as if Gen could read her thoughts. There was a palpable silence, a bubble, waiting to be popped. One of those silences that no one seems to make a sound in, not even to breathe, where everyone involved is just waiting for it to end, for what needs to be said, to be said.

"Does she make you happy?" Gen finally asked. Bea raised her eyes from her lap to Gen's face, and she melted into the familiarity of those stony grey eyes, round and magnified slightly by her thick glasses. "I mean, obviously, she's bloody hot but, like, is she *fun*? Fun enough to wait for?"

"You know, she's barely messaged me? Like I know she's away and busy but she has enough internet to post three

Instagram posts a day, and she just doesn't message me to see how I'm doing? If Coco's been found yet? Or even just to check in? That's pretty crazy, right?"

"I don't think I'm qualified to give you an unbiased opinion but she seems like a total sack of shit girlfriend, to be completely honest."

Bea chuckled. Their words were a strange break in the quiet of the since emptied dining hall. It seemed that since Gen had sat next to her, everyone in the room left without Bea noticing until that moment, when she noticed how quiet it had become, how Gen's words reverberated off the walls. It was far too easy for them to talk like this, for the spell of eternal silence to have been broken by one single tear so immediately, so effectively. It felt like sinking into an old chair that had moulded itself to Bea's frame. Comfortable, familiar.

"I know you're trying to be funny but, Christ, you're right."

"In times like this you need people around you who want to listen and want to help. You need someone who knows that you're not coping, even when you insist that you are. I'm not saying it's me but…"

Bea was shocked to find her lips meeting Gen's, but the familiar taste of Carmex made her pull her closer.

"Bea…"

"I know. I'm sorry."

"This isn't the time for ultimatums, I know it isn't, but I'm happy to be your *friend*, for now, yeah? Until things become a little…clearer? I'll be here for you, but I'm not going to help you cheat on India because you're in a messed up place, you understand?" Gen said, her voice stern and clear. Bea placed her head on Gen's shoulders. It was like nothing changed.

Gen made an exasperated sound and as she sighed, she appeared to deflate like a balloon running out of helium.

"I've missed you, Gen. I've missed just, you being around, your presence, you know? My life feels weird without you in it."

To this, Gen offered a wry smile. "I thought your busy life with the beautiful people kept you too preoccupied for thoughts of me," she said.

"They're all great, actually. Complicated but, well Coco's one of the best people I've ever met, and I know we used to make fun of her all the time, right? But she's such a good friend, such a good person... Shit, I hope she's alright. If something's happened."

"I'm sure it'll work itself out, I'm sure. I'm sorry I made fun of them, if they're such good friends to you. It's pretty rich coming from me."

"It's been a long time since we last talked," Bea said, and nodded.

"Yeah..." Gen gave Bea a searching look, drinking in her features as though she was seeing her again for the first time. "You're different."

"I am?"

"Yeah, you're a lot more sure of who you are. It's nice."

"It's funny. You haven't changed at all. I feel like we're fifteen again, sat in your bedroom, watching Netflix."

Gen offered a mischievous grin and elbowed her in the ribs. "Easy, girl." She giggled. "I know what you mean, though."

Bea nodded. They sat in a contemplative silence for a while, that thought hanging over them in a dense and threatening cloud.

Bea placed a hand gently on Gen's forearm, which was resting on the table. "Let's be friends again," she said.

Gen sighed, and her small smile didn't quite reach her eyes, which were shining and wistful. "I'm not sure we can be."

"Why?"

"Well, look at us, one conversation and we're already back where we were. We aren't 'just friends'. We're more than that, or significantly less. We can't be somewhere in the middle."

"Maybe being back where we were isn't a *bad* thing," Bea said, not knowing where this confidence, this boldness was coming from. Maybe it was Gen being back, and feeling like she always did. That was always her main concern, that she would risk everything for nothing to ever really feel quite right again, but here, on this bench, talking about all of this, she felt that they were still on the same wavelength, still connected, somehow, even after all this time. Or maybe it was the image of India and that arsehole ex of hers, Chris, frolicking around on some beach somewhere. Or maybe it was just that she wanted to feel like she was back in time, when things were easier.

Gen frowned. "You're in no state to decide that today." She stood, avoiding Bea's gaze. "Give me a knock if you need me, Bea. I mean that, but I need to go, for now."

Gen walked away hastily. Her sensible shoes clunked on the wood and left a ringing in Bea's ears. She sat for a few minutes, taking in what just happened. This reunion made her realise that things needed to end with India, and that all of this was only because Coco was still missing, anyway. She woke up yesterday morning in a state of serene complacency, happy with her friends, with her girlfriend. But in just a day it felt as though everything was thrown into question, tilted on its axis, wonky. *She* felt wonky.

Bea decided that she needed to distract herself for a while, watching Netflix in her room or reading or painting, or anything that wasn't sitting around thinking about Coco. She walked towards her dorm slowly, playing a supercut in her head of her and Gen's relationship, of just the good times, the bad times long forgotten. She walked past her own door, and found herself instead knocking on Gen's, not even knowing if she would be in there, but something told her she would be.

When she opened her door, Gen's eyes were red. She had been crying.

"I need you today," Bea said, with no time for pleasantries. "You said to knock, and, well…"

Gen pulled Bea close by her shirt, slamming the door behind her, and then pushed Bea against it. Stood on her tiptoes, Gen kissed her hard on the mouth, her hands resting on her waist. Bea ran her hands through her hair and down her back. All of a sudden she was transported, fifteen again, she travelled through time and was discovering herself again, discovering Gen, discovering who she was and who they were together. Bea felt electric as long lost feelings stirred within her.

She broke apart to open the collar of Gen's school shirt to allow her to kiss her neck. Bea lead Gen to her own bed, and gently pulled her glasses off her face and laid them on her bedside table, remembering the fight they had had years ago when she accidentally broke Gen's favourite pair in her enthusiasm, and decided that she didn't want to ruin the moment by doing it again. Bea climbed upon the bed and lay on top of her, kissing her again. She began unbuttoning Gen's shirt when she stiffened.

"Bea, wait…"

Breathing heavily, Bea tore her eyes away from Gen's body and focused on her face. Gen reached to her bedside table and placed her glasses hastily back onto her nose. Her eyes were magnified again and she was back to her normal bookish self. That's what Bea fancied so much about her when they were together; the fact that she could go from librarian chic by day, to a completely different person by night.

"What's wrong?"

"You… have a girlfriend." Gen was annoyed as she buttoned her shirt. Bea sensed that it was at herself more than at her. Gen lost control, and Bea knew that if it was anything she hated, it was that.

Bea lay next to her on the bed. Staring at the ceiling as Gen sat up beside her, her knees under her chin, reading Bea's expression.

"I do, yeah," Bea said, and closed her eyes tightly. "*Fuck*, I never thought I could cheat."

Gen smirked. "You didn't get that far, I didn't let you," she said.

"But if you didn't—"

"We can't think about what would have happened if I didn't stop you."

"Why?"

"Because if I think about that for so much as a second, I'll have no choice but to carry on. It's been a long time, Bea."

Bea propped herself onto one elbow, and ran her free hand down Gen's prickly calf. Gen closed her eyes and rolled her neck before drawing a deep breath.

"We can't."

"I'll finish with India. I've been meaning to anyway."

"It's not just that, though. The timing's all wrong. I don't want to be something you regret."

Bea sat up next to her, placing an arm around her shoulders. "I get it, we should wait until this is sorted out, but when it is, can we talk then? Maybe… more than talk?"

Gen smiled another smile that did not reach her eyes. "We can 'more than talk' until the sun comes up when that happens, but what if it never does? What if the timing is never right? What if we made the right choice ending this?"

"But what about today?"

"Yeah, maybe…" Her voice was vague, dreamy, the voice of someone thinking a million thoughts at once.

"I should go, then. Maybe we'll talk soon."

Gen smiled again and waved goodbye, still thinking deeply. She called out as Bea's hand grabbed the door handle. "Bea?"

"Mhm?"

"There's something else."

Bea turned towards her. Gen was fiddling with her shirt sleeve, unable to look her in the eye. She was quiet for a long time, until Bea cleared her throat.

"The tweets sent to Coco, they were me."

"What?"

"You know the ones - telling her to stick to what she knows, calling her dumb. They were me."

Bea's heart was racing, her hand shaking. "You told her to kill herself?" she said.

"No! I wrote a lot of them, but not that one. I think I sort of opened the troll floodgates and it got out of hand. I'm really sorry."

"They upset her. More than you could know."

"I wasn't thinking. I would always see you with them, always having so much fun, always joking and laughing. I missed you and I was lonely and miserable and I took it out on her. I'm an idiot. A vicious little idiot. I should never have done it and I regret it so much now, but I can't take it back and- ugh." She wiped her eyes impatiently. "I'm such a fucking idiot."

"You're not an idiot. You're a lot of things, but not stupid." Bea surprised herself at how angry she suddenly was, at herself, mainly, making this mistake when she knew better. "Maybe you're right. Maybe today isn't the right day to make any big decisions. I'll message you, if you've bothered to unblock me yet, that is."

"I'm so sorry."

"Yeah."

The door clicked as Bea stepped out into the grey corridor, and walked towards her room. When she passed Coco's door, she saw that it was wide open.

PART THREE
CONRAD

Chapter Nine

Conrad left Bea and Harrison in the dining hall and shuffled slowly to the library with Ella. His head was still ringing from the thoughts that were haunting him since the morning before. *Where the hell is she? Why hasn't she told us anything?*

He was tired, so damn tired, fuelled on nervous energy and strong coffee, not from the non-existent sleep he had last night. He wasn't able to sit still, and the assembly that morning made it feel so much more real. He spent the morning online, frowning as people who didn't know her shared Coco's photo with stupid captions calling her a 'friend', when they probably couldn't even recall her middle name. They meant well, he reasoned, but he wished they didn't seem to revel in the drama. It sent a wave of revulsion rippling through him every time he saw some faker feign their concern.

He missed her. She was the glue that held them together and they just didn't work as a unit without her there. She was the shoulder to cry on, the ear to tell all to, the lips to kiss, if you were Harrison.

Grateful for Ella's solemn silence, he thought about the year they all became friends, year nine, the year everything changed. They were placed in different classes that September, ranked again on their academic ability, and placed in more fitting classes based on how clever, or not, they were. The top set was a small one, consisting of up to only ten students, depending on the subject. Harrison, Coco, Ella, and Conrad were placed in the same class for most of their subjects, and were sometimes seated next to each other.

They were fourteen. It was the age of pimples and growth

spurts, of first kisses and general awkwardness. All the boys fancied Coco, of course they did, she was gorgeous. They said a lot about her in locker rooms and behind closed doors but, for most of them, their behaviour in front of her was vastly different, most of them daring to barely speak two words to her, for fear of speaking the wrong ones. That was, of course, because they were so focused on her being 'theirs', that they forgot to actually get to know her. There was no uncertainty about it, she was an intimidating girl. Loud, devilishly smart, and beautiful, she seemed to leave everyone in her presence shivering in her shadow.

But then Conrad started talking to her. They were sat together for maths class, and whilst Harrison scribbled down equations on the opposite side of the room, sat next to Genevieve, thanks to obligatory seating plans, Conrad and Coco scratched their heads and giggled uncontrollably at the hopelessness of their situation. They laughed at the look on Mr Davies' face when he realised how little they knew, when he explained things to them for the second time in an exasperated tone (*slower please, sir,* Coco would say) before running and making his second coffee of the lesson. They helped each other through their problem sets, sat behind the cramped desks that forced them to sit elbow to elbow, that forced him to breathe in her coconutty smell, and for her hair to tickle his arm, sending shivers down his spine. He would flirt with her every lesson, theatrically enforcing his side of the desk.

"Coco, you're on my side again!" he declared dramatically, and she giggled. "It's unbelievable that someone as tiny as you can take up so much room." He gently moved her arm to 'her' side, always wishing it would venture over again, giving him an excuse to touch her once more.

Then he started chatting to her outside maths. She stopped him in the hallways, in the queue at mealtimes, even when they couldn't be bothered to put in any effort during their Monday morning PE class. By Christmas time of that year, he considered her a friend, and the boys all groaned with jealousy when he hung back to chat with Coco between classes. Conrad grinned every time she stopped him in the corridor.

It was the first time he'd ever felt that way about a girl, but what he didn't notice in his blind state of euphoria at thinking he might have a chance with the most magnificent girl ever to have lived, was that his best friend was feeling the same. What he didn't know was that the period after maths class, after he and Coco giggled and flirted, she was made to sit next to Harrison in history. History was Coco's best subject, and the methodical Harrison could never wrap his head around the chaos, around the blood-splattered timeline of the subject. They, too, were pushed into a small corner in that class, as Coco gently explained ways to help Harrison remember the facts he needed to, and he too felt her blonde hair tickle his arm, and that electric reaction running through him, he too noticed the waft of coconut that was always so conspicuous whenever Coco was around. Harrison, too, fell in love with her.

When they returned after Christmas break of that year, Conrad discovered an acne-ridden Harrison pacing his bland dorm room, unpacking his bag in a chaotic, manic fashion. In an uncharacteristically deep conversation on their first night back in January, he clumsily confessed to Conrad exactly what was on his mind.

"I really like a girl, and I need to ask her out, like, as soon as I can, because it's driving me mad."

"Excellent! Who is she?" Conrad asked, excited for his friend.

And then Harrison explained how he barely had the courage to speak to Coco for the first three years at school, but when they were sat next to each other, he could hardly ignore her. He was worried that she thought he'd stared a little too long, but they seemed to laugh a lot, over almost nothing, and she once said that she thought he had a kind face.

A weight fell in Conrad's stomach. "Oh," he said.

"What? What's wrong?" Harrison asked.

"Nothing, I just had no idea, that's great! So when are you going to ask her out?"

"At the dance later," Harrison told him, as though announcing his own execution. The weight in Conrad's stomach increased. He was going to ask Coco out then himself. There was always a welcome back party after the Christmas break, and all the borders put on their best clothes, their sparkliest dresses and sharpest shirts, and made a fuss for it. It was always a good night, the perfect opportunity to ask out a girl you liked, and evidently Harrison had the same idea.

Conrad got ready slowly, all the while thinking about why he was bothering, who he was trying to impress. He sighed as he angrily fumbled at his shirt buttons and knocked on Harrison's door down the hall.

Harrison sat on his bed, with ten minutes to go before the party, his brow furrowed and shining with sweat. "I can't do it," he said, "I can't just go up to her and ask her out. That's madness."

"Jesus Christ," Conrad said, and stared at him. He'd never seen Harrison like this. "Just ask her to dance. I dunno, go from there." He said it simply, bluntly. That was what he planned to do, and he wouldn't have made as much of a performance of doing it, either. But he supposed that Harrison's overreaction was just because he was really into Coco, but then again, so was he. It was unfair, but Harrison was his best mate, he couldn't just swoop in and ruin this for him, or could he? His mind was like a pendulum, swinging between one way and the other.

"What if she says no?" Harrison said, his eyes wide, his face slack with terror.

Conrad sighed a long, drawn out breath. He could dissuade Harrison from doing it, he could let him bottle it, let him mess it all up. He could do it. But could he? Really? *No*, he resolved, *not to Harrison*, not when he seemed even more worked up about her than he was, he couldn't let him down, he couldn't betray him like that.

"But what if she says yes? Mate, you've got to ask her. If

she does this to you, you can't sit by and wait until… someone else… asks her out. Everyone fancies her, *everyone*, yet the only guys she seems to talk to are in this room, so I'd say you have a chance."

He stared at Harrison, and Harrison placed his head in his hands. Conrad realised he probably emphasised the fact that Coco was the object of all the boys' affections perhaps a little too much. He sat next to Harrison on the bed, who raised his head and looked up at Conrad.

"Go for it," Conrad said, emphasising every word.

"I can't just go up to her and ask. She'll laugh in my face."

"Alright, I'll ask her for you. She can laugh in mine instead." A small smile grew upon Conrad's lips despite the disappointment that seemed to sit on his now heavy chest.

"Is that not a bit… pathetic?"

"You're being a bit pathetic!" They laughed as Conrad sprayed some of Harrison's cologne on himself. He opened the door, and held it open for his best friend.

They walked nervously to the party, and found Coco stood in the corner with Ella. They both looked pretty, but Coco radiated that something extra. Her sparkly top drew eyes from across the room, her angelic face kept them there. She watched them come into the party with shrewd, big eyes. Harrison stood rigid in the entrance to the room, looking as though he were about to walk to his doom. His face was pale, green even. Conrad marvelled at his friend's complete inability to hide his feelings, he was always a canvas, emotion splattered across him messily, in a Pollockesque fashion.

"Alright, follow me," Conrad said, his voice overly hearty in his attempt to brace himself for what he was about to do.

Harrison looked alarmed. "We're not going over to them!"

"No, just follow. You'll see." His eyes barely leaving Coco, Conrad guided Harrison to the refreshment table. He poured them a glass of pop.

Harrison, eying him suspiciously, drank quickly. "What now?"

"Coco watched us walk over here. I guarantee she'll be

inexplicably thirsty in a minute or so, and when she does, play along." He felt it unnecessary to tell Harrison that Coco watched him cross the room, not both of them. Nevertheless, Conrad's prediction came true, and quickly enough, they saw Ella and Coco head their way.

"Here we go," Conrad said, a little nervous himself. Setting his cup down, he called out. "Hey girls, fancy a dance?"

Coco and Ella looked at each other, giggling. Ella started towards Harrison, and Coco towards Conrad, but Conrad quickly grabbed a flummoxed Ella's arm, and grinned at her as he spun her to the dancefloor. It was one of those moments that changes the course of your own little history, the butterfly flapping its wings and causing a series of mini hurricanes in the years to come.

Ella pretended as though she assumed nothing, too polite to say anything.

"Don't tread on my feet now," he said, winking.

"Only if you don't tread on mine."

"I'm a prodigy of dance. I don't tread on feet."

"You could have fooled me," Ella said, laughing. She kept stealing glances towards the other couple.

"He really likes her, you know," Conrad said, catching her staring.

Ella blinked in surprise. "He does?"

They stopped dancing, too focused now on watching the others. Coco and Harrison were swaying closely, he was saying something into her ear. She was listening intently. The fairy lights and soppy pop song playing in the far distance made it seem to Conrad as though they were two characters in some cheesy fairy-tale musical, and he half expected Harrison to start belting out some slow sappy acoustic song. He looked at them, the class genius and the queen bee, both so perfect as individuals. He made his peace that would probably mean they would be perfect together.

An astonished look came across Coco's face before she placed a hand upon Harrison's scarlet cheek and kissed him. Conrad knew it was Harrison's first kiss. Ella knew it wasn't Coco's. Ella and Conrad stared at the ground, before raising their heads and somehow managing to smile awkwardly at each other. As the song ended, Harrison and Coco went for a walk in the grounds. As they left, Ella stepped away from Conrad, to find some other friends to talk to and he was left, alone on the dancefloor, feeling that all the girls seemed to scatter around him whenever he was too near.

He made his way over to the football boys, feeling mute amid their incessant gossip about the fact that Harrison Fletcher had managed to run off with a girl, no, not just a girl, *the* girl.

When Coco and Harrison returned to the party they were both radiating happiness, both grinning from ear to ear. Harrison grabbed Conrad and taken him to a quiet corner in the corridor just outside the common room.

"We're going out on Saturday!"

"Yes, mate. Knew you could do it!" Conrad clapped him on the back.

"We kissed. Did you see? Well, we kissed loads actually," Harrison said, grinning.

"Nice one. Well, I think it's safe to say she likes you back then."

"What about you though? Ella's sweet. Did you ask her out?" Harrison asked, beaming so sincerely that Conrad almost forgot his own disappointment.

"Nah, she's nice, but not for me."

"Oh, right. Well, thanks, Con."

"No problem."

That evening, Harrison and Coco went to their beds happier than they could have imagined. Conrad closed the door to his room and exhaled the long sigh that he was suppressing for the entire night. His mind whirred as he tried to sleep, and he was unable to shift from it the image of Coco kissing Harrison in the middle of that godforsaken dancefloor.

Coco was the first girl he truly liked, and now she was dating his best friend. A selfish part of him hoped it wouldn't last, but then he noted that even if they didn't, he still could never go out with her after she'd been with Harrison, when

Harrison liked her so much. He resolved himself to the fact that she would never be his, thinking that, surely, another girl would come along who he liked even more.

The trouble for Conrad and Ella was that Harrison and Coco became quickly glued at the hip, and, wanting to remain close to their best friend, they were forced to hang out with the pair together. This meant they both spent three years wistfully watching on as Harrison and Coco snogged at every opportunity, held hands between lessons, laughed too loudly at each other's worst jokes. They were both constantly reminded of what could have been.

Conrad held the heavy library door open for Ella, and they slunk inside to find a table. They placed their already thick philosophy folders on the table, and Conrad pulled out his notebook.

"So, the cosmological argument… shall we start with the uncaused cause?"

"Sure," Ella said and shrugged. She pulled out that poly pocket, rubbed her tired eyes, and scanned her neatly written notes. "So Aquinas says that everything in the world has a cause, a series of events that leads to one thing happening."

"Yeah, so that means, according to him, that one day there must have been an uncaused cause. Something that was always there, eternally, as a product of its own accord, coming from nothing, and as a result of nothing, A contingent being, which he thinks is God," Conrad continued, nodding. He condensed the notes he already took in the lesson, which were a little jumbled thanks to Hunter's erratic teaching methods, which, during that particular lesson involved him making the entire class watch an irrelevant YouTube video from his favourite skit show.

"Some of the criticisms of this are…" Ella started, her eyes scanning her rounded, neat handwriting, but Conrad didn't hear her as he stared out of the window and someone caught his eye; a tall, blond, sloping boy, sheepishly walking towards somewhere he shouldn't be.

"Wait a minute, why is Harrison going into the girls' dorms?" Conrad interrupted her, after watching him walk across the grass and failing to turn onto the path that led to the boys' building. He and Ella exchanged a worried glance, before wordlessly ramming their folders into their bags and rushing towards B Block. When they got there, they saw Harrison standing outside Coco's room, his hand awkwardly hovering above the handle.

"Think about what you're doing," Conrad said, his voice soft and gentle. "If you rearrange the room, you could make it more difficult to find her. Don't go in, Fletch, it isn't right."

"But we could see something. We could find something and know what it means. We could figure it out sooner than someone who doesn't know her could."

"Harrison…" Ella began tentatively, but he opened the door and walked in.

"Firing Christ," Conrad whispered, rushing in after him. They wedged Coco's door open, not wanting to feel claustrophobic in the atmosphere that was surrounding them, the palpable feeling that this room held secrets of which none of them knew, but were so important that they could suffocate them, trap them at any given moment.

"I- I don't even know where to start," Harrison said, stood in the middle, looking around to the desk at his side, then turning to glance at the unmade bed.

"Me neither," Ella said, her face gleaming white, as though she had been given a great fright. Conrad thought he understood. Stood in that room, it was like they could see a ghost, and he, as well as Ella, knew that the walls encasing them held all the answers. It seemed to Conrad that Ella was questioning whether she actually wanted to know them.

"It's so odd, though," Harrison said for what felt like the three hundredth and sixteenth time, casting a significant look at Ella. "You know everything about her life, El, and she knows everything about yours. You live in your own little bubble, to the point where it's even a bit weird, but none of us have any idea where she could have gone."

"I know," Ella said, dropping her gaze from Harrison, and sharing a second of eye contact with Conrad, before hastily looking at the wall.

Harrison wandered over to Coco's desk and started rifling through the few notebooks and files and papers that were neatly arranged around her laptop. Conrad and Ella held their breath. They knew that they shouldn't be there, that Harrison was out of his mind with worry, and that they should stop him. But they didn't. Harrison sighed and tutted as he turned pages and scraps of paper over and found only homework or random ideas and other things of no consequence. He slumped into her desk chair. Harrison's eyes widened as they passed over Coco's desk. Being too preoccupied with the haphazard papers, he hadn't initially seen what was right in front of him.

Shaking, Harrison's hand stretched towards Coco's lamp. Draped over it, was her H necklace.

"She took it off," he said quietly, in a hollow voice.

"Maybe it was irritating her. Or maybe it's broken," Conrad said. Harrison turned the necklace over in his hand, inspecting the chain closely.

"No... it's not broken." His face was ashen, he looked faint. "She always wore it, even during our worst- she never took it off."

"Let's not jump to conclusions. There's a million reasons she might have taken it o-"

"Was she mad at me, Ella?"

Ella jumped at the sound of her own name. "I don't know. I told you, she didn't tell me."

"She told you everything. Too much." His voice was forceful, his fist whitening as he clung tightly to the necklace.

"She said she didn't know. This might be something Coco didn't want to tell her, or something that wasn't even worth mentioning," said Conrad.

"We didn't tell each other everything. There were things we kept to ourselves. Like you and Conrad, you don't tell each other absolutely everything, do you?" Ella spoke diplomatically, tentatively, like a hostage negotiator.

Harrison looked between them both.

"Sure we do," Conrad said, looking away, feigning interest in Coco's photo wall to his left, but only seeing the flashes of

126

clothes being thrown, of hair flying around playfully, of hushed, eager whispers and tanned, naked bodies, that were coursing through his mind. Harrison shrugged vexatiously and turned back to Coco's desk, picking up her laptop and opening the laptop bag that was beneath it.

Bea appeared in the doorway, frowning upon discovering that it was only them, that Coco hadn't returned. "You shouldn't be in here," she said.

They ignored her. Conrad finally plucked the courage to look Harrison in the face once again, to find his pallor ashen, as white as the paper he held in his hand, as he sank into Coco's desk chair.

"What's that?" he asked. Without looking at him, Harrison cleared his throat and began reading aloud.

"Dear Harrison,

I doubt I will ever send you this letter, but I've written it anyway, to get my head together.

Whatever I say from this point onwards, you should know that I love you like I never imagined I could love anyone. You have made my life a fairy-tale for three years, and for that I am so thankful.

But I know what you did.

You were the perfect boyfriend. You made me feel special. You gave me everything I could have wanted. But you've done something unthinkable, and you've ruined it all.

I know I've been difficult to handle, I know I wear you down, but to want to hurt me so much, to want to cause so much damage in your anger, I don't understand how the Harrison I have been with for three years could do that. I don't understand how you could look me in the eye and so shamelessly profess your love, as always, to me, every day, knowing what you had done.

Or perhaps I do. I don't know. You might have a terrible secret that you're keeping from me, but what you don't know is that there's a huge secret that I'm keeping from you, too.

There's someone else, Harrison, and you know him too.

I've meant to tell you, I promise, but I"

127

He turned the page in his hand and found the back empty. Tears streaked down his face as he frantically shook the laptop bag, as he ripped open her notebooks, as her desk drawers crashed as he yanked them open.

"Where's the other page? Is has to be around here…" he said. The others looked on in shock.

"You have to stop! Listen-" Bea pleaded with him, but he was hysterical, senseless in his horror.

"Fletch, stop it, mate," Conrad reasoned.

"I don't want to hear it, not from you."

"What's that supposed to mean?"

"You know him well also? It's you, isn't it?"

"You *what*?" Conrad was incensed, his face an angry red snarl as he stepped towards Harrison, who stood up.

"Oh come on. You've always had a soft spot for her-"

"Stop it. Think about what you're saying."

"I saw the way you looked at her, heard that way you spoke to her, you loved her, and what? You were shagging her?"

"Don't you fucking dare." Conrad's fists were clenched.

Harrison looked as though he were about to protest and Conrad held up a shaking hand. "I'm telling you, shut it," he warned.

Conrad couldn't believe what he was hearing; that his best friend thought he was running around with Coco, when he spent nearly three years fighting with everything he had, against himself, to avoid doing just that.

"Do you know where she is?"

"Of course I don't," he spat angrily.

"Did anything happen between you lately? Did she love you? Did you love her?"

Conrad's only response was a long, cold glare into Harrison's thunderous face.

"Well?"

His anger turned to sadness as he replied slowly, his head bowed. "No. At least, I don't think so. I mean-" Conrad took a deep breath, squeezing the bridge of his nose with his thumb and forefinger, before squaring up and staring

Harrison in the face. If he was going to do this, he was going to do it properly. "No, I wasn't sneaking around with her. There was a time, a while ago now, when I thought about it a lot, I admit. But I never did, because you're my best mate, I don't think I ever could even if I wanted to do that to you. I can't believe you'd think I would."

Harrison looked ashamed. Still breathing heavily, he placed a large hand on Conrad's shoulder.

"I'm sorry, I-"

"She tried once, though." Conrad blurted it out. He was sick of the secrets he was holding, of the feelings he pushed down for so long. The words seemed to crawl themselves desperately from his throat.

"What?"

"Yeah, it was last year, before Christmas. You know we'd spent a lot of time together, after Mum… One night we were alone, talking, you were revising in the library, and… well, she kissed me. That's why we stopped being so close."

He could remember it as though he was still there. He could feel the heat from the radiator that stood, boiling hot, on the wall next to him, making him sweat. He could almost feel the lumpy common room sofa underneath him, and he could hear Coco's laugh. She had been laughing at something dumb he'd said, a stupid joke that he couldn't remember, but she had stopped suddenly and given him a lingering, thoughtful look. As he had begun to redden under her gaze, she had leaned in and pressed her lips against his. He had kissed her back, only for a minute, albeit a fantastical minute that at that point was perhaps the best minute of his life, before gently pushing her away.

"Coco-"

"Shit…." She continued to give him that look, a look that made him sure she was hearing his thoughts. God, he hoped she couldn't. "I know, Con, I'm so sorry, I-"

"I can't. I can't do that to him." He cut her off, he couldn't let her continue, he was in a precarious enough situation. The less that was said, the better.

"I love him. You know that, right? Like, I know I just did

129

that and it was awful. Not the kiss, obviously…" She giggled nervously. She was babbling. "But I do. I love him so much but sometimes I feel like he doesn't open up to me, I always feel like he has this shell that I just can't crack and I've been trying but he doesn't ever really confide in me, he never tells me his problems, and I know he has them. It's just hard, I worry about him, I worry about what he isn't telling me, and it puts me on edge. And now you're here and you've always been so open and it's so refreshing and new and…" She glanced into Conrad's eyes, pausing mid-sentence, deciding whether she should say what was coming next. "And this is going to be weird, and I shouldn't say it…"

"So don't," he said weakly, softly, although of course he wanted her to. Her face was still so close to his. He knew he should sit further back, but his body would not allow him to do so. He needed to savour the moment, Coco's breath tickling his face, the smell of her perfume lingering between them. He knew he would only be in this position once, dancing with himself, with his head and his morals screaming at him to run away but with everything else, with every impulse he possessed, screaming at him to grab her and never let her go, teetering on the hilt of a double edged sword, of what he wanted most but the worst decision he would ever make.

"I liked you, you know," she said, well aware that his feeble protestations meant nothing. "Before that dance, before the first time Harrison kissed me at that disco, I liked you. And I thought you liked me too, but you pushed Harrison towards me, and it was all so confusing and now it's two years later and I just caught myself wondering what if, you know?"

"Coco, this isn't fair."

"I know. But it's out there now. I actually don't think I have any secrets from you anymore. You're one of my best friends."

Conrad frowned at the hand she tentatively placed on his forearm. He moved his arm away, folding them tightly across his chest. "As far as I'm concerned, this didn't happen, yeah?" he said. "He doesn't have to know about this." He paused, his sharp, shallow breaths the only sound in the almost deserted common room. Coco stared back at him, wide-eyed. The lamp on the table directly behind her gave her a glow, as though she was a dream, a vision, and Conrad was only 90% sure she wasn't either of those things at that moment. He was trying to think clearly after that kiss and it was hard, but the idea of him betraying Harrison like this kept him grounded, kept his head from flying among the stars like it wanted to, kept the victory parade standing by at bay.

"He doesn't have to know because you made a stupid mistake in the heat of the moment and I didn't reciprocate. In comparison to what he feels, and what I know you feel, too, this was nothing, a typo in the long and tooth-achingly-sweet love story that is your time together. This is nothing, I am nothing to that, so we forget about this and move on, yeah?"

She nodded slowly as he stood up. "I'm so sorry," she said.

Conrad nodded and then walked fast to his dorm without looking back.

He paced his room for an hour or so, wondering if he made the wrong decision, if he should throw caution into the wind and be selfish, if he should walk through the pouring rain across the path to her dorm, knock on her window and kiss her as his hair dripped rain onto her nose like this was a romcom and Harrison was just a hurdle between him and the girl he was supposed to be with. But life isn't written by Richard Curtis, it's not a romantic comedy. The reality is somewhere between him and George R R Martin, but without the cool wolves and dragons.

When he checked his phone a while later, he saw from their photos online that Coco and Harrison were together watching a movie in her bed. The decision was made for him. That was fine, easier even. So why did he throw his phone across the room so it smashed his mirror?

When they all met for breakfast the next morning, he and Coco pretended that nothing happened and Ella and Harrison were none the wiser. They had no idea that for the entire day, maybe week, in fact, probably month, all he could think about was Coco's lips on his, Coco saying that she wanted him, and imagining what would have happened if he never exercised that level of restraint.

"But I pushed her away. I told her to stop it, that she loved you. I didn't tell you because it wasn't worth ruining what you have, not for me, when she never really cared about me the way she cared about you. So I told her off a bit, and agreed to put it behind us. I'm sorry I never told you, I just- I didn't know what to do and it seemed like it was for the best."

To his surprise, Harrison hugged him, hard, tightly.

"Oh, for God's sake." Bea ran her hand down her face, shaking her head.

"What?" Conrad whirled towards her, jutting his chin. He felt defensive, wishing that he had only told that to Harrison. Bea's judgement wouldn't make this any easier. But she wasn't looking at him.

Staring Harrison dead in the eyes, Bea continued, her voice venomous, her fists clenched at her sides. "You see, Harrison, that's what a good friend does, it's what a good person does. They turn away when they have the chance to do something wrong. My God, what a mess."

"Bea, don't."

"Don't what?" Conrad asked, his mouth open, staring between them both. He heard Ella retire a small squeak somewhere to his left.

"Tell him, Harrison."

"Tell me what?" he said confrontationally, his eyes darting between them, already preparing to be angry.

Harrison was backed into a corner, the truth was out, or it would be in the next few minutes.

"Harrison…" Ella started weakly, but Harrison shook his head.

"Alright!" he inhaled deeply, looking as though he was about to faint. "They day before Coco went missing, I cheated on her."

Conrad's jaw clenched, his heavy brows knitted together.

The words hung in the air above them for the couple of seconds of pregnant silence as the force of this admission hit Conrad like a runaway train.

"You've got to be fucking joking," he hissed. He couldn't recall ever being this angry with Harrison in his entire life.

Harrison explained it all in excruciating detail. He slumped again onto the chair, speaking into his hands, as the other three leaned in to listen. All the while, with every detail, with every description, with every twist and turn, Conrad tried with all his might to resist the urge to vomit.

"It was a fucking horrible night," Harrison said. Conrad remembered the storm that had taken place a few nights before, the rain lashing against the windows as the thunder roared above them, the whistling and rattling windows illuminated with the flashes of lightning. But that wasn't what Harrison meant.

"We just got back from half term, but Coco stayed at school. She was getting weird with me again, like she was over the summer. She didn't talk to me at all, for the week before and it worried me, I thought I was losing her.

But I get back and she acts like nothing happened, but she doesn't want to be alone with me, and we ended up arguing in her room that night. I don't even know why she got so angry. I only asked her what was wrong, but she got all defensive and she told me to get out of her room, that she didn't want to see me that night so I opened the door and, well, Ella's door was open, and she was stood there. I'm guessing hearing me storm off.

She was just wearing her little dressing gown, and she was telling me that I didn't have to put up with that shit and she came onto me and... and we hooked up. It happened, and it was so good to be with someone else, and I did it because we both wanted it and I- I don't even know why else. We weren't thinking. But I left, and Bea saw me."

"Buttoning up his shirt, yeah. Thinking he was the man," Bea interjected. "He babbled and spluttered at me for a bit before running off but then I went into Ella's room and told her that if she wouldn't tell Coco, I would. The day Coco went missing I was texting the pair of them, telling them to face her and tell her. But then, well, she wasn't there the next morning."

"You cheated on her, with Ella?" Conrad was dumbstruck. Slapped across the face with the impact of the truth that was imparted upon him. Once it sank in, a couple of long moments later, his eyes narrowed, and he whirled to face her.

"What the fuck?"

"Con, I-" Ella spluttered.

Conrad went on as though she hadn't spoken. "Did you always hope I was Harrison? What was I? The next best thing?"

"It wasn't like that."

"Then what the fuck was it like? I give you everything I can, everything, and you go and do that?"

"What do you mean?" Harrison said, his breathing heavy.

"I mean that we've been together. I mean that we started getting together in Miami and now we're taking it slow. Or at least that's what I thought, I didn't realise we were taking it quite so slow that we were going fucking backwards," Conrad seethed, and Bea's hand flung to her mouth.

"I had no idea, you have to know that. If I knew you and Ella…" Harrison began, panicked.

"You wouldn't have cheated on your girlfriend who loves you?" Bea snapped. "You think the wrong thing here is that you slept with your best friends sort of girlfriend? You cheated, Harrison. And from the sounds of it, so did Ella."

Everyone whirled towards Ella, who seemed to shrink beneath their gaze. "I- it just happened," she said lamely. They all scoffed, mocking in their anger, in their exasperation at Ella's inadequate explanation.

"You waited for him to leave her room? You knew he was angry at Coco, and saw an opportunity to spite her and fuck the guy you've always wanted in the process, right? That didn't 'just happen', El. That's called being a goddamn sociopath," Conrad's voice was bitter and uneven with emotion.

Tears ran down Ella's face as she shook her head. "It

134

wasn't like that-"

"It was though, wasn't it?" Harrison added. "You stood there in your tiny dressing gown with nothing on underneath, telling me that you're not like her, that I didn't have to put up with her."

"Enough," Conrad said, staring into Ella's face, which hadn't left his since Harrison started talking, her eyes pleading him to forgive her.

"Why?" he asked. It was all he could say. For the first time, he was almost at a loss for words. This one word was the only one that mattered. He tried to keep his voice even. He tried to stop the emotion from seeping out, but even though it was only one, short word, he couldn't manage it. He frowned at how sad it sounded, at how the pain in his chest and the nausea in his stomach seemed to find itself so unsubtly in this one syllable.

"I don't know," she whispered, furiously shaking her head, her eyebrows furrowed, her face crumpled in disgrace at what she did. She heard it too. "I was angry, so damn angry, all the time at her. I figured I'd go out there so we could talk together, so we could rant about how difficult she was being and get it out, and I wouldn't feel so bitter about her when she hadn't really done anything wrong. I was just so sick of being angry and on my own and finally it felt like Harrison might understand my side of things. But then he was there and he was looking at me in this way and he kissed me and it all happened very fast and-" she started to sob. "I know you don't believe it but it really did just happen."

Conrad looked away. Her tears made it worse somehow. "The police don't know?"

Harrison shook his head. "I can't see how Coco would have known. This can't be anything to do with why she's not here, right?"

"Don't be a fucking idiot. It could be everything to do with where she is right now." Conrad whirled around. Bea should have told someone about this, the police are least, but also him. On top of everything else, he felt left out. "Bea?"

"I saw them, sure, but I wish I'd hadn't," Bea scowled,

crossing her arms. "It's not my secret to tell. This is on them, not me. I thought they'd be sensible enough to tell them, but obviously they're not."

"This is important, guys. You both realise that this could be the reason, right? She might have found out and…"

"And what? Ran away? Killed herself?" Harrison frowned, his voice booming in the solemn, quiet room, and reverberating off Coco's walls.

"Don't say those things, Harrison," Ella said in barely a whisper, but Harrison ignored her, and turned to face Conrad, his face a furious mask of rage.

"Is that really what you think Coco would do? You know that if she found out, everyone would know about it, there would be a massive drama. She'd post on that bloody blog of hers, putting Ella and me in the stocks for everyone to take her side and hurl their thoughts at us online. You know that's how Coco would handle this. Unless she's doing this specifically to worry us- I- I'm not sure what it is that's telling me that, but I don't think she knows."

Harrison gripped the desk for support, his knuckles whitening as he gritted his teeth. Conrad stared in shock. This wasn't the Harrison he knew. This was some gnarled, hardened, twisted version of his soppy best friend, a version that denied all responsibility for his wrongdoings and slept with girls who weren't his girlfriend.

"I'm not sure it is, you know," Bea chimed in. "She's a lot more sensitive than you give her credit for. If she knew about this, everything would have crumbled. I mean, she loved you two more than anything. She loved this group, right here, more than anything, which, if you haven't noticed, has fallen apart because of what you have done. If she knows about this, it's destroyed her, like it's destroyed us as a unit."

"Yeah!" Conrad said, his voice rising to a shout. "You threw a knife in her back, and she's missing because of it. This is *your fault*, Harrison! She was happy, so disgustingly happy with you! And now she's God-knows-where, upset and alone because you couldn't control yourself." He paused for a moment. "You too, El," he added, this time with less enthusiasm. All his anger was aimed at Harrison, but not so much at Ella. If anything, he was just sad at the thought of not being enough for her, of throwing everything he had at someone who didn't want it. "You fucked it. You screwed everything up." Conrad's voice broke. He was distraught, but he didn't feel as weak as he sounded. He was feeling a devastation that was a forest fire, ripping through him without caring much about what it destroyed. It was anger at that moment, not sadness. A desperate, powerful anger.

Harrison stood, squaring up to Conrad, his face red and angry, his nostrils flared. Conrad appreciated just how huge he was in that moment, an absolute bull of a boy, but he wasn't afraid. The way he was feeling at that moment, he hoped Harrison would come at him, would give him an excuse to unleash upon him. He wouldn't even mind if he got punched a few times, a few bruises, a broken nose and a split lip would be nice, a refreshing change from the substantially more painful feeling that was tearing through his insides, constricting his breathing, making it hard to stand, making it hard to think.

But then Harrison relaxed, his shoulders sank and tears filled his eyes, and he looked much smaller.

"You're right," he said quietly. "This is my fault, it's all my fault. She's gone off and we don't know where she is, and it's because of me."

"Yeah, probably," Conrad said, still frowning, still fuming.

Harrison sank onto Coco's bed, his hands covering his face. "Shit," he groaned.

Bea sat next to him, rubbing his arm supportively. Her face wore an odd expression. "But do any of you know who she was, you know…"

They shook their heads.

"I think I have an idea of how to find out," Ella said, as she pulled open Coco's MacBook.

"We shouldn't, El," Bea started.

"No, go on. Do it. If we know him well too, I want to know who it is," Conrad said, his breathing still sharp, still shallow, his face still hot.

They all turned towards Harrison, his ashen face grim as he nodded. "Okay. I want to know, too," he blushed for a moment as he paused. "Her password is CLSlovesHF080116."

Ella raised an eyebrow.

"Hey, it's a strong password!" He said it indignantly and, for a second, they all smirked except Conrad. They were acting as though they were sat at their lunch table on any other day and Harrison and Coco were being embarrassing.

But Conrad couldn't see it that way. He couldn't look at Ella, look at Harrison and bring himself to smile, even momentarily. None of these feelings were going away that quickly. He was still seething, still filled with hot, burning anger that he knew was only going to be fuelled more as they discovered the slimy bastard who caused all this. Despite his anger, his fury at Harrison at that moment, he was still his best friend. And the guy that cheated with Coco was another enemy.

Ella unlocked Coco's laptop as they gathered round. She sat at Coco's desk chair as Harrison sat on the end of her bed, and Bea sat next to him, her arm still around him, keeping him upright.

Conrad stood back a little, staring at Ella's hair as it fell towards the desk when she typed. Her hair gently brushed Harrison's forearm. Harrison glanced momentarily at her face, before turning quickly to Conrad, and hurriedly placing his arm rigidly by his side.

"Alright, I'm into her iMessages."

"This feels so wrong," Bea started. "What if she comes back and finds out-"

"Look," Ella said, pointing at the screen. "This number asked to see her two nights ago, or even told her, by the looks of it," Ella turned to face Conrad. "Con, come and see."

He took a step closer and leaned over the desk to get a better view, resting his hand next to Ella's, closing his eyes momentarily, gathering himself before reading what was in front of him. It was an odd moment. Even though more important things were at stake, everyone paused. He could feel Harrison and Bea watching him, and Ella determinedly looking the other way. He read the message.

I need to see you. Tonight. 12.

Monday, 11am.

"Who is this?" he asked quietly.

"That's what I'm trying to find out," Ella said, frowning at the messages. "She hasn't saved their number, and I don't think this would be the first message, she deleted the others, I'm guessing. It would be weird to send this out of the blue." She squinted as she looked closer, inspecting the date. "It's probably someone at school, who else would she meet at 12 on a Monday night? They have to be here, right?" Ella said it tentatively, casting Harrison a wary look.

Harrison sighed, shaking his head. "I knew it. I knew something was going on."

"I'm sorry," Bea said, patting his arm.

"Don't be," Conrad added bitterly.

"I know what I di-"

"I don't want to hear it, not right now at least. Coco's obviously been dealing with stuff. You said yourself that she started being strange, and now this has happened. We're setting in stone that she's done something terrible, and she's not here to defend herself, to say it *just happened*, that she didn't mean to." He said those last few words through gritted teeth.

"You might be right," Bea said, and Ella looked wounded. "I mean, we don't know what happened for sure."

"But…" Harrison started.

"It's bad, I agree. But we don't know everything. When she gets back, she might be able to explain, it might be okay."

Conrad shook his head. "How can it be okay? Whether she knows about those two, or whether she has yet to find that out, I don't see how you're coming back from this, mate." The word burned his throat and come out bitter. "Not after how long this has been coming. If- When she comes back, things won't be the same. You know that, right?"

"We'll cross that bridge when we come to it," Bea said. "The important thing now is getting her back safely. With respect, the three of you, your fucked-up love square isn't the most important thing here. Coco could be hurt, she could be ill and doing something reckless. We've already broken into…"

"Her door was open!" Harrison said, red in the face.

"We've already broken into her room and invaded her privacy. We might as well do something good with it. I'm sorry, Con, I know all you probably want to do right now is scream, but we need to find Coco first. We have good information here, we have a number of someone who met with her the night she went missing."

"They definitely saw her that night?" he asked quietly, ignoring Bea since she made too much sense.

"Yeah, or they tried at least," Ella said.

"I'm going to call it," Harrison said, grabbing his phone.

Bea looked sceptical. "Maybe we should tell the police first."

"I want to speak with him. I want to find out who it is. I don't want to hear it from the police." Harrison angrily tapped the keypad on his screen, and put the call on speakerphone.

They all stared at the phone, waiting for all the answers to fall into place.

"You've reached the AC Mobile Voicemail service, the number you have called is unavailable to take your call. Please leave a message-"

"Shit," Harrison said, slamming his fist on the table.

"Right then. That's that," Conrad said, turning on his heel to leave and go… anywhere that wasn't B-block, anywhere that wasn't the same room as Ella. "I- I need to get away from here now, let me know if you find out anything else."

"Con, wait…" Ella began.

"Save it," he said, before leaving the room, slamming the door behind him. He didn't know where he was going, but he knew that he couldn't stay there. He couldn't look at Harrison and Ella and hear their excuses, their reasons and their apologies. He couldn't stand in Coco's room, looking at the photos strung up on her wall, of them all smiling happily, past versions of themselves completely oblivious to the shitstorm that was brewing, blissful in their ignorance, sat at their fancy meals, on a sunny beach, or in their school uniforms pulling silly faces. It felt wrong that those naive parallel universe Ellas, Harrisons. Beas, Cocos, and Conrads should see this, that they should see what they become. They were always so good to each other, they always treated each other well, or so he thought. The Harrison and Ella that stood before him in that room weren't the ones he knew as the supportive friends who had brought him through a time no child of nearly fifteen should ever experience.

The memories of those dark days made him want to see Coco, to hug her, to comfort her, for all she did for him. If he felt like this, then God knows how she felt. But he knew that at that moment, he was the only person qualified to comfort her, he was the only person that began to understand being torn apart, being so betrayed and feeling that hurt so deep in your stomach. And, at any rate, he owed her a good few makeshift counselling sessions, after the many she offered him.

She was always so good to him, and when his mother died, it only strengthened their friendship.

Chapter Ten

Conrad's mum, Marie Huntington-Peakes, was diagnosed with cancer just as he finished Year 10. He was fifteen when she gave him the news. They were in Hawaii on a summer holiday, and Conrad and his older brothers, Michael, Solomon, and Harley, squinted in the sunlight at their parents who sat underneath the umbrella. Their mum told them she needed to make an announcement, and their dad, the big, boisterous CEO of a construction company, started weeping. Donal Huntington-Peakes never cried. The boys were startled, and Conrad felt a brick fall in his stomach. His tonsils seemed to swell, and his heart was trying to escape the confines of his chest. He knew this was nothing good.

"My lovelies, so the thing is, only the week before last I was given some pretty shit news, and you're going to have a lot to deal with. I'm poorly, and the doctors keep telling me I'm not going to get any better."

"Poorly how?" Solomon asked, trying and failing to stop his chin from wobbling. Conrad always thought his middle two twin brothers, Solomon and Michael, eighteen and at uni, seemed so much older than him, but their shell shocked expressions left them looking just like kids that felt just as he did.

"Cancer, darling," mum said, leaning over and squeezing Sol's knee as she did so. "And the trouble is, the bloody thing's gotten everywhere. I went to the doctors and they had an impressive list of things wrong with me. It seems that even at being ill I need to be the best." She offered a small smile that no one returned. Conrad marvelled at her ability to joke on a day like this.

"So this is how it's all going to happen. I'm not taking

anything to try and get better, and that means I probably have a couple of months. We're talking weeks here, boys. We've caught it too late. Chemo wouldn't kill it, and would just make me even more ill. So I'm on painkillers, and we just have as much fun together as we can until, well…"

She started crying, and dad placed an arm around her, kissing her forehead. Harley jumped up and sat next to her, hugging her tightly, sobbing. In no time at all, the rest of them joined in and they just sat like that, on the public beach, crying their hearts out as a family.

It was a terrible summer. Mum booked all sorts of surprises on their holiday; jet skiing, skydiving, a hot air balloon ride, white water rafting, coasteering, and kayaking through caves and discovering magical places. It should have been the best holiday of their lives, but the four boys barely stopped crying all week, even though they were kept busy, even though mum kept up a determinedly upbeat attitude, they couldn't stop thinking about how she soon wouldn't be around, and they needed her.

When they got back to England two weeks later, she was exhausted, and her decline was far more obvious in her own house. She kept becoming tired, and the fun days out she planned became dangerous to her, putting her out for days afterwards. They saw her shrink into herself, saw her clothes start to balloon around her. She was getting minuscule, and she was spending more and more time in bed.

It wasn't long before they converted their drawing room into a bedroom. A hospital bed was delivered that sat up and lowered to the ground for her, and she spent her last few weeks watching movies and reading books in that room, watching summer pass her by through the vast window that looked out onto the lawn.

The boys did the best they could to help. They picked up prescriptions, they walked the dog, they made dinner and brought cups of tea to the 'friends' their mum hadn't seen in years but who all seemed so suddenly close to her. Conrad deliberately left the sugar out of their teas. He couldn't understand their desperate need to see her now that she was

143

almost gone, when they hadn't bothered when she was alive. They managed all these years without her, but he hadn't, yet they sat with her and cried like they had any right to do so.

He realised that was what people did. They liked being able to say that they knew the dead person, that they saw her 'only a week ago'. There was a sort of morbid fame in it, and it made Conrad feel sick to his core.

Mum was home at the end of the summer, but they knew that as September came around, she only had days left. Conrad argued with his father until he was red in the face, refusing to leave and return to school. But then the last night of the summer was upon him eerily quickly, as though time was mocking him in being so limited but so wasteful. He still stubbornly wore his jogging bottoms and nothing else, like he always did around the house, refusing to pack, determined that he would not go back to Lainsbury, not when mum was like this. And then his mum called for him.

He walked into the horrible room in which the curtains were always drawn and was always so quiet lately. He sat beside her bed and she turned her head, smiling the same, wide, wicked smile she wore all his life.

"I hear you've been stirring up quite a bit of trouble for your poor dad, dear." She said it in a whisper, in a ghost of her voice.

Conrad hung his head and nodded like a naughty child.

"Why don't you want to go to school? You usually can't wait to leave."

"I'm not leaving you, Mum." He sounded so childlike. He wanted to act mature about this, but the lump in his throat garbled his speech and sent tears running down his face, which his mum weakly brushed away.

"And what are you going to do here? I'm sorry, Conny, but unless you've found a magic cure for me, you're going to be pretty useless." She grinned at him as he stared at her in horror.

"I can make tea! I can help! I just want to be here when… when…"

He couldn't finish his sentence. Mum placed a skeletal

arm around his shaking shoulders and whispered soothing words.

"Listen to me. When I go, it won't be pretty, it won't be nice. Honestly, you don't want to be here for those last few days. Everyone will be sad, I probably won't even be conscious. And I'm telling you, darling, I've thought a lot about it and I don't want you here. I don't want you to go through that, and I don't want you to see me like that. I don't have a choice about any of this, but damn it I'm still your mother and you're still my baby boy and I still get to tell you what to do. Go to school, get your good grades, see your friends, play some hockey. You're not staying here, do you understand me?"

He nodded. He couldn't understand how nonchalant she was being, how normal she still was even when facing death. It was a strength he hadn't seen before, strength that he never thought a person could hold so well.

"But I won't see you again."

"That's… probably true, yeah. But a lot of emphasis is put on people's last moments, when they don't really mean much. Our whole entire lifetimes mean so much more than those last few sick, sad moments. They don't matter. I've had so much fun with you, Conny, for all these years, and these last weeks mean nothing compared to all that." She clasped his hand in hers and stared into his eyes.

"I want you to listen to me now, and I want you to remember this. You're the brightest and the wickedest of the four of you, but don't tell Harley and the twins that. You got all that from me. But you also have such a good heart, and you have to let people into it, you understand? Don't take any shit, and don't be shit, that's all you have to remember." She looked so small, so weak, but her grip was strong. She frowned then, a pained expression, as though this conversation cost her the last of her energy. "Now go, get out. You've got lots to learn, little one."

He hugged her the next day for a long time before telling her he loved her and picking up the bags his dad had packed, knowing that she would persuade him, and he left for school in a grey daze, the permanent headache that accompanied the constant crying pressing on his mind.

Harrison sat with him all night that night, and they played video games and talked about anything that wasn't his mum. He appreciated it. He appreciated the distraction. He found that going to classes and playing sports again helped too.

But then mum died the first week he returned to Lainsbury. The phone rang on that first Saturday and, after the call ended, he sat on the edge of his bed after hanging up, not knowing what to do. His dad wasn't picking him up to take him home until the following day.

Harrison knocked on his door and broke the silence. As Conrad opened it, he was reminded that they were going to go to town to see that new superhero movie everyone was talking about.

"I can't," was all Conrad said.

The good natured smile ever-present on Harrison's lips disappeared as he registered the look on his face. "Your mum?" he said.

Conrad nodded and sank into Harrison as he hugged him fiercely. "She's gone. I wanted to be there but she told me to leave, and now she's gone," Conrad said, his face passive, wide-eyed and vacant, far away, as though he had fallen so deeply into himself that the real Conrad was somewhere behind those green eyes, shouting out from afar, as though trapped down a well.

He couldn't summon the energy to cry in that moment. It was a grief, a pain that went beyond the tears that fell for the weeks before this. He felt numb, shocked, even though he knew it was coming, even though he tried to prepare for this moment for weeks.

Harrison sat in his desk chair beside him, dumbfounded, at a loss as to what to say. Conrad sat on his bed and stared out of the window at the clear sky, and Harrison stared at him.

Conrad briefly heard the ring of Harrison's phone. It was an odd sound in the silence. It felt disconnected, as though from afar, an alien sound that did not belong in this new world.

"Coco, yeah, We're not coming. It's Conrad's mum…" Harrison whispered, and Conrad could hear Coco's muffled voice on the other end of the phone. "Yeah."

"Oh, I'm not sure you…" Harrison sighed. Coco hung up.

Harrison moved onto the bed and sat up next to Conrad. "Come here," he said.

Conrad rolled towards him, lying in a foetal position, his head across Harrison's legs. He started to sob then, hard. Harrison said very little, unable to find the words. It was enough for Conrad that he was present, offering his silent support, awkwardly stroking his arm.

Coco knocked on the door, and she and Ella came inside without waiting for an answer.

"Oh, Conrad," Coco wailed, climbing onto the spare few inches of the bed the other side of him, and started stroking his hair gently. Ella sat on the end of his bed, patting his leg like a spare part. Conrad himself didn't know what he would have done if it was one of the others in his situation, but he couldn't offer any better way of handling it than his friends did. They were there, and that was all that mattered.

After lying silently on Harrison's legs for a long time, he sat up, sniffling. His face was red and wet, his nose streaming. His back ached from lying in such a stupid position. "Can I get some water?" he said in a hoarse voice, and Ella grabbed a glass from his bedside table, then took it over to the sink in the far corner of his room.

She handed it to him, concern etched on her face. The three of them watched him sip, mesmerised.

"What a day," he said weakly.

"It'll get better," Coco said, putting an arm around his shoulders. He sat up straight between Coco and Harrison, and he let his heavy, sore head drop onto Coco's shoulders. Her curly hair tickled his face and he could smell her perfume. Chanel. Always Chanel. He knew that smell like he knew his own face. "I'm so sorry you have to go through this."

"She was just always so good, you know? In our house of five fucking men, all of us horrible and loud and shit, she looked after us, she cared for us. She never said a bad word

147

about anyone and then… How is that fair? How is it fair that of all the terrible shitstains in the world, it's my fucking Mum that has to go through that?"

"I know, I know," Coco whispered, stroking his hair, her arms wrapped around him. She made him feel better, she made him say what he felt, before it boiled up inside him and exploded. She was good at comforting him.

He left the next day, still dazed, still lost. He went home, but it didn't feel like home anymore. It felt cold, his house too big without her to fill it. He realised almost immediately that he had been wrong. He was better off back at school.

The funeral was awful. He expected it to be, but it still all felt so real. The vicar, the flowers, the weird parade people do afterwards where you line up to be told that you're 'so brave' by people you've seen twice in your life. He nodded and shook hands with these people because it's what his mum would have wanted. But if she had been standing right behind him, he knew she would be making silly comments about their messy lives and laughing at them.

It lasted forever in the way that the things Conrad dreaded always seemed to do. It was long. It was tortuous. And Conrad needed to get out of the house, to escape people. So he left the wake early.

Three hours after the funeral, Conrad found himself walking alone on the rocky cliff path in his ill-fitting funeral suit and inappropriate shoes. He always liked the path, and he must have walked his dog along it a thousand times, but he never realised how lonely it felt. He never realised that he felt like the only person in the world when he stood on top of the cliffs, gazing out onto the vast expanse of the ocean.

He obviously knew that it was a fact that he lived on a planet suspended in some vast nothingness, almost all of which he had no knowledge of, but it was only until he stared out onto the sea on that day and pondered the clear, curved horizon, that he realised he actually did live on a giant rock rolling around through space. He was living in an infinite universe, which was comforting since his own tiny universe collapsed. He never used to see the tragic beauty of that path, of that feeling of insignificance, like he was an ant in a football field, but it was what he needed on that day.

He wandered for a while, ignoring the dust from the path that was ruining the trousers of his best suit. Instead, he walked, all the while staring out to sea, watching the glittering waves and hearing the sounds. The sounds of life, the sounds of a world turning, the birds, the distant waves crashing, the rustling of the wind in the grass. It drowned out the pounding in his head.

He walked until he came across a memorial bench and sat down. *'For Charity, Simon and Oscar'* he read. *'The summers of our childhood lasting forever in our hearts.'*

He wondered how many others were sat at that very second staring out into the sea or sky or mountains, their own lives shattered into a million pieces. He supposed it was lots. He wondered if they had their own Charitys, Simons and Oscars, their own Cocos and Ellas and Harrisons. He hoped they did.

When he returned to school two weeks later, Coco sat with him and talked for hours. Harrison and Ella's complete inability to talk about feelings rendered them poor candidates for the monumental task Coco took on - operation help-Conrad-get-through-this, and so they stepped aside as Coco took the reins and it meant that they became close friends, probably even best friends for a while. They carried it on all year, and it became so easy for them to spend time alone together.

She listened to the stories that he wanted to say aloud when he was ready, not so she heard them really, but so they were out there, in the air. It felt good, for some reason, that those memories were outside his own head, were shared with another person.

He couldn't say why exactly, but Coco smiling as he told her the wickedly fun things his mother had said or done for him growing up, made all the difference. It made it bearable. She was content to just sit and listen, and in a world of talkers and very few listeners, in a world of noise, Coco's silence was important.

Harrison didn't know what to do or say. He was awkward in those intimate situations. But Coco did it well. She liked stories, she liked memories, even if they weren't hers. She knew that they were important, they were our mark on the world, the stories people will tell about us when we're gone, the things we said that changed people's lives, the things we did that we had no idea meant so much. She assured him that it was nice to sit and listen, it was nice to honour his mum in that way, by knowing her, even if she had never met her, and even if it was after she was dead.

"Although, of course," Coco said one day near Christmas, "she's only technically gone. She lives on, through everything she passed onto you, and through the grandchildren she will have, who will be taught the same things, they'll be shaped by her, too. So in a very real sense she's not altogether gone, is she?"

He could have kissed her then. She had such a way with words, such a way of expressing exactly the abstract concept that needed to be said aloud. She knew exactly what needed to be said, and he needed to hear that. She made him cry when she said that, but he stopped crying every day after then. It was no hyperbole to say that Coco got him through it, through the walks they took together, and the long conversations they had. They weren't always about his Mum, sometimes just about life, about any subject, deep or not, but she made him express himself, and he knew that he wouldn't have gotten through it without her.

That was why it was so outrageous to him that the two people closest to her decided to deliberately hurt her. Not because he was once in love with her, but because she was, at her core, good throughout, and Conrad believed that her friendship made him a better person too, by association. Harrison and Ella took that for granted.

Chapter Eleven

Conrad was halfway down the downstairs corridor of B Block, walking fast, his feet stomping beneath him, when he heard her hurried, gentle footsteps behind him.

"Wait, Con, please," Ella said quietly. He stopped and took a second to breathe.

"What?" he said, closing his eyes. He didn't turn to face her. Instead, he felt her move in front of him, her hand touching his arm. He wanted to yank his arm away, but he couldn't. He couldn't move, he couldn't ignore her. Even in his furious state, he couldn't walk away from her. There was just something, and he couldn't explain what, that kept him there, that stopped him from walking off and screaming into the mountains. He opened his eyes and saw her standing right in front of him, her huge, damp eyes staring up at him imploringly.

Why does she have to be so damn cute? he thought.

"I'm sorry," she began, speaking quickly when he showed signs of protesting. "And not because I feel guilty, not even because you're upset, although I am sorry about that, but mainly because I did that and it didn't even mean anything. I'm sorry that I ruined this because of that, because of just him. It was such a stupid thing to do, and that's why I'm sorry. I'm sorry because I was such a fucking idiot, because I did something that a past version of myself would have wanted and that's not who I am, not now. You've been there for me, Con. You stood beside me. You've had my back, and you've wanted me when I thought no one else could. I know I royally screwed this up, I know that, and if you can't be with me anymore, I understand, but I just want to say… well, thanks, for everything."

"Really? *Really*? You cheat on me, and you say 'you can leave now if you want, cheers for a good run'? That's all I get? That's all I get for putting myself out there for you, for going along with your weird rules, for watching you outright lie about me to our friends, for accepting all your hang ups and obstacles that you placed in front of us? I go along, taking it slow, when all I wanted to do was to tell everyone how in love I was- I *am*, with you, for you to cheat and casually just say 'Sorry, thanks though.' That's not good enough, El. That's not nearly good enough. I deserve more than that. I deserve you begging me to take you back. I deserve you telling me you'll do all you can to make this right, if I just stay with you. I deserve you telling everyone that we're together. I deserve *you*."

"I-" Ella stuttered.

"And, for that matter, so does Coco. You haven't mentioned her once. She's out there somewhere, probably thinking over what you've done, probably going through every godforsaken second, picturing the both of you in her head, like I am, and you can't even do her the good grace of pretending like you're worried, that you feel just a little bit guilty at all. It's all just so wrong. She's missing, and it doesn't even seem like you care."

"I care," she croaked. "I care a lot. I've not stopped thinking about it. I haven't mentioned her because I can't, because the thought of her- of her-" Ella started sobbing, her words catching in her throat. "I can't think about what I've done to her because it's eating me alive, the thought of her so upset at me, I can't handle it. I'm not handling any of this. You're right, she's missing, and her hating me so much that she can't even look at me is the best case scenario. How do I even start to be able to think about that?"

Conrad and Ella stopped. They heard footsteps coming from around the corner. Genevieve was hurrying towards them, her pale face, tinged green and her face waxen, almost inhuman. Her eyes were wide, The sight of her sent a jolt through Conrad's spine.

"Where are the others?" Genevieve asked, her voice

panicked.

"In… her room. What's happening?" he asked, his heart hammering against his chest, surely as loud as any of their footsteps, and they hurried towards the door. Gen stayed quiet until she opened it, and her eyes met Bea's.

"I was wandering around outside just now and I saw Coco's parents. They're here, and Miss Hardy's with them. I think-" Genevieve took a deep breath. "I think something bad has happened. If I were you, I'd go and see what's going on."

They looked at each other for a moment, and then they hurried out of the dorm. Without thinking, Conrad grabbed Ella's hand, guiding her to Hardy's office, jostling younger students in the hallway as they made their way through the school. The panic was rising through him, a tidal wave ready to come crashing down, destroying everything in his wake. He had a bad feeling, one that niggled in the depths of his stomach. Something was very wrong.

Chapter Twelve

It happened in Miami. After all the drama of the garden party, and after everyone went to bed, it was just Conrad and Ella left. They sat on opposite sides of the same sofa, chatting happily.

They always got on well. They needed to, since Coco and Harrison had a habit of getting lost in their own little world, where no one else existed. In the long lunch times, when the couple whispered in ears and sat on laps, Conrad and Ella talked and laughed. Knowing the other two better than anyone else in the world gave them a powerful connection. They were brought together because their best friends had fallen in love. They shared inside jokes about the weird little moans Coco made when she kissed, and the doleful look that came across Harrison's face whenever Coco spoke. They referenced films that the four of them watched together in the common room, but only Ella and Conrad paid attention.

Conrad and Ella obsessed over the sitcoms they watched as a group, ending up watching them alone when Harrison and Coco couldn't be relied upon, since they were too invested in each other. They spent hours discussing which series of The Office was the best, what they thought happened to the Friends characters after the finale, whether the last season of How I Met Your Mother was a complete let down or a stroke of genius, and why the hell they decided to carry on That Seventies Show without Ashton Kutcher.

Ella proofread all of Conrad's essays. Being the top English Literature student she was, she always bolstered him by saying she was amazed by his creative reasoning and interpretation of the world around him. She told him that she had never met anyone with such a unique view of the world.

She had covered many of the essays in notes, so many that to write them in and do her changes would sometimes take as long as to write the essays themselves, and sometimes they would still only get a B. When he told Ella about those essays, though, her genuine rage and disbelief, that Mr Davies or Miss Jenkins would mark him so low, made the grade worth it.

Ella had the ability to make Conrad feel special, truly one of a kind. That night in Miami was no exception. They talked for hours, until the effects of the alcohol wore off, and they began to feel tired.

The house was quieter than usual. Without the others to join them, their conversation was a lot less loud, more serious. They, well, he, talked until there was a thoughtful, sleepy pause which lingered in the stillness of the house.

"What you did for Bea, that was good, Con, noble of you," Ella said. "There should be more guys like you around."

"I still made you uncomfortable, though. About that, earlier…" Conrad said, his anxious face staring into hers.

"I know. I didn't have to freak out. I'm sorry," Ella said, looking down at her lap, her long lashes dusting her cheeks.

He looked at her, perplexed. "For what?" he asked.

"For being so weird. I just didn't want to make things complicated, you know, for a bloody game."

"No, I'm sorry. I shouldn't have just come up to you like that. I shouldn't have assumed you'd be cool with it. That wasn't right." He shook his head angrily, annoyed at himself. "For future reference, though, I wouldn't have been awkward about it. If we kissed, it wouldn't have bothered me. I wouldn't have expected anything. You know that, right? There was nothing for you to… worry about." Conrad paused for a moment. "I'll always look after you, El," he added, and squeezed her hand. Conrad worried about her, a lot. She was going through so much, and it was so obvious that she wasn't coping well. She was screaming at Coco for little things, she was snogging guys at parties just because they liked her, he could see that she wasn't herself, and in hindsight, Conrad knew that getting her to play spin the bottle was idiotic, childish, and thoughtless.

"I know. I'm just… in a strange place at the moment, and I don't know, it just stressed me out. I feel like, if I'm going to kiss boys, it has to be thought out, not because a bottle told me to," Ella said.

Conrad squeezed her hand again and smiled. He stared so intently into her eyes that she blushed. "You're going through a lot," he said. "You can always talk to me.

She nodded, tears filling her eyes, and he hugged her tightly.

"You're incredible for going through all this. I mean it, I couldn't do it. Just, don't let it ruin you, don't let it push your friends away. Don't let it change who you are, because you're pretty damn fantastic."

"I'm pretty damn awkward." Ella laughed now, wiping her eyes.

Conrad laughed too and stared down at his knees. He raised his head and looked into her face once again, deciding if he should say it, his head whirring with the possibilities.

"You are, yeah," Conrad said, laughing a little harder, but for once he wasn't joking. "But so am I."

Ella gave him a disbelieving look.

"No, really, I'm shite with girls. When have you ever seen me chat one up?" Conrad went on. Ella frowned, and he made an impatient sound, batting her disbelief away. "Alright, apart from Rosie today but, in all fairness, I didn't do anything, she was just into me for no reason. Or maybe it was just because of, you know…" Conrad pointed to his cheek and grinned his most 'handsome' smile at her, and she chuckled. He could see the cogs whirring in her mind.

"Come to think of it, you never talk to girls," Ella said, running her fingers through her hair.

"Nope. Well, I guess not never, there was the Erica Lovelace whirlwind, remember?"

"Isn't she going out with Angus Stanstead now?"

"Yeah, exactly. See, I can't talk to girls. No, honest. I can do public speaking, I can do being an arrogant dick, but I just don't know how to flirt, like, at all. Although, in all honesty, don't think I've met a girl that could put up with me yet, guess that's why I'm still a virgin. Maybe I wasn't bothered enough."

Ella choked on her water. "You're a virgin? Really?"

"I'm only seventeen, El!" he said, his face pink and indignant.

"There's nothing wrong with that! It's just... I didn't expect it. I mean, you were quick to try and get it on with Erica, and you're always talking the big talk, I just figured... and, well, look at you!"

He looked at her, raising an eyebrow. "Do I look like someone that's had sex? It can do that?" He made his eyes wide in faux horror as she laughed. He liked Ella's laugh, a light, carefree sound. It was about the only carefree thing about her in those days, and he tried to bring that laugh out of her as much as possible. "I just mean...your face..."

"My face?" Conrad asked, laughing quietly, now sat nearly nose to nose with her on the sofa.

"Yeah..." Ella answered, her voice soft. She ran her fingers along his jaw. "You always say how handsome you are." She chuckled before carrying on, pulling her serious face. "The chiselled bone-structure..." She ran her finger along his cheekbone. "Your big, serious eyebrows..." She smiled. "Your lips..." Her face now set, she traced his lips with her index finger. Shivers shot through Conrad's spine as he kissed her. She sat on his lap, her lips frantically moving against his. He kept a steady hand on her back as his other touched her face, pulling her in closer. It might have been awkward, perhaps, that he was kissing such a close friend, but a part of him had been waiting for this to happen. It was always the two of them who stood on the side-lines, the pair of them seemingly cursed when it came to love. It was weird that after she shocked them all that day, months before, with her terrible news, he realised how much he cared for her. His protective instinct surprised even him, and it made him see Ella in a different way, he realised that he was wasting his time yearning after Coco when there was another incredible girl at his side, distinctly not shagging his best friend at every available moment. Kissing Ella simply seemed the next step, a completely natural thing. Far more normal than it had any right to be.

Breathless, they broke apart, and she slid off his lap to sit next to him, her legs resting over his. He looked into her flustered face as he tucked a strand of her long hair behind her ear.

"I am, too. But I think that's a little more obvious." Ella was talking fast, her wide eyes peering into his. "Should we, you know...get it over with, with each other? Somewhere we can keep it quiet, with someone we know won't screw us over?"

Conrad rested his forehead against hers and grinned. "Isabella Constance Fitzpatrick, are you trying to seduce me?" he said.

"You know what I mean," she breathed, rolling her eyes. "If you don't want to...."

"No, no, it worked. I'd love to 'get it over with', with you. You're so romantic." Conrad was already on his feet, his hand outstretched. He kissed her dainty hand as she placed it in his. He hoped to God his palms weren't too sweaty. He led her to his room and locked the door. She sat nervously on the edge of his bed.

Ella couldn't hear the thud of his heart, the only evidence of his equally strong nerves. She never heard the roaring applause, a rowdy orchestra, a mariachi band, celebrating this huge moment in Conrad's life. But he would have to hold back, he would have to check that she was really okay with this. She trusted him, he knew that, and for good reason. This was between them, a sacred moment, a shared confidence that he would never make her regret.

More to the point, this was the first time for him that it felt right. All the other girls were great, but he'd always reached a moment of clarity where he would think *this isn't it*. Then he would freak out and abort mission. But now, he was excited, fluttery and flustered, sure, but not nervous, not exactly,

Conrad sat next to her, mimicking her straight, rigid

position, and they awkwardly laughed. "Are you sure you want to do this, El?" he said.

"*Yes*, I am." Ella rolled her eyes.

"I mean, you're sure you're sure, like actually, really, one hundred percent, this is the greatest idea in the history of the world sure?" he said, and Ella laughed at his concerned face.

"Yes, Con. In a weird way, this feels right, yeah?"

He smiled at that. He didn't want her to regret the decision that he didn't have to think twice about. "We can stop at any point. I want you to be absolutely totall-" Ella kissed Conrad to shut him up, knocking him onto his back in her enthusiasm, and sitting on top of him.

When they broke apart for breath, Conrad started talking again. "Are you ok?" he asked.

Ella nodded and he noticed that she was smiling now, her nervousness seemingly gone. She placed his hands on her chest, which was now bare, naked, after she yanked her dress above her head and threw it aside.

She kissed him again, and he grinned against her lips as he flipped himself on top of her and took off his own shirt. After that, it just happened. It was a little fumbly, a little awkward, and there were a couple of condom-related issues, but nothing too devastating, and it was... good, for both of them, he hoped.

From the smile on Ella's face as they both lay, shocked and breathless afterwards, he knew it couldn't have been a complete disaster, or maybe not even a disaster at all. He'd been worried. There were a lot of things to it, a lot of things to get right, or very, very wrong. It was daunting. When he was all set to run off with Erica, he was drunk, he felt like he needed to be. But Ella made him feel as if it didn't matter so much, that he could relax. She was new at this too, and they got through it together, and it was good, really good. He didn't expect to go quite that well.

He was thinking all this when Ella spoke into his chest.

"I thought it wasn't meant to be good the first time, but that was. Like, I get it, you know? I thought I'd have to get used to it, I thought it'd take a while to actually enjoy it but that was, like, *good*," she told him.

Conrad smiled at his ceiling. "No, that wasn't good. That was bloody splendid."

Ella laughed, hard. "I'm not sure you're really supposed to describe sex as 'splendid'.."

"Delightful?" he suggested.

She shook her head again, grinning.

"Fucking fantastic then," Conrad said.

"That's more like it." Ella smiled, nodding enthusiastically.

"So I haven't put you off it?" he asked tentatively, rolling onto his elbow to look into her face.

"Most definitely not."

"So, same time tomorrow?"

Ella thought for a moment. It was a long pause, a long couple of seconds, his heart, only now retaining its usual rhythm, sped up again, hammering against his chest, against her cheek.

"Yeah. And maybe the night after that, and every night until we go home?"

"That's the best plan that has ever been made. Ever," Conrad said.

When they woke up the next morning, after Ella snuck back into her own bed late the night before, things were different. They kept catching each other's eyes and grinning, both of them still in shock after what they did, so spontaneously, so fast. But they had to keep it quiet.

He knew she was a flight risk, Like a scared bird, one wrong move, and she'd be gone, he'd have blown it. And something inside screamed at him not to blow this one. His brain shouted at him to tread carefully.

So, when they sat next to each other on the sofa the following morning, eating toast, he kept a distance between them, a distance in which the air seemed thick. He could almost feel an invisible barrier, a wall keeping him from putting an arm around Ella's delicate shoulders and feeling her soft, tanned arms. He gulped and tried not to think about her tan, about the white lines upon her skin that they had laughed about the night before. He tried not to think about

160

her long hair which had got in the way so much, about the fact that he would see her in a bikini for the millionth time in a matter of only minutes.

Conrad wondered if she felt the same, if her heart hammered a tune against her ribcage when she saw him, if she wanted to touch him, too, or if the night before didn't mean as much as he thought it did.

"Conrad!" Harrison shouted, making him jump.

"What?"

"I asked if you were finished. We want to head to the beach already."

"Oh, uh, yeah," he said, vaguely.

"Really? You've only eaten one piece of toast. I swear you usually have four," Bea said, eying up his plate.

"Alright, the food police. If you must know, I'm saving room for one of those club sandwiches at that place on the beach. I've been dreaming about them since yesterday." He wished he hadn't said it. He hated those club sandwiches.

They shrugged and grabbed their bags. Coco and Bea walked fast in front, and Conrad walked slowly with Harrison and Ella, Harrison standing between them.

"El, I want to talk to you about last night," Harrison said, and both Ella and Conrad whirled around to look at him.

"What do you mean?" Ella asked, her face scarlet. Conrad realised that she was an even worse liar than him.

He racked his brain, trying to think how Harrison could know what they had done, how the secret they thought they hid pretty well was now out in the open. He felt nauseous. "Coco's pretty upset about your argument. She needs to talk to you some more, I need you to meet her halfway," Harrison said.

The relief on Ella's face was fleeting, but it turned into an angry grimace. "Maybe I'm pretty upset, too. Maybe she just needs to think a bit more sometimes, Harrison. Have you considered that?" she said.

"Yeah, but, she didn't really do anything wrong, did she? You just…" Harrison valiantly ploughed on, his messenger boy duties not going quite as planned.

"I just *what*? rounded on her like a crazy person? I was annoyed at her, and if you remember correctly, so were you, and so was Conrad."

"But I was annoyed with her for humouring that douche who was obsessed with her, and Conrad was annoyed because…"

"Because she made us hang out with those arseholes, because I had to throw down my gauntlet to defend Bea's honour, which I really didn't want to have to do. Yeah," Conrad said, reluctantly brought into the conversation, and only now remembering the antics from the night before which now felt like trying to remember a past life.

"Coco didn't know any of that was going to happen," Harrison said tentatively.

"If she opened her eyes once in a while, she would," Ella snapped.

"I- alright. I just don't like seeing her so upset. It's stupid that you're fighting so much over something so meaningless," Harrison sighed.

"As long as Coco's happy, nothing matters, right? It doesn't matter how anyone else feels, how many toes she's stepped on and probably fucking broke, right? As long as *dear* Coco is seen to, everything's just grand."

"You're not being fair, El. You're in her house, and you're supposed to be her best friend. Let it go."

Ella shook her head and stormed off in the opposite direction.

"Why do they have to fight so much? We never do this shit," Harrison groaned.

"I dunno, Fletch. She's just sick of everyone taking Coco's side," Conrad said, watching Ella storm off into the distance.

"I have to take Coco's side. She'll kick off if I don't." Harrison was shocked, appalled at the suggestion that he disagree with his girlfriend.

Conrad rolled his eyes. "Look, who do you think is right here?"

"Coco was pretty obtuse," Harrison reasoned.

"Did you tell her that?"

"I tried to when she came to bed, but she was already so upset over Ella, and she gave me those sad eyes, and I couldn't shout at her then."

"Maybe you need to focus less on being a good boyfriend, and more on being a good friend. One will make two of you happy, one will make all of us happy. There's a lot more people that need you. That's all I'm going to say."

"But…"

"Is Ella your friend or not?" Conrad asked impatiently, eyeing the direction Ella headed in, but unable to make her out in the distance. *Her little legs can carry her fast when she's in a mood*, he noted.

Harrison hesitated, looking down at his shuffling feet. "Yeah, of course she's my friend. You're right," he said.

Conrad clapped him on the back. "Always am," he grinned, and Harrison shook his head, smiling back.

The day was awkward. They lay on the beach, a fraught silence hanging in the air when Ella joined them a little while later, the atmosphere icy despite the weather being so warm. He wanted to comfort Ella, wanted to stick up for her and be there for her like Harrison was for Coco, but he knew that if he did, he would cause more problems.

Conrad felt that Coco's house, whilst idyllic, was claustrophobic, and if they all found out about him and Ella, it was big news that would cause the group to implode. It was odd, they always all got on so well, so effortlessly, even when Bea started hanging out with them. Within a week it felt as though she had always been there, or had always been what they were missing, the voice of sensibility in their group. Now they were so delicate, one small move could tip the balance and spill their contentment everywhere. It was as if they were dancing around a mine field, especially with Ella and Coco constantly at each other's throats, and now all the secrets caused an even bigger strain.

Ella didn't help things. Clearly bored without the girls to talk to, she went down the route of taunting him instead.

"Con, can you suncream my back, please?" she asked him, sitting up abruptly on her deckchair and nudging him in the back with her big toe.

"Uh. Sure," Conrad said, gesturing to her to move into the space he made on his own chair, under the umbrella.

"Factor 50 alright?"

"Jesus," Ella laughed, Harrison chuckled too. "Use this," she said, handing him her own bottle of Factor 15.

"Are you planning on frying yourself with this oil? Cos I don't think you'd go well with chips, to be honest."

Conrad felt her shoulders shrug under his hands, which were shaking at the touch of her silky skin.

"Stick some salt and vinegar on me and I'd be alright, I reckon," Ella joked, and Conrad chuckled softly. "Your hands are soft," she said, rolling her back under his touch, and his jaw clenched under the strain.

"Thanks." Conrad giggled ominously. "It's just my right hand though, actually. I go through so much hand cream but my left hand never seems to get any softer."

Harrison took a badly-timed sip of beer and started choking with laughter, spitting out his mouthful over the side of his deckchair.

Coco rolled her eyes under her pink Chanel sunglasses.

"Oh, for the love of God," Bea murmured through a reluctant smirk.

Conrad's joke broke the ice a little, and they talked some more when he was done with Ella's back, but he noticed the girls still avoiding each other's eyes.

Later on, everyone headed off for an early night. The others stood up around them and left Ella and Conrad alone to watch the rest of the movie they projected onto a sheet outside. They were forced to sit next to each other on the sofa when everyone piled on next to them, and Ella shuffled a little further away when they all left. He wished she hadn't.

It was odd how it always seemed to happen, that Bea would run off with India, Coco obviously with Harrison. It didn't hold any significance to Conrad before these last few days, but now it was important that they left. It offered a world of opportunity that he was keen to pursue. He craved the moments he could spend alone with Ella.

He crossed his fingers and hoped that his best mate would get bored and desert him, because for that last week in Miami, the only person he wanted anything to do with was Ella. He sympathised with Harrison at that time. He understood what it was to feel that pull, to be unable to keep your hands off someone, to be itching to run away to dark rooms and be alone.

Ella looked sweet. Her hair was wet from her shower, and she sat in her thin pyjamas with the tiny shorts, so damn tiny, determinedly watching the film and ignoring the feeling that he was watching her, drinking her in. He found himself watching very little of the film and an awful lot of her.

She smiled when she finally turned her head and caught him staring. "What?" she asked.

"You're just beautiful, that's all."

Smirking, Ella nudged him with her foot. "Well, if that's all…"

Conrad slid along the wicker sofa, which he found surprisingly comfortable for patio furniture, and sat close to her.

"Can I help you?" Ella giggled.

He leaned in, smiling into her face, and noticed her eyes widening as he left just an inch between their lips. "There are a lot of things you could help me with," he said, before kissing her gently.

She broke them apart, her hands resting on his chest. "Not in the garden!" Ella gasped, her eyes dancing with excitement.

"Well then, get your arse inside!"

They stood, giggling, running around, and turning off all the lights, before locking the French doors and pulling the curtain, turning the lights off in the open kitchen and living space.

Ella snuck up behind Conrad as he bent over the counter. She turned off the little spotlights from the overhead cupboards. Wrapping her arms around him, she stood on her tiptoes and kissed his neck. She gasped as he turned her around, and he pressed her against the countertops, her body arching into his. He let his hands wander around her torso, and she moved into him for a couple of seconds.

"Not here," he whispered, and she laughed. He kissed her, nipping at her bottom lip, allowing his teeth to bring up the goosebumps in her skin. "Then again, everyone else is in bed."

"They might…" Ella started, smiling, showing her bright white teeth, as the door opened and Conrad pushed her away unceremoniously. She threw him a glare as she steadied herself, and he tried to convey his apology with a look before opening the door to the freezer.

"What are you guys doing down here in the dark?" Coco asked, surprised to find herself with company.

"Just about to go to bed. Film just finished. We fancied a bit of ice cream first. Your mum's carbonara was about a million hours ago now," Conrad said, without missing a beat. He placed the tub of Phish Food on the counter. "Get the spoons, El."

"I know what you mean. It's so hot tonight. I can't sleep. Harrison's already out cold though, obviously. One for me too, please," Coco said, eying Ella's back, who turned to get the cutlery from the drawer behind her.

"It sure is," Con said, avoiding Ella's gaze.

They bent over the countertop with their spoons and chipped away at the hard mass of ice cream.

"Today was fun," Coco small-talked.

"Mhm," Ella said, her eyes not leaving the marble countertop.

"I'm sorry, El," Coco said out of the blue, and Ella's face shot up. She stared into Coco's eyes.

"You are?"

"I'm sorry I put you in that position, that I made you uncomfortable. I'm sorry for not thinking, and for not seeing your side. I take you for granted and I shouldn't. I need to stop that. I need to start thinking more about the people I love and less about myself. I'm sorry, El."

Ella rushed past Conrad and pulled Coco into a fierce hug.

"I'll leave you guys to it then," Conrad said, grinning, and made his way to the door.

"Later," Ella mouthed over Coco's shoulder, and he nodded.

Conrad reached his room and lay down on his bed. It had been a long day, and as soon as his head hit the pillow, his eyes fluttered, and he drifted off into a dreamless sleep.

Some time later he woke up to a sinking feeling on his mattress, and to the touch of a kiss on his cheek. He lay on his back to get a better view, and saw Ella leaning over him in her tiny pyjamas.

"You snore terribly, you know that?" Ella asked.

"I'm not snoring anymore," he mumbled sleepily, pulling her under his arm.

She giggled as she manoeuvred herself into a comfier position and began to kiss his neck. She escaped his embrace and pattered kisses on his chest, down his torso.

And it carried on like that, midnight wanderings, gently closing doors, torn buttons, and disregarded clothes littering the floor. Conrad had never felt so alive, watching Ella wander around his room, wearing nothing but the slim beams of moonlight that the curtains failed to block. He'd never felt better. It was all he could do to stop himself from grinning every second of the day. He wanted to carry on feeling like that. He wanted to be with Ella and tell the world how happy he was, how fucking fantastic life was and everything in it, how things had gone from absolute crap, the worst of the worst, to significantly better, just because of one person.

But then came the last night. It went as usual, Ella ran in, locked the door, jumped on top of him. She was giggling, her clothes flying, heavy breathing. And then she stood, wandered around his bed, and tried to find her pyjamas from across the room. He watched her, the light from the streetlamp outside illuminating everything, her silky hair shining in the darkness.

"Have you seen my shorts?" Ella asked, frowning in his direction.

He pointed. "On the chair."

She pulled them on quickly and unlocked the door.

"Hey, El. Stay a minute, will you?"

She gave him a confused look before making her way over to him and snuggling under the covers.

In the last couple of days he had felt her change, felt her holding back, pushing away. He was worried. He knew what she was like; that she was erratic and unpredictable but he needed to know where he stood. He wanted to talk properly about them as a couple, but he never had the chance, and now he was running out of time. Every time he saw her alone she was always so naked, and they were always so busy. Whatever they were right now worked. It was efficient, but it wasn't enough.

He pulled her close, so that their faces were nearly touching. She looked up at him with big, wide eyes.

"You don't have to do this, Con," Ella whispered.

"What do you mean?"

"You don't have to look after me. If you want it to just be this week, it can be. I'm not sure I'd be good for you."

Conrad's face flashed with astonishment before darkening into a thundering frown. "You want me to just pretend it never happened? Keep it a secret forever? Because screw that."

Ella sighed. "I didn't think would get this complicated. If it stays here, no one else has to know. Nothing."

"What if I want people to know? I like you, El. I don't want it just to be this. If you want me too, I want to be with you."

She shook her head. "You don't. I'm not myself right now. I'll just push you away and piss you off."

"I want you to piss me off! Please piss me off, every day if you like," Conrad said, unabashed at the pleading in his voice. They both laughed, but Ella still shook her head. Before she could say anything else, he kissed her, and then spoke quickly. "Okay, one date. When we get back to school, we'll go to town one weekend, we won't tell anyone, and go on a date. Fully clothed, low key, something basic like fighting seagulls for our chips on the beach and we'll be normal. Please."

"I don't know…"

"If you're trying to use me for my body, you can at least eat some bloody chips with me once! If the others find out, we'll tell them we're just meeting up to talk about them. Come *on*, give me a chance. I won't tell anyone. I'll keep my mouth shut, but I don't want this to end like this. Please," Conrad said, trying to keep that plea from his voice.

Ella hesitated, seemingly inspecting the duvet's thread count thoroughly, before raising her eyes and looking into his face. "Alright," she said. "Take me out. Not for chips though, gross."

"Anywhere you like." Conrad grinned.

"It'll be expensive," she teased, standing up and slowly making her way to the door.

"I'll order the best wine."

"I'll complain about the food."

"Sure. If you do, we might get it for free," Conrad said, and a chuckle reluctantly escaped Ella.

"I'll complain about *you*."

"Everyone does, anyway." He wove her away.

"You can't be deterred, can you?" Ella asked, her eyes narrowed playfully, but he sensed the insecurity behind them. Conrad knew that her reluctance to take a chance on him wasn't personal, not to him anyway. It was because she never thought anyone would like her for her. And he wasn't about to prove her right. He knew she needed to see herself as she was; smart, beautiful, funny, and he was going to help her see it, too. He realised that what he wanted most in that moment was for her to see herself as he saw her, and he would as long as he needed trying to make that happen.

"You're not going to scare me off, Ella."

Her hand rested on the door handle, and she sighed gently.

"That's what you think," she murmured into the door.

"You won't. I get you. I know you, and I like you for it." It was a promise. She shook her head, smiling, and left. Conrad grinned as he fell back onto his pillow.

Chapter Thirteen

They arrived at their headteacher's office breathless and red in the face. Coco's parents left the room, sobbing, too stricken with grief to notice them. Hardy walked beside them, a supportive hand placed on Harriet's back.

"Go in," Hardy said quietly, nodding towards her office door.

There were only three chairs in front of her desk. Bea stood and leaned against Conrad's. They waited nervously for a couple of minutes, all jiggling legs and biting nails, and cumbersome hands that had no idea of what they wanted to do.

Hardy slowly made her way across the room. When she reached her desk chair, she sat heavily, and took off her glasses. "What I have to tell you next is the most distressing thing I have ever had to say to students in my thirty-five years of teaching," she said. "All I can say is that you have my continued support at this time, and I am always more than..."

"What's happened?" Harrison interrupted.

Mrs Hardy took a deep breath and closed her eyes. "Early this morning, Coco's body was found at the bottom of the cliffs, near our beach."

Bea made an awful yelp of pain as she clung to the chair in front of her. Conrad brought his hand to his mouth as tears started rolling down his cheeks, a stream of uninterrupted emotion.

Ella and Harrison did not react.

"Her body? But that sounds like she's dead," Harrison said, not comprehending the awfulness of Hardy's words.

Mrs Hardy looked down upon him with pity, tears shining

in her heavily bagged eyes. "Mr Fletcher, we do not yet know the cause of her death," she said. "But it seems that Coco took her own life."

"No!" Ella wailed. The sound she made was a cry of such pain that she made audible the agony felt by the others.

Harrison covered his face with his hands, which were shaking violently. Conrad absent-mindedly placed a hand onto his shoulder. Harrison shrugged it off.

They sat in shock for a moment as Mrs Hardy said words into her handkerchief that Conrad doubted any of them registered. He stood a couple of minutes later, swaying, as the blood rushed from his head. Harrison did not move.

Ella stood as Conrad did, and glanced at him, and then at Harrison, before sprinting out of the room. She sobbed into her hand.

It felt to Conrad as though the world was moving quickly around him. Hardy was moving in and out, and the receptionist, Elaine, brought in tea and biscuits, crying herself.

Conrad shook his head to try and clear his thoughts, and held his hand out to Harrison, who did not acknowledge it.

Bea knelt on the floor and put her arm around Harrison. She gazed up at Conrad and told him he could go. And he did. He walked towards his dorm and checked his watch. It was 6pm. Everyone was heading to or from dinner and staring inquisitively at the red headed guy with bags under his eyes and tears streaming down his face. He reached his door and shakily pulled his keys out of his school bag, sobbing harder as he dropped them and they clanged to the floor.

Conrad threw his school bag across the room and sat on the edge of his bed as he did the moment he found out about his mum. Only that day he had three people waiting to be there for him. Now he had no one. It was becoming too much to bear, and he was hyperventilating. The gasping for air made him see sense for a moment. His elbows resting on his thighs, he placed his hands behind his neck, closed his eyes, and focused on breathing steadily. He thought practically. If he was going to deal with the next day, he would need sleep. He stood and unsteadily walked to his sink cabinet, pulling out the prescription sleeping tablets he had started to take two years earlier. He knew the nights would be the worst, and made a note first to renew his prescription, and second, to advise the others to do the same. He took them with a pint of water, which he refilled for when he needed it later. He took off his uniform and curled up in bed in his pants, cocooning the sheets around him as he sobbed into his pillow.

Conrad rose from bed, impossibly early, the next morning. He thought bitterly that the only person he knew who was emotionally accomplished enough to deal with the feelings overcoming him was Coco.

He wanted to call her. He sat on the edge of his bed, at 6.30, already dressed ready for school. He stared at her number, at her name. He wanted to speak to her so badly, he wanted to hear her voice, he wanted her to tell him what to do, since she always did know what to do. But she couldn't. She was elsewhere, unavailable, behind a heavy locked door to which Conrad had no key. Or, she was simply dead, lost to the world. A massive loss.

Conrad stayed like that for a long time, until he went over to his sink and washed his face with cold water. He saw himself in the mirror. A haggard, ill version of himself, with heavy, angry purple bags under his eyes stared back.

"Fuck," he said aloud. He dabbed his finger in his moisturiser and felt the silkiness mask his face. The clean smell made him aware of the stagnant state of his room. The drawn curtains and the dirty sheets suddenly made him feel ill, so he made a coffee with three spoonfuls of coffee and two sugars, and stared at the sunrise through the window of the kitchen.

It was strange that the sun should rise when the world might as well have ended the day before.

Mum, Coco.

But, nevertheless, the sun still rose, as he still walked and thought, and the world still turned on its axis. Odd.

No, devastating.

172

How dare it? How dare it pretend everything was going to be normal when it wasn't.

Conrad looked down at the uniform he had put on at six in the morning and realised he was pretending that everything was normal too, and he suddenly sympathised. Maybe the world was in mourning too. Maybe it was just trying to get through today just like him. Maybe it couldn't wait for the moon to take over, for it to be able to fall back into bed again. Maybe the sun looked in the mirror this morning and said 'fuck', too.

He closed his eyes and felt the warmth on his face. He found it comforting. It made him think of happy memories, of Coco laughing on the beach that summer. It almost drove out the image he had in his mind of Coco, cold and broken, and whatever the hell happened to her before that.

He picked up his school bag from beside him and walked across the grass to registration. Conrad thought that Mrs Turner looked tired, too. Everyone was quieter than usual, trying their best not to glance towards the table at which he sat alone, staring at Coco's empty chair.

She only called Conrad's name. She didn't mention Harrison, or Bea, or Ella, and she didn't mention Coco. She would still be on the register, he thought, and he would bet that there wasn't an absence note for 'dead'. No, there was no need for that, because no one could ever expect something so catastrophically awful to happen, no one ever did, he realised.

As Baz Luhrmann once said, the really bad things in life are those that surprise you on some idle Tuesday, and whether you worry or not, they're still going to hit you like a bus when they happen. That's why there's no 'dead' note on a register, it's because the death of an eighteen-year-old girl who probably would have conquered the world, was something no one would have the morbid foresight to predict.

So whilst, with an ache, he knew that her name was on that screen in black and white, he was almost glad it was a shock to the computer, as much as it was to him.

Conrad made his way to history, his first lesson of the day, and sat listening to Mr Graham explain the contents of today's lesson when a familiar voice caused him to sit bolt upright and turn to the door.

"I'm sorry I'm late, sir."

"Not at all, Mr Fletcher, not at all. It's good to see you," Mr Graham said with a forced, far too jovial voice.

A better teacher, a better human being, would have taken one look at him and insisted that Harrison go somewhere else, talk to a counsellor, go for a walk, go anywhere that wasn't his lesson about World War Two when Harrison's own version of Nagasaki dropped the night before.

But alas, Mr Graham was neither of those things, and Harrison sat down near the door, as Conrad watched his red eyes and pallid face as he dropped his schoolbag down upon the desk, and he wondered what on earth he was doing here.

Conrad was in lessons himself, of course, but that was because he knew how he dealt with things, he knew that grief only festered within him if he stayed in bed. He needed to get out of his room. He had to get away from his dark little nest, now damp with tears, and filled with a sense of hopelessness. He needed to leave the dark, smelly room he had been in all night, and he needed the everyday mundanity of school.

Harrison, however, wasn't him, and Conrad knew him well enough to know that he was ticking away, awaiting an explosion that could happen at any given moment.

Mr Graham droned on for half an hour, and Conrad privately commended Harrison's valiant effort in quietly attending, but he still held his breath every time Harrison made a substantial movement, like a scratch of his nose or the stretch of his arm.

Mr Graham was beckoned out of his class by Miss Jenkins, who gave a startled look at Harrison when she opened the door and saw him there. Mr Graham left the room and the seven students were alone.

"I'm so sorry about what you're going through, Harrison. Coco was very...unique," Genevieve said, leaning back in her chair.

Oh for fuck's sake, Gen. Conrad thought. *You hated her,*

174

and you're not even pretending any differently.

Harrison nodded.

Rose Tindham-Jones, a girl who had perhaps spoken to Coco twice in her life, then decided that it was her place to speak. "When I woke up this morning, I couldn't believe that it had actually happened, that she wouldn't be here today. She was such a nice girl."

Conrad was building up to say something himself, but then Harrison spoke. His feeble voice was loud in the grim quiet of the classroom, of the whole school. It felt as though the walls themself were listening. "Nice? She wasn't nice. At least Genevieve had the decency to not pretend she knew or even liked her. No, she wasn't nice!"

Harrison stood up, arms flailing around him as he now began to shout. "She was funny, she was thoughtful and sweet and completely barmy, and despite what Gen thinks, she was good. She was wild and dramatic and never boring. Nice is boring, nice is normal. She was a load of things before that. So don't pretend like you know her. Don't pretend like you care that she won't be around ever again because you don't. Don't talk about waking up without her being here because I haven't slept in days, knowing that it's all my fault. All my fucking fault."

His voice broke, and he punched the desk before he buckled over, sobbing.

Conrad jumped out of his seat and placed an arm over his shoulders. "Come on, Fletch. You shouldn't be in school," he said quietly. Harrison stood and hugged him. Conrad hugged him tightly back, now crying himself. The rest of the class watched in stunned silence.

"Let's get out of here," Conrad said as he wiped the tears from his cheek and opened the heavy classroom door. It took all his strength to hold it open.

They walked together to the dorm in a quiet daze. Nothing felt real. They were woozy, a mixture of sleep deprivation and total and complete devastation.

"It was my fault, Con, I did it, I…"

"Listen, we don't know what happened, but if she did,

well… a girl doesn't do that as the product of one thing. Doing that because your boyfriend cheated on you is not a normal thing to do. We all should have noticed that something was up. But we didn't, and she didn't tell us either. What she did was her decision, it wasn't ours. It's awful that she felt that way, that she felt that that was the only way out of whatever situation she felt she was in, but she did it. She deserved better. She did. From you, from me, from the girls, and we failed her. But this isn't all your fault, Harrison, not at all."

They reached Harrison's room, and he immediately jumped on his bed.

"I'm sorry," Harrison said into his pillow.

"What for?" Conrad asked as he sat beside the big Harrison-shaped lump in the duvet.

"For Ella. For being with Coco when you liked her. For throwing it away. For being a dick. I'm sorry, for all of it. I don't understand how you could even be sat here with me now, I know I couldn't."

"You didn't know that I liked Coco to begin with, and you didn't know I liked Ella. As for the being a dick bit, I've gotten used to it these past few years." Conrad shrugged, catching Harrison's eye. They both exchanged unenthusiastic watery smiles, nothing more than a small acknowledgement of the lack of hard feelings. "I'll always be your best mate, Fletch. Sometimes reluctantly, sure, but we'll never not be friends. I've got to say one thing though - I think we need to talk more. Not just me and you, the girls too."

"Even Ella?" Harrison asked.

"Even Ella, yeah. She made a mistake, but she's been having a hard time too. I feel like that needs forgiveness. We all need each other at the moment."

"So we're just all going to be friends again, like nothing's changed?"

"Everything's changed, there's no denying that. But there's no one else that can help us through this. We need to go through this as a unit, not alone. I know that it takes an army of people to make really bad stuff hurt a little less, and we need to help each other, or it's just going to get worse." They pondered Conrad's words in silence for a while.

"I think I need to try and get some sleep," Harrison said, his voice weak.

"That's a good idea. If you need me, give me a call. I'll come and visit you in a bit."

"Where are you going?"

"B Block."

"Oh."

Conrad cleared his throat. "I need to see if she's alright," he said.

"Yeah. I get it. I- I hope she's okay too. And Bea."

Conrad nodded, perhaps a little curtly. "Course you do. I'll see you in a bit."

He walked across the wet grass to the ugly outbuilding hosting the girls dorm. He punched in the number on the keypad that the girls gave him and Harrison years ago, and walked along the downstairs corridor to Ella's room. In the otherwise silent B-block, Conrad's footsteps echoed on the floor, the sound booming against the grey walls.

Trying his best to ignore the door beside him that seemed to scream for his attention in the silence, Conrad knocked on room 8, and Ella opened it a crack, squinting in the light.

"Conrad."

"I came to see if you were okay," he said

Ella opened the door wider and stood aside, allowing him into her dark, musky room.

He walked over to her sink and poured her a glass of water.

"You need to drink," he told her, as sat on the bed that Ella returned to.

She drank the entire glass of water in a few seconds, gulping and gasping. Conrad briefly wondered how long she would have gone without drinking anything if he hadn't come to visit, if he decided that he couldn't stand to look at her, if he decided that he couldn't put out of his mind the fact that she and Harrison had slept together in this bed, in this room, Jesus, maybe even on these sheets for all he knew, as

177

Coco was next door, to vanish a day later. If he couldn't get over that enough to visit Ella, he dreaded to think what would happen to her. But some things were more important than who was sleeping with who, like life. He was confident Ella had made a mistake, and, above everything, that she needed him. Perhaps not him exactly, but she needed someone, and he was willing to be someone, he thought.

"I thought you hated me," she said, her voice hoarse.

"Don't be daft. Of course I don't," Conrad said, and put an arm around her shoulders, kissing her head as she leaned into him. She felt soft, comforting.

"How are the others?"

"I haven't seen Bea. Harrison tried going to school, but he's a total wreck, obviously. I left him to nap."

"You tried going to school, too," Ella said, gently tugging the lapel of his blazer.

"When the sun came up this morning I felt like I needed to leave my room. I needed the normality of putting on my blazer and tie and doing my hair and going to lessons, but then Harrison showed up and, well, absolutely fucking lost it. And I realised that history was not where I needed to be today either. I needed to be here, checking you were all alright."

"How are you doing so well?"

"I'm not. I'm in shock, if anything. I'm just the most functional, which means I'm the one that has to make sure you're all okay."

Conrad supposed that's what adults do in times of need, pushing their own needs to one side for those who needed them. He sympathised with his dad who, for all his cock ups after Conrad's mum died, always made sure his sons were doing as well as they could be. Only now did he realise how much strength that must have taken, although he knew that his mum would have told him to do so, sternly. Conrad knew that Coco would have made sure that he, Ella, Harrison and Bea were looked after if she could have done, and so Conrad took on that responsibility in her place.

He stood up. "I'm making a cup of tea, I'll be back in five minutes," he said.

He walked quickly past Coco's room, to the small kitchen at the end of the corridor. Their dorm kitchens didn't have anything for real cooking, like a hob or oven, just a microwave and toaster for snacks, and a kettle for hot drinks.

Conrad grabbed two mugs, not really caring if they were Ella's, secretly hoping they were Genevieve's and Rose's, reminding himself not to wash them as a scheme of dumb revenge.

He put extra sugar in Ella's mug, figuring she needed the energy, and definitely wouldn't eat.

When he opened her door with his hip, she was cocooned in her bed again.

"Leave them on the bedside table and come here," Ella said. Her eyes were wide and red, blinking at him from over the top of the duvet.

He hesitated for a moment, staring at the duvet she was wrapped under, but now holding open for him. He took off his blazer and tie and shoes, and got under it with her, pulling her close.

"Oh, El," Conrad whispered, as she started sniffling again.

"I was awful. A terrible friend."

"No, you weren't yourself. You still probably aren't right, and you won't be for a while."

"That doesn't change how I made her feel, how she felt that she had to..." Ella's voice broke off into a deep sob.

"I know. But it's understandable. You're not a terrible friend, or person, El."

"You really think that?"

"You're a bloody headfuck of epic proportions sometimes, but you're a good girl, really," Conrad said, smiling down at her. At a time like this, when Ella was crying, and Coco was dead, those huge brown eyes, that earnest, solemn face, still made him smile, even if to do so cost him every ounce of enthusiasm he had left.

"I really don't want Harrison anymore, Con. I mean it. I know I did for a long time, and that happened a few days ago but..."

"Shh," he said, and hugged her tight, the smile wiped off

his face at the idea of Ella and Harrison. "That doesn't matter right now."

He stroked her hair and whispered soothing words as her emotions escaped her. Ella started crying harder, her body shaking in his arms.

"I can't believe she's gone," she sobbed, and Conrad nodded, swallowing hard.

"I know," was all he managed to say before joining her, the pair of them lying together, holding each other, her sobbing into his chest, him into her hair.

They stayed like that for a few minutes, and then Ella stopped and looked into his face, her eyes burning into his. She kissed him. It took him a moment, but he knew that it was pointless resisting, that he was inexplicably drawn to her, that he was always going to end up going along with whatever she did. He was enthralled by her, and no matter how tentative he was, he had no choice but to push aside all his scruples, all his anger and jealousy, because to be with her was so much better than the alternative, no matter what she did, how much she messed up.

"Shh, now," he said, pulling her in close, as she nuzzled into his chest.

They lay together as the darkness fell upon them, and as Ella fell asleep. Conrad did not smile as he pushed her curtain of hair out of her face, and as he gazed upon her pouty lips, her cheeks, puffy and innocent in sleep, and her long eyelashes that dusted them. Here with her was where he knew he needed to be at that moment.

PART FOUR
HARRISON

Chapter Fourteen

Hardy told them all that Coco was gone, but Harrison couldn't understand. There was a tinny ringing in his ears that meant he couldn't hear properly, and he couldn't think. He felt lightheaded and slow, unable to comprehend what was going on. *Why were they talking about Coco as though she was dead when that couldn't be the case, when nothing that horrendously bad could ever happen, could it?* he wondered. *Coco couldn't be gone.*

This couldn't be happening. But then, why would Mrs Hardy lie about such a thing? It had to be a mistake, an awful, terrible mistake. That poor girl wasn't Coco, because if it was then Harrison would never see Coco again. If that girl was Coco then she was gone forever and that absolutely could not be the case because she was going to live to be an eccentric old lady who insisted on skydiving at 82 and celebrating her achievement with a bottle of champagne. That girl was not Coco.

She couldn't be.

But then, why did every mention of her name, whether spoken or in his head, cause his whole body to feel an agonising ache, a thousand burning knives puncturing his every inch of skin, every organ? Coco being gone was the only explanation for this pain, he concluded, because she always did her best to keep him from hurting. She protected him, and nothing could hurt this much so long as she was around.

She was so good.

Was.

Coco was now a was.

For a few minutes, it didn't seem real. For a few glorious minutes, the full force of the news that was just imparted onto Harrison had not yet hit. He sat, shocked, briefly aware of Bea's presence next to him.

He blinked, and all of a sudden Harrison saw the room. He saw the cold cups of tea left on the desk, and the discarded biscuits next to them. He saw the calm sky through the long window in front of him. He saw Bea's tear sodden face blinking up at him, and Conrad's foot disappear around the door.

He could hear the silence in the usually loud and busy school. It was a roaring, violent sound, that signified that something was truly, horribly amiss.

Then he found himself falling apart. He felt as though he shattered on the old, dusty, seat, crumpling to only a fraction of his size, his body shaking with sobs.

Bea's hand rubbed his back. "I know, Harrison. We feel it too," she said softly, her voice weak and broken.

He could hear her sobs next to him. He sat up and hugged her.

She was kneeling on the floor so they were at awkward heights but feeling her arms around his waist felt comforting.

He and Bea sat like that for a minute, until she stood and offered him her hand. He took it, thinking that wherever she was leading him, it couldn't be worse than the hell he found himself in at that moment.

They walked together, arms linked, until they reached the point at which the paths to the dorms split off. Block A for the boys, and B for the girls.

Bea hugged him tightly. "Get some sleep. I'm not sure what else will help. Come and get me if you need me," she said.

He nodded and wandered to his dorm. He was briefly aware of flinging off his shoes before lying on top of his bed.

He thought about Coco, and how he treated her. He thought desperately about all the things he should have done differently, all the things he should have said. It was too much to bear, and his head was spinning. He closed his eyes.

184

He let himself take her for granted, but he didn't always. He used to be good to her. He used to make her feel special. He used to do all the things to make her aware that, to him, she was the best person in the world. He knew he didn't deserve her, that Coco was infinitely stronger, funnier, smarter than him, and he tried to narrow the margin of their brilliantness slightly by making up for that in grand romantic gestures, when he would once spend all his pocket money on flowers and meals out, even though she had her parents' credit card and infinitely more accessible funds than he did. He would take candid pictures of her and endure his friends making fun of the soppy captions he would post, like when he took a photo of Coco in Paris with a gigantic box of macaroons, and wrote something about them being nowhere near as sweet as she was. He would take pictures of historic monuments, of works of art, with Coco in the shot, and make a point of her being the most magnificent thing in front of him. It was silly, contrived, but not altogether dishonest, and as much as she giggled and rolled her eyes, he could tell she loved it. She loved their relationship being broadcast like that, and he knew it made her happy to see that it wasn't only her posting everything they did together online. But the best thing about him and Coco was that they didn't have one of those relationships which are *only* happy online. For so long they weren't one of those couples who took and edited and posted the perfect picture and argued all night. They were happy, and as happy as they seemed to all their friends and followers.

That wasn't to say, though, that they didn't have any fights at all. All couples did. But they had worked through them in the past because he tried his hardest to make it up to her.

There aren't many sixteen-year-old boys who, after their girlfriend storm off at lunchtime because he spent his fifth break time in a row playing rugby with the boys, would organise the school orchestra to play *I Want You Back* by the Jackson 5, and put on his most ridiculous Michael Jackson impression to serenade her as she walks into music class.

There aren't many boyfriends who would succeed in

planning a surprise trip to Paris for their girlfriend's sixteenth birthday, liaising with her mum to find a hotel with a balcony that overlooks the Eiffel tower and, on the night of her birthday, set his watch to tell exactly when it would sparkle with those twinkly lights, as it does at night, every hour, and record him kissing her at the exact moment it lit up, under the guise of taking a photo. It may have been Harriet's idea, but God, it was a good one.

He was meticulous. He knew what she wanted. He knew what made her happy. He knew what it was that made her grin her ridiculous toothy grin that only ever appeared when she was completely and utter overwhelmed with happiness, and he had to admit that he neglected that side of himself for a while during their last year together.

He was grateful to Coco. She gave him an escape. She was his place to run to, where he could be himself and forget about everything that worried him. When he was with her, at least until things started to change, he could forget about school, forget about his piano recitals and violin gradings, about his rugby finals and football matches. When he was with Coco it was only her that mattered, and when she stopped being that, when that magic ended and Coco became one of his problems instead of his answer, their relationship started to flicker in the wind, until eventually it would blow out, or maybe catch the curtain and set the house alight. One or the other.

As Harrison lay in his dark room, uncomfortably, on his tear-sodden pillow, he knew that he wanted nothing more than to have a chance to make it up to her, to organise more trips to Paris, more scavenger hunts and serenades, or even just the chance to apologise, to fall on his knees even for just a minute, and tell her how damn sorry he was for everything, for every fight, for every little thing, and evidently massive things, that he didn't notice, but should have. He would apologise for Ella, for how stupid he had been, when it meant absolutely nothing at the time and now would be singularly the worst thing he had ever done, and probably would ever do. In that moment, he would have traded places with her, with no second thought, and no hesitation. He wanted to be as far away as possible from the agony of loss and guilt that he felt.

For so long they were so good, never able to get enough of each other, much to their friends' disgust, especially the single ones.

Harrison remembered standing on that dancefloor when he was just a kid, and Coco wrapping her arms around him for the first time. He remembered thinking that his heart would stop. They giggled awkwardly for a second as they swayed in the crowd, before he gulped and decided to bite the bullet, and whispered in her ear. "I like you, you know," he began, and he could see her eyes widen as her cheeks pinked and a radiant smile grew across her lips. "Well, saying I like you is a bit of an understatement, really. If I was being honest, I'd say that you're actually the most perfect girl I've ever met, and I know that you have hundreds of guys wanting to go out with you, but I wondered if you wanted to go out with me, on Saturday, please."

Coco stared at him for a long moment, and he was just about to stress that there was no need to give an answer then and there, when she kissed him.

There was lots of tongue and saliva, but they both grinned at each other when they broke apart, and hastily walked through the crowd hand-in-hand and out onto the grounds.

It was a clear, starry night, and he gave her his jacket he shivered as they wandered around the grounds. They embraced on the set of rocks that they would find themselves sat at for much of their school life, and they kissed some more.

It was so instant, so set in stone. That first kiss was like a switch, turning the light off on his life before Coco, and turning it on for his life with Coco. It was a contrasting moment, and things were never the same after it.

Harrison ate lunch with her the next day, and Ella and Conrad joined them. It was the start of their group that was now made up of only four. None of them really talking to anyone else.

He and Coco kissed constantly. He found he yearned to be upon them again whenever he wasn't. He convinced himself at fourteen that they were the only lips he would want to kiss for the rest of his life, and he stayed sure of that for a long time, until Ella.

As Harrison and Coco got older, most nights he found himself clandestinely roaming B Block, or climbing through Coco's window to spend the night with her. That went on for months, from the day Coco turned sixteen in Paris, until around the time of their exams last year, and then they felt a lull.

The summer before, Coco would hardly let him touch her. It went on for almost two months, and the panic, the worry that there was something wrong with their relationship nearly killed him. There was the odd time, the day of their last exam, the night of their summer party on the last day of term, but he felt a gaping chasm between them that hadn't been there before, and he longed to find out what he had done. He couldn't figure out why, but somehow he could feel her slipping away from him.

He was distracted, he knew that. He felt the pressure, the absolute and serious need to achieve, in a way that he hadn't before. He withdrew, spent far too much time in the library and far too little time eating, sleeping, or with Coco. He felt the stress of exams, of coursework, of unis in two years' time, of his job in six years' time, for his house and family and kids and dogs in God knows when time, and he knew he wouldn't be able to deal with failure. The weight of his future rested heavily upon him, and that pressure had killed far greater men.

And the thing was, for Harrison and everyone else that was told they could achieve the best marks, those who were told they could go to the best universities and get the best jobs, and would be the best their school could offer, failure wasn't about not passing. It was about getting an A, or even worse, a B, when there were A*s to be had. It was about going to a brilliant university when he could have gone to the best, that niggling feeling that you could always do *better*.

It was exhausting, damaging, and, well, shit. It took its toll on Harrison, and Coco couldn't understand it. She couldn't understand his desperate need to be the best, she couldn't understand his obsession with success, because she found that it always came so naturally to her.

They were having problems, and he assumed it was the stress. But when their summer exams were finished, and he spent every moment he could with her, she was still distant, she was still off with him, and she wasn't one to hold grudges. That wasn't like her. She would always crack her icy exterior in a second. He would make her laugh, or say or do something to make it up to her, and they were back to normal, all within the hour. But at that time, she held back from him, she avoided any intimate moments, and it was unsettling. The last few weeks of the school year were busy, and they'd had no opportunity to talk it through together, beyond him asking if everything was alright and her telling him she just wasn't in the mood.

She wasn't constantly brushing him off, it seemed, to flit between normality and distance, usually when he had done nothing wrong. Their usual bickering was so much more intense, leaving them screaming at each other in private, and it was taking the energy out of him.

It was little things, like him embarrassing her in front of the others, giving out too many details and leaving her red in the face. Before then, she would roll her eyes and giggle, or else mildly tell him off when they were alone, and he would make it up to her in a way she would definitely prefer to keep secret, but she wasn't having any of it that summer. After their end of year party, when he sent her into fits of embarrassed giggles for revealing too much, as usual, at the breakfast table, she went back to his room to help him pack and yelled at him for forty five minutes.

"You just don't respect me at all, do you? You used to be with me because of who I was, but now you're with me because you want a quick fuck, aren't you?" Coco's hungover frown made her look vicious, her unbrushed, air-dried, wild hair, made her seem like a lion, ready to tear him limb from limb.

"Hey!" Harrison interrupted, astounded by her revelation. "That's ridiculous, babe. I love you. You know I do. I was only teasing."

"I was mortified, Harrison!"

"Because of a silly comment like that? I'm sorry that I said it, okay? But, I mean, don't you think you're overreacting a little bit?"

She glared at him and stormed out of his room, slamming his door behind her. She didn't answer his texts or calls for hours, until, when Harrison and Conrad were sat down to lunch, she eventually turned up in the dining hall, and perched on the chair next to him.

"Where the hell have you been? I've been worried about you! You haven't been answering your phone," Harrison said.

She shrugged. "My phone was turned off. I was only at the beach. I sat there for a while," she said in a quiet, miserable mumble.

"You could have told me," Harrison said, and put his arm around her shoulders.

She stiffened for a second, before resolving to let him pull her close. "Alright, I'm sorry," she said without feeling, and he kissed her. She kissed him back softly, almost mechanically, as if the action was habitual, from muscle memory. He ran his fingers through her hair and traced her jaw with his thumb. It was a kiss of desperation, Harrison's bid to bring her back to normal, to revive what seemed to have spluttered and died. All he wanted was for them to be happy again, and he was so aware in that moment of his half-arsed attempts at fixing things that should this be the end, and it felt it. He would only have himself to blame.

"Uh... I'm gonna go and get dessert," Conrad said, causing Coco to break apart from him. Harrison could have killed him for ruining the moment.

"I need to get food anyway," she said glumly, and wandered over to the food counters.

He watched her walk heavily along the space between the benches. She didn't strut like she used to once, and he didn't know if it was the hangover, or something else, but she seemed to *blend in*, and if there was once thing that Coco Lyndham-Smith never did, it was blending in.

"That was cold," Conrad said, eyeing him with interest. He wished he wouldn't.

"Yeah. She's been like that a lot lately."

"Well, like, are you okay? You can't split up. I'm counting on this holiday."

Harrison offered him a reluctant laugh. "Your guess is as good as mine. She's not telling me anything," he said, as Coco came back with Ella and Bea, and was almost back to normal again.

A couple of weeks later they arrived in Miami, and things were still weird. Harrison went home to his dad's for a week, and then to Conrad's, and Coco stayed with Bea and spoke to him on the phone in the mornings and evenings. They were both with friends, so had no chance to address the weirdness between them. He felt that it would be a long argument, so he tried to avoid bringing it up, only talking to Coco in brief, shallow bursts.

And then Harrison saw her again and he thought the distance would make Coco pleased to see him, but he was met with a brief kiss on the lips as they all met at the airport and she shopped for the rest of their wait, barely saying twenty words to him.

When they landed and they dropped off their bags in Coco's room, he decided then to address it, unwilling to spend a month with her when she was like this.

"Have I done something wrong?" Harrison asked as they were searching through their luggage for swimsuits. The question seemed to erupt from within him, out of his control. It sounded angrier than he wanted it to, and he adjusted his face to show that he wasn't. Coco looked up from her suitcase with her huge blue eyes, in shock.

"Like what?" she asked.

"I don't know, baby, but you've been... distant lately, different."

"I have?"

"Come on, Coco. We've barely had sex in two months. You don't talk to me anymore, you're yelling at me for nothing, what's going on? Have I screwed up?"

Coco looked down at the floor and mumbled something inaudible. She shook her head, as though shaking some sense into herself, and walked closer to him, placing a hand on his cheek when she reached him.

"I've just been stressed with exams, Harrison," she said, "And so have you. I'm fine. *We're* fine."

Harrison nodded, but he was still unsure. She gave him a discerning look before kissing him like she had not kissed him in months, her hands eagerly undoing the buttons on his shirt. They kicked off their holiday by truly breaking their drought on her bed, splayed over their suitcases.

But even then, they didn't feel the same. That afternoon was incredible, but more because of the wait before it. Harrison had been drunk the time before that and could hardly remember, so that afternoon the passion and the clarity that Coco seemed to have was like a homage to how they were a few months before. But, even still, he still felt an indescribable distance between them.

He could tell that Coco had something on her mind. He could see the cogs whirring, but she would not tell him what she was thinking. And when they were around Bea and Ella and Conrad, she wore her usual grin and evoked her usual carefree exterior. But when she and Harrison were alone, she didn't smile. She snapped at him for the slightest of inconveniences, and she spent her evenings getting drunk and running off into bathrooms or to the beach to cry about the smallest things. It was as if anything could tip her over the edge.

In a way, Harrison preferred that, because the alternative was her other tactic of not speaking to him for hours at a time. He felt like he was sharing a bed with a stranger, and for the first couple of weeks in Miami, hardly anything changed.

And then the night of the garden party came and Coco seemed so back to normal in front of that idiot, Brad, giggling bashfully at his inappropriate comments, and staying notedly quiet when he clearly stepped over a line.

It frustrated Harrison so much that Brad, of all people, should get to see Coco at her best like that, when he was dealing with her ghost.

And it built up, and he found himself playing a montage in his mind of the couple of months before, of all the fights and shitty moments they faced, and he lost it with the guy and Conrad's fist, and Bea's knee ended up bringing an end to the crappy little party they found themselves having.

After they left, Coco sent Harrison and Conrad off so she could have some sort of a domestic with Ella, and they wandered to the house together.

"Can you fucking believe it?" Harrison growled.

"What?" Conrad asked, wincing as he gingerly ran his thumb against his sore knuckles.

"Just *her* and that fucking guy, letting him say all that shit to her as I had to watch. That wasn't on, right?"

Conrad looked up at him, frowning thoughtfully as they reached the French doors into the kitchen. The sounds from the party, of the drunken women slurring their arguments and ordering even more drinks, from the other side of the house, felt distant, as though miles away.

"I think it's more his fault, though. I mean, it's not like it was her saying those things to him, was it? And he was quite clever about it too, they were subtle digs," Conrad said.

"What, so I just let it go?" Harrison asked, his face red, his breathing fast. Conrad fidgeted sheepishly. Harrison knew it was unlike himself to be so angry, but the angry thumping in his chest was not slowing down.

Conrad shrugged, sensing that he was facing a losing battle. He opened the freezer door and placed some peas around his hand, before turning to face him Harrison across the counter.

"What do I know, mate? Girls aren't exactly my area, are they?"

Harrison sighed and shook his head, walking towards the door. "Alright. Tell her I'm in her room and I want to talk,"

Harrison mumbled, and Conrad nodded, his eyes following him, filled with concern.

"Hey, Fletch," Conrad called, as Harrison had one foot through the door.

He turned and saw that Conrad was already lounging across lazily. "Go easy on her, yeah? Calm down a minute before you talk."

Harrison's response was to give a weary look, and then he turned and stomped up the stairs. He flopped onto the far too many cushions on Coco's bed and sighed heavily. He was lying across the width of the bed. His tall frame meant that his calves and head were dangling in the air when Coco gently opened the door to her room a few minutes later. He looked at her upside down for a second before sitting up and frowning. At the look on his face, she burst out crying.

"Hey, hey!" he said soothingly, before patting the space next to him. She sat there and he pulled her in close. "What is it?" he asked.

"E-Ella j-just went off at me," Coco gasped between sobs, fanning her face with her hands as the tears rolled down her cheeks.

"Really? Saying what?" Harrison asked, surprised. He knew that of the four of them, Ella had the least reason to be mad at her.

"That it's hard being my friend when all I think about is myself and that I need boys to like me to feel good about myself, something like that. She's furious it was my fault she had to deal with James. She doesn't get how awful I feel and that everyone's mad at me and…" She broke off, sobbing.

Harrison stroked her hair and shushed her, whispering, "it's okay," over and over again.

"It's so annoying that she can't see it," Coco said a few minutes later, emerging from his chest, her eyes dark, her makeup smudged. He sighed as he saw the state of his white shirt.

Coco went on. "She had James *and* Conrad falling over her tonight, but she still says to me that she's ugly and no one wants her. She's really out of her depth with all she's dealing with. It's turning her into something she's not. She's not okay, babe, and I don't know what to do."

"She'll work it out, she's tough," Harrison began, his voice slow and sleepy. He slouched down on the bed and propped himself up on his elbow. "Wait, *Conrad*?"

"Yeah, he's crazy about her, it's obvious. Don't you see the way he stares, the little inside jokes they always have? The *weirdness* when they almost kissed earlier?"

"But that was just a game, it was weird 'cos they're friends. They're close."

Coco shook her head. "It's different now, he likes her. I know it," she said.

Harrison's eyes widened in Coco's dim room, her fairy lights casting long shadows on the wall as the light was blocked by the tower of discarded clothes on Coco's desk chair.

"Weird," he said, as Coco stretched over him into her bedside drawer and retrieved a pack of face wipes, wiping her makeup off, her eyes closed and her lips pursed as she sighed through her nose. It was maybe the longest, and definitely the nicest conversation they'd had in weeks, which was ironic considering how angry he had been only minutes before.

He sat up next to her, and she jumped when she opened her eyes and he was inches from her face.

"Come here," Harrison said, pulling another wipe from the packet and gently wiping the parts Coco missed, finishing by kissing her forehead.

"I'm sorry," she said. "Brad was ridiculous tonight, and I should have said something. I know I've been in a weird place lately, being worried about Ella and school and stuff, but I think now that school's over and we can relax again, things will get better." She looked into his face and rubbed his shoulders with her delicate hands. "I love you," she told him.

Harrison kissed Coco, gently lowering her onto her back. She wrapped her legs around him and he smiled against her mouth as she did so. She moaned a little as he kissed her neck and chest, before wriggling out from under him, and she pinned him beneath her with her strong thighs.

"I missed you," he whispered as she peeled off her red lacy top.

"I'm back now," she whispered too, leaning into his neck, nibbling his ear as she did so.

And she was. For the rest of the summer they were back to normal, even better than usual, it seemed. Once again, she couldn't get enough of him and he was validated once more. It was as though they made up for lost time, sneaking off in the middle of the night for walks on the beach and skinny dipping in the sea, even to her room in the middle of the day, leaving the others sunbathing by the pool.

They were more Harrison And Coco than ever before and it was great. Even when they started school again, it was only three days into their new term that they were caught red handed at midnight, when Mrs Brown, the usually very oblivious B Block guardian, noticed the lamp shining in Coco's room at 1AM on a Thursday morning, and then heard the giggling. She knocked the door in a rage and sent Harrison off immediately with a host of threats that he dealt with the following morning. They had, not for the first time, been summoned to Hardy's office, who had decided she had put up with their shenanigans for long enough and called their parents.

Mercifully, Harriet explained to their headmistress that she regularly and severely instilled upon Coco the importance of safe sex and that Harrison was an exceptional boy who had only ever treated Coco with the utmost respect and, further, that they were both of legal age and, frankly, it was their decision.

Harrison's Dad, Marcus, called Harrison to tell him that he would pull him out of school the next time he mortified him in such a scandalous way. But he knew it was an empty threat. Lainsbury Hall School was Harrison's best chance of success, so really, they got off easy.

And it wasn't just the fact that they were together physically again, they talked about rubbish like they used to, they joked around and had fun and it was easy again. For six weeks they carried on as normal, grossing their friends out with never-ending public displays of affection. But then came October half term, a week before Coco went missing.

For the first two days, Harrison couldn't get Coco to stop messaging, calling and tagging him in memes. His dad constantly yelled about the incessant notifications, and then, suddenly, he was faced with radio silence. For the last few days of the break he received, at the most, three or four messages and replies from Coco. For the last two days she hadn't sent him anything, and the bombardment of messages that he sent her went unread.

He was anxious when he returned to Lainsbury, expecting her to have decided that he wasn't worth her time, that she fell in love with someone else. But she greeted him as casually as she would any other day.

Coco kissed him normally, and they spent that Sunday with Ella, Conrad and Bea, in the common room watching movies and playing video games together, as they usually would.

She got weird when he whispered to her to try and leave.

"Let's get out of here," Harrison whispered, and she forcefully pushed off the hand that was stroking her thigh.

"I'm watching the film," she whispered too, her eyes not leaving the screen.

Harrison remembered that they already watched this film twice before and she was always far more interested in him. He felt that familiar devastation once again, that worry and disappointment that he had become so accustomed to falling slowly into the pit of his stomach.

For the next thirty minutes, Coco sat there, rigid, cold, next to him. Her eyes never left the TV, seemingly she failed to notice his subtle, but desperate bids for attention, him nibbling her ear or kissing her neck. Ella and Bea decided to leave as the movie ended, so he went back with Coco to her room.

She was still silent, and seemed unnerved that he joined her, offering him an anxious sideways glance as she unlocked her door, but she didn't turn him away.

"I'm tired, I'm going to bed," Coco said as she quickly changed into her pyjamas and curled up in bed. It was 8pm.

As Harrison removed his shoes, he noticed her shiver. He crawled, fully clothed, under the covers behind her, and wrapped his arms around her as the windows rattled in the wind and the thunder echoed outside. They lay like that for a few minutes, before she told him to turn off the light, which he did. Out of nowhere lightning filled the room, and he saw that her eyes were wide open. He kissed her neck and nibbled her ear again, but when his hands roamed under her vest, she stood up and walked across the room.

"What's wrong?" he asked.

"I'm getting water," she said quietly, her back to him.

"You know what I mean."

"I- I don't know, babe, I just…"

"Is it me? Have I done something?" Harrison's voice was loud, the sadness making it sound unlike his own. He turned the lamp back on, and the warm light made them both squint.

"*No,* Harrison, it's nothing," Coco said wearily.

"It doesn't feel like nothing. You haven't talked to me all week. And now you're being weird with me again? *What is up with you,* Coco? It's hard to keep up with you lately. One minute you're normal, the next you're ignoring me, and you're not telling me how to fix it. I'm going out of my mind here, babe!"

"Please, just…"

"No, I can't keep up with you!" Harrison's deep voice filled the room and changed the mood. He stood, scowling at her.

When Coco said nothing and only stared at him, still with that withering, weary look on her face, he continued. "And we still haven't talked about you ignoring me all week. You've no idea how hard it's been, the things that have been going around my mind."

"Yeah? Like what?" Coco said, and folded her arms, tendrils of hair that escaped her bun floating in front of her eyes.

"You… deciding you didn't want me, cheating on me."

"You really think I would do that to you, after all this time?"

"I can't think of any other explanation. You don't want me, so who do you want?" Harrison said. He had never fought with her like this before, he was usually chasing after her as she stormed off into the distance, angry at some sort of neglect or thoughtless words, but they were rounding on each other, their words filling the quiet room in a definite, unpleasant way.

"You think that because I don't want to sleep with you once that means I'm sleeping with the entire school? *Really*?"

"That's not what I'm saying, I just…"

"Is that all I'm good for, Harrison? A quick fuck?" Coco's hair, escaping from the bun she had thrown it up in, seemed to grow with her anger. Her face was red with incandescent rage. Harrison had never seen her look quite so mad.

"Babe, I'm not…"

"Get out," she said icily, a harshness to her voice that he had rarely heard. The momentary silence in which they stood was thick, enveloping them both, waiting to be broken.

"What?"

"Get out of my room. I don't want to see you tonight." When Harrison stared at her, dumbstruck, she shouted. "Go!"

Coco rushed him out, hastily grabbing his shoes and thrusting them into his chest. She slammed the door behind him, leaving him out in the corridor, shocked, staring at the number 9 on her door, as she blared angry rock music from her speakers inside. She had never thrown him out before.

Ella opened her door and raised her eyebrows when she saw Harrison kneeling in front of Coco's door, tying his shoelaces. Her characteristic massive sloth mug was clutched in her hand. She was heading to the kitchen to wash it.

"Rough night?" she asked. Harrison eyed Coco's door wearily before standing up and running his hand down his face, turning towards her.

"Yeah."

199

"She's hard work. You knew that ages ago," Ella said tentatively, diplomatically. It was only his knowledge of the tension between them that allowed him to hear the subtle bitter bite to her tone.

"She's been difficult lately. That's for sure."

"So what are you going to do?"

Harrison blinked at her for a moment. Her eyes bore deep into his. Their doors were only about a metre apart, meaning that he and Ella were even closer than that. "I don't know, what can I do?" he asked.

"Well, and I'm telling this to you, my friend, not her boyfriend, so don't tell her I said this, but the way I see it, you have a couple of options. You can stay with her and try and sort this out, but you've been trying to do that for months and have just been screaming at each other constantly and still haven't figured it out yet. Or... I mean, there's got to be plenty of people who won't give out this shit all the time, right?" Ella said it all quickly. She knew she shouldn't be saying this.

He moved closer to her to hear over the music, and now he looked down at her face. He could count the faint freckles on her nose.

"She's been giving out enough shit lately, that's true," Harrison said, his jaw set.

"It shouldn't be this difficult. I'm not telling you what to do, but you have to do something. Objectively, it's a little bit ridiculous."

He gulped and noticed that there was no trace of pyjamas under Ella's dressing gown. He closed his eyes momentarily and looked into her face, wondering if she caught him staring.

"It can't carry on like this, you're right," Harrison said, and took a step back. He shook his head. He knew that he was in dangerous territory. Actually, that was an understatement. He knew that he had just jumped out of the trenches and was in No Man's Land, and he knew that he had no chance.

Ella nodded, and he thought back to what Coco told him in Miami. She struggled being so close to Coco, too. And then he thought about Conrad fancying her. Looking at her in that moment, he could see why. He thought she was gorgeous.

"Some girls won't be like this, you know," she said quietly, her massive brown eyes alive with mischief, with danger. Neither of them knew what was going on, what was making them say these things, but a current was building between them, he could feel it.

He stared at Ella for a moment, then looked at his feet, and took a deep breath before responding. "And what are some girls like, Ella?"

Harrison took a step closer again. He saw her tense as he said her name. She liked the way it sounded on his lips.

"Understanding. Easy going. Won't scream at you for every little thing," Ella said, her face and chest scarlet now. He could feel the heat radiating off her in the cold night.

"And where are these other girls?"

She gulped as he edged ever nearer. Her lips were parted. Her eyes hadn't left his face since she opened her door.

"Right in front of you, if you just look," she said. In one fluid motion he kissed her intently, his hand in her hair as she grasped for her door handle behind her. They stumbled into her room. Harrison kicked the door shut with his heel and, when they broke apart, he locked the door. The music was still blaring from next door, and the flashes of lightning from outside preceded the roaring thunder. It filled Ella's room, illuminating her slight figure, waiting for him to approach. She looked luminous, ethereal.

He swept across the room and pulled apart the belt of Ella's robe. It fell to the floor as they fell onto her bed.

If he stopped to think, he would never have done it, he would never have gotten that far. But he didn't stop. Harrison started looking at Ella differently since Miami. He started seeing her as more than a friend, picturing her in all sorts of precarious situations. He didn't know what it was that changed, but their sarcastic banter in the face of Coco's apathy or tedious drama intrigued him. He knew she would be easy to be with, and if he was honest, that really turned him on in comparison to Coco having just screamed at him, or to Coco brushing him off for months at a time.

He wished he could say that he regretted it instantly, that it was a terrible mistake. But Ella's longing for him manifested itself, ready to be released that evening. Every unsaid emotion she felt for as long as she loved Harrison she expressed in an almost completely non-verbal manner. Her body was hot to touch, almost electric, responding to him in a dramatic way.

Harrison felt exhausted as he collapsed onto Ella's pillow, the same one she was lying on. She breathed heavily next to him, some time later.

"That wasn't your first time, was it?" Harrison asked her, not nervously or curiously, more stating a fact.

She smiled and shook her head.

"Who…?" But his question was lost in her lips as she kissed him once again. She only had limited opportunities to do so. They both knew that. He ran his hands through her uncharacteristically ruffled hair.

They kissed for a while until he became aware of the lateness of the time. He couldn't risk falling asleep in Ella's room, for Coco to knock on her door to head to breakfast the next morning.

The music next door was still blaring. He thought that was a good thing since he doubted neither he nor Ella would have been able to remain silent, to avoid detection. What they were doing, the terrible, truly horrendous act of betrayal, felt better than anything either of them ever felt before.

Once he eventually retrieved his clothes from all four corners of Ella's room, he kissed her for what he knew would be the last time. With more swagger than normal, with a bounce in his step, and a guilty smile on his face, he opened her door.

He would never have felt like such a man, if he knew that some time the following night, Coco would just vanish. He would have stayed, he would have stayed by her side forever. He would have stopped her leaving the next night, would have stopped whatever happened to her. But it was too late and instead of cherishing every moment he had with Coco, he had spent that time angry with her, screwing her best friend. He couldn't live with it. He couldn't live with the fact that she could have been out there, hating him, upset because of him, because he had acted on an angry impulse. He was disgusted at himself, devastated at what he had done to the poor girl he really did adore, but couldn't appreciate when things were difficult. He was immature, fickle, and careless with her heart, and he would have to learn to live with that. If he could ever live with that. He knew he wouldn't.

But, of course, he thought all of this in hindsight, and not at the time.

As he had one foot out of Ella's door, he noticed that he buttoned up two of his shirt buttons in the wrong hole, and stopped, still smirking, to fix them.

Ella laughed from her bed. She hadn't taken her eyes off him. She stared as he walked out of her room as though she would never see anything as brilliant ever again.

He looked down at his chest and did up the buttons, one leg still in Ella's room, as Bea's door opened across the corridor. Ella's door clicked shut behind him as he jumped in shock.

Bea looked at him quizzically. "Harrison?"

He turned puce.

"What are you…" Bea went on.

"Ella was helping me with, uh, English coursework. You know what Coco's like about English though. She'd go mad if she thought I was focusing on anything other than physics if I want to get into Cambridge. So do me a favour and don't tell her about this, yeah?" Harrison waffled, feeling and probably looking like a deer caught unaware, as though Bea's gaze was a gun pointed at his head, ready to shoot.

"Shirtless? Huh. Sure," she said through gritted teeth. He stuttered and left quickly as Bea side-stepped him and knocked on Ella's door.

He didn't hear the end of it the next day. A message group that included just him and Ella and Bea was going off non-stop the next morning. Almost all of the messages were Bea urging them to tell Coco, or threatening that she would do it herself. He prepared himself to tell her, but now she was gone, and he would never be able to explain.

203

Chapter Fifteen

On top of everything else, Harrison felt the guilt of what he had done to Conrad. He had never expected him to be affected by him and Ella. He was too panicked about Coco finding out, too caught up in his own affairs, to notice anything out of the ordinary with him, to notice any clues about some girl now occupying his time.

He couldn't quite believe that he had cheated. When Harrison thought about that night with Ella, it was as if he was watching the scandal of someone else. He felt strangely disconnected to that boy from his memories of that night.

When he had confessed it all, stood in his then girlfriend's room, back when she was missing, but at least still possibly somewhere, he had seen Conrad's face. He had heard the hurt in his voice as he asked Ella why she had done it. He had rarely seen Conrad so vulnerable. He was the most resilient person he knew, and he admired that about him. To have a hand in the downfall of that, the guilt was overpowering.

He felt sick. He felt sick as Conrad had glared angrily at him and spoke to him in a bitter, waspish voice. It was a terrible act that he had done, a terrible betrayal. Coco going missing had pulled the dustsheet off a whole host of lies, of secrets between them all, and it was him that was the common denominator. Everything he touched seemed to turn to ash.

Harrison thought all of these bitter and terrible thoughts as he lay in his bed. His world was crumbling, he was falling into a black hole where things were only getting worse, and he could think of no way that anything would get better.

He wondered if Coco knew it was Ella. He supposed she must have, to go so soon afterwards was too much of a coincidence. He realised that he knew so little, with no information to help him understand why, all of a sudden, he was losing everything.

He barely moved all night, and he squinted as the sun rose and touched his face through the gap in the curtains. He was still in his school uniform.

Rubbing his sore eyes, he padded across the hallway and showered, the hot water reddening his skin, reminding him with venom that he was not in some sort of horrendous dream.

Afterwards, he absentmindedly changed into clean clothes and left the dorm, figuring that perhaps he needed to take his mind off this, and the only thing he could think that would occupy his thoughts of anything other than Coco at that moment was his lessons.

He was late to History and sat in the back. From the corner of his eye he could see that Conrad was there, too. Harrison dared not look at him, as he didn't think he could cope with looking into Conrad's face and seeing such hurt and anger again. Conrad hated him now, and rightly so. Overnight he had lost the two people who were the most important to him in the world. He was alone.

He swallowed hard and tried to focus on what was written on the board. He took good, detailed notes.

It all went pretty well until that girl, Rose, pretended she was sorry that Coco was gone when she knew nothing about her, when she pretended that she was upset, but she had no idea what it felt like to be there at that moment, desperately trying not to fall apart.

And then he actually did fall apart. Before he knew it, he was shouting and hitting the table, and then Conrad was hugging him.

He always thought he was a little more grown up than Conrad, perhaps because he had a girlfriend, perhaps because he took his responsibilities in school seriously, perhaps because he was generally better behaved. But the Conrad who had taken him away to his room and sat with him was an infinitely better man than Harrison.

He closed his eyes, just for a minute, feeling a peaceful

sense of weightlessness, feeling the dark envelop him like a well needed hug. He was so tired.

He was suddenly on a train. He missed his stop and was panicking. He couldn't get off and he was already late. Coco was panicking too, shouting at him, telling him it was his fault they were stuck. She was screaming that she was going to write a letter to his dad about how useless he was and he would deal with him.

She pulled out wads and wads of paper and scribbled furiously. "*And* I'm going to write about this on my blog!" she shouted manically.

Harrison sat bolt upright. It was dark out, the middle of the night. He didn't know how long he had been asleep, if this was tonight or tomorrow night. He didn't know when he last drank or ate, or brushed his teeth. But he had an idea, and if it worked, it could give him all the answers, but even still, Harrison knew it would be a pretty stupid thing to do.

He changed into his grey hoodie and black jogging bottoms and walked out of his dorm. As the heavy fire door clicked behind him, the chilly night hit him like a bucket of icy water, but his skin was still hot to touch. He had a fever.

He turned and checked that no one was watching and, seeing the coast was clear, he bolted across the grass to B Block, to Coco's window, and pushed it open.

As he rolled through the window he fell, as he knew he would, onto her bed. It was strange to think that the last time he did this was weeks ago, and it was to see her, to have fun. Now he felt like he was intruding, that he shouldn't be here. And he was right about that, of course.

He stood in the middle of her room, and now he was here, his stupid plan seemed even more juvenile. There was no reason it would still be there, he thought, and he knew that he could risk going to jail for this. It was a crime scene. But if it was being looked at so closely, why hadn't they found it? Why hadn't they found *anything*?

Two years before, Harrison and Coco were fooling around, wrestling on her bed, when he fell off and sat on her floor, unable to move for the laughing that caused his ribs to ache. He heard a thud next to him as a notebook fell from under Coco's bed. Presumably it had been wedged between the frame and the mattress. He picked it up, and saw Coco immediately blanche.

"Put that down," she said seriously, still breathless from laughing, although now her face was solemn.

Harrison dramatically gasped and teased her. "Coco, is this a *diary*?" he asked.

"Harrison, no. Don't read it, please."

He sat down next to her, and handed it over. She clutched it tight to her chest, her gaze not meeting his. He felt a little guilty about her embarrassment, and tried to diffuse the tension. "What does it say? *Harrison is the best boyfriend in the world, I can't believe I'm lucky enough to be with him*?"

Glaring at him, Coco smirked slightly before responding, deadpan. "It says *I am a good person. What in God's name have I done to be stuck with an immature piece of work like Harrison Fletcher?*"

"Oh really? Is that how it is?" Harrison poked her in her belly and she giggled.

"Yeah. It then goes on to list all of the people far nicer and better looking than you that I should be with. Boys who don't tease me for documenting my thoughts."

"Now that was just mean," he said, moving over to her desk and sitting up straight, grabbing a pen from the little vase in which she kept her pens and pencils, and a piece of paper from the delicate wooden tray that held all her stationary.

"What are you doing?"

"*Dear diary. Coco was horrible to me today. I don't know how much longer I can take her cruel jibes…*"

Coco swept across the room and put her arms through his. She grabbed the pen from his hand.

"*She is the most entertaining person that I have ever met though, and my life would be so dull without her, so I should probably be far kinder to her from now on.*"

He laughed as he read the words appearing on the page

from her delicate hand. They were both giggling as she dropped the pen, and she pulled him closer to her, hugging him from behind. She rested her chin in his neck and nuzzled into him a little. He raised his arms awkwardly so that he could touch her face.

They stayed like that for a while, each quietly taking in the warmth of the other in their arms. They couldn't escape the feeling, the awareness of that bond between them, which at that moment encapsulated them both. They were both suddenly struck by it, by how much they meant to each other, by how, even though they were only fifteen at that point, they were so decisively, undeniably in love, even after a year of being together, ten times the length of most of their peers' relationships.

He didn't know if that moment was as significant to Coco, but for Harrison, it was the first time he had been really struck with the fact that he was in love.

He was too afraid to turn on the light, so in the darkness around him, he reached under Coco's bed, and he felt it. What he pulled out was a different notebook. The last one, he remembered, had flowers on it. This one was plain, but her hiding spot evidently hadn't changed. He quickly grabbed his schoolbag and stuffed it inside, escaping through the window again and slowly making his way over to his dorm.

He sat in his room, the main light casting a harsh hue over everything, over the mess, over the cold cup of tea left by Conrad as he had been asleep, over the notebook.

He stared at the pink and sparkly book as though it was a bomb ready to explode. He knew he wouldn't be able to deal with what was inside, but he needed to know. He had to find out what it was that led to this.

So reluctantly, knowing that there was no way that this would end well for him, he opened the first page.

January 8th, 2019

School started back today, Harrison arrived with me. Somehow, the long train went quickly with him with me. We made backstories of all the people in the carriage.

The woman sat opposite us is off to kill her ex-husband and his new girlfriend.

The little boy kicking Harrison's chair is actually the spawn of Satan sent to test our patience...

Harrison laughed. They had spent that train journey whispering and giggling, and despite the humid, overcrowded train, he had fun.

He flicked through a few pages. He saw that she had only written once a week, until he arrived at the summer.

May 24th, 2019

Something happened today. I'm not really sure how, or why, but I kissed Mr Hunter. Well, I guess he's Daniel now.

I'm panicking a little, if I'm honest. If anyone finds out, I've ruined two people. I don't know what I'm going to do.

I don't think it means anything, not really. I arrived at our revision session all in a huff because I've barely seen Harrison for two weeks, and he isn't eating or sleeping, he's just studying obsessively. He needs help and he isn't listening to me. He got a bit nasty, actually, when I told him to get some help. He's never raised his voice before. I know it's the exams but it shook me up a little.

Daniel asked what was wrong, and I told him. I ranted, and he listened and was gentle and kind, and the sort of lovely that Harrison can be when he isn't stressed.

Daniel told me that I deserve the world, that I shouldn't be ignored or spoken to like that.

I don't know what came over me, but I kissed him. I thought he'd stop me. I thought he'd tell me that I was a student and this was crazy and shout at me to get out of his office, but he kissed me back.

It was different. I don't know if it's just been a while for me or what, but I was spinning. I could feel it heating up and I told him I had to go. He called me beautiful and kissed me again as I left.

Harrison frantically turned the page. It was dated only two days later.

May 26th, 2019

I stayed late after Daniel's lesson today. I told the others I wanted to ask about my essay. I wanted to say I was sorry.

He locked the door and kissed me straight away, against the wall. Before I knew it, we were having sex. It happened fast. I didn't mean for that to happen, but the way he looked at me and the way he kissed me, it sent me reeling. Around him, I can't think straight.

Again, I don't know what I'm going to do, how I'm going to do philosophy anymore.

I can't bear to look at Harrison. I can't live with this. I can't tell him. Daniel would lose everything.

It keeps running around my mind and playing over all my thoughts. I'm trying to act normally, but I can't. I freak out every time Harrison tries to touch me. I feel tainted, dirty. Perhaps I am.

June 5th, 2019

I had another coursework session with Daniel today. He had written down all my amendments and gave them to me at the start. They were detailed. He even stapled on some extra pages. I think it was to avoid needing to talk about them, because he explained nothing before he started kissing me.

He kissed my neck, and I told him we should stop. But he didn't listen. He popped off the button on my shirt and I was sat there, in my skirt and not a lot else.

Then Miss Jenkins walked in the room. I jumped away from him, but it was too late. She already saw me. I pulled my jumper on and ran out of the room. I feel mortified.

I realise that I actually hate her a little bit.

Nonetheless, that put a stop to that.

11pm

I sent him a text asking how he was. I knew he'd be freaking out.

He told me to stop texting him. He told me that what happened between us was nothing, that it was just a mistake.

Rationally, I know that that's all it is. But when I was around him, I felt different. I felt wanted. I felt listened to. He's an adult, he's sexy as hell, and he wanted me. I know it shouldn't, but that meant a lot to me. I feel so stupid. I can't look Harrison in the eye. I can't go to into philosophy now.

In a way, though, it might be a good thing. It's over now, at least. All it will be is a strange fever dream, and now I can move on.

July 10th, 2019

Last exam today. Thank God it's over. Thank God I can get away from here, at least for a little while.

I feel weird, panicky, anxious. I haven't really eaten much in days. Not surprising, I guess, considering what I've done, but I still think this is something more. I'm two weeks late, too. I'm staying at Bea's after we leave next week, and I think I'm going to have to take a test there.

I can't tell Ella. I can't, not after all she's been through. And I worry what she would say. Fuck, I've been so damn idiotic. So fucking stupid.

July 10th, 2019.

I couldn't wait. I took a test tonight, on my own. Negative.

And breathe.

July 14th, 2019

I went to see Daniel this evening. I don't know why. I just wanted to see him.

Jenkins was in his classroom. He told me to get out.

She smiled at me as she left, and I started crying.

I think Jenkins panicked. She rushed me into her lab. I sat on the stool and sobbed for ages. She stared at me all the time. It was awkward.

She asked me what was wrong, and I knew I couldn't tell anyone else, and she knew about him anyway, so I told her everything.

"You've gotten yourself into a bit of a pickle, haven't you, Coco?"

She said that, word for word. A bit of a pickle.

At the look on my face at her sheer stupidity, she shut up. I realised I didn't need her help. I don't even know why I did this.

I told her that, and she said that I should think about the consequences of my actions in the future. As if that's going to help anything, as if I don't feel fucking dirty and used and awful anyway.

I don't know why I told her. I wish I hadn't.

I went to leave and she told me to think hard about what I was doing, as if I wasn't doing that anyway.

I could have done without her fucking Catholic guilt.

Harrison could see that the next entry was written differently. It was untidy, scribbled, as though her hand had been shaking.

July 30th, 2019

Harrison is devastated, and I haven't even told him anything. He knows something is wrong, of course he does. I couldn't bring myself to tell him about last week, and telling him about Daniel is out of the question.

My only choice is to try and forget, to push it all down and hope I don't explode from within.

But he looked so heartbroken, standing in my room. He asked if he'd done something wrong. If he had done something wrong.

212

Harrison, I can't tell you this directly, but you're perfect. You always have been. It's me, stupid, fucked up me that's ruined us. I love you so much, and I think I might have broken this beyond repair. I'm sorry. I'm so sorry.

Harrison saw that there weren't any more entries until the following school year, a few weeks into term. He supposed before then that she had little time to write in secret while they were sharing a room in Miami.

October 14th, 2019

It's been a while. I've been busy. Miami was a bit up and down, but ended well. Things are a little better.

Although, someone has been in my room. I'm sure they have. My chest of drawers is open, and my desk is messed up. I can't see that anything was taken, but I think that makes it worse - if they took something I'd at least know what they are after.

I'll have to wait and see. I'm nervous, but that's not really new. I've been constantly anxious for months. Miami was nice, I felt I had escaped a bit, but coming back here, I have to see him, I have to take his classes, it's hard.

I'm trying hard with Harrison, and we feel almost normal again but I can't shake what I've done. I can't forget.

Everyone's left today, and I'm here on my own for a week. Harrison asked me to go to his but I can't. I think maybe I need time to myself. I'm going to try jogging.

Or, there's a bottle of expensive Merlot under my bed... I could drink that.

October 15th, 2019

I went for a run this morning, and I've done half of my homework already. I'm reading Moby Dick. Anything without a romantic plot device.

I feel good. Better than I've been in a while. I'm going to catch up with TV until bed.

October 17th, 2019

I was doing well. I was doing so fucking well, and then I went to dinner, and he was there. He was eating with her and she grinned at me. Every time she smiles at me I swear she's gloating somehow.

I could tell he was deliberately not looking at me, as if I'm the issue. He's just to blame as I am. He's just as guilty, if not more. In fact, definitely more. He should have stopped me. He shouldn't have pulled my clothes off me and kissed me. I'm sick of feeling guilty. I'm sick of being the bad guy. It's him. He's the terrible person.

He's the arsehole who decided he wanted a quick fuck and used me. I was with him, I was vulnerable. He should have stopped it before it became anything of any substance. He used me.

Why is it me that's sat alone on my bedroom floor, crying into a glass of wine? Why isn't he hurt? Why am I protecting him? What has he done to deserve that? I don't owe him anything.

I need help, and I'm going to get it. He can go to hell.

October 18th, 2019

I might not be as okay as I thought. I might have drunk a whole bottle of wine to myself. I might have text him.

He's furious at me.

I don't want to be alone anymore.

October 20th, 2019

Harrison came back today. I can't cope with the stress. Any minute I'm afraid my phone will go and he'll know. I feel like this secret is a ticking bomb. I'm waiting for it to explode in my face.

I can't believe I was stupid enough to text him again. I feel like I'm back at square one. I can't look Harrison in the eye, I can't bear him touching me. And he knows. He's impatient.

He suspects that I've done something.

I threw him out, and now I just wish he was here. But if he comes back I'll end up telling him, and then, well, that's it I guess.

No, I can't say goodbye. I can't not have him. It's not fair, but I need him.

I can't stop crying.

October 21st, 2019

A lot has happened today.

Harrison knocked on my window early and apologised. I'd calmed down after last night, so we were okay for about three hours.

Weird, but Daniel accidentally pulled a pair of knickers out of his pile of work today, and I swear they were mine. They're my favourite red ones and they've been missing for a while. But I didn't put them there. I was never wearing them with him.

I don't really know what happened with that. But I don't think he does either, because he texted me, furious, asking what the fuck I was playing at, and that I needed to see him at midnight tonight.

I don't know if I should go. He's not going to believe me. Also, he's so angry that I'm actually a bit afraid. Someone's trying to screw with me, I can feel it. I don't feel safe.

Nevertheless, I've cast that out of my mind because something even worse has happened, something big.

Something's gone on with Harrison and Ella. Bea's laptop was open in philosophy class, and I could see the messages as they came through, drawing fucking straws about who was going to tell me.

I'm shaking with anger, but how can I blame him? How can I be angry that I can't let him go yet I can't be me anymore, and now he's searching somewhere else? But Ella, I guess her little crush has finally paid off. I know so little, when or where. Oh God, what if it was in her room, when I was just here? What if I was sat alone as they were fucking on her bed? What if she ran past my window to his?

My head is spinning. What the fuck has happened to my life? What has happened to me? I'm cheating. I'm cheated on. This is everything I never thought I would have to deal with.

How could Ella do that? Knowing I love him. Knowing he doesn't love her.

Ha. Maybe I do know. I guess he gave her that look, the look he gives me when I know he's not listening to a word that I say and I'm already naked in his head. I bet he ran his fingers through her hair. I bet he kissed her neck. I bet he was fucking fantastic, he's always been good.

I bet she fucking loved it.

I wonder how she feels now. I wonder how she felt as he left her alone and ran, stressed out, to his room. He's not a bad person, he'll be freaking out.

I can't decide how I feel. I can't decide if I can get over this. I know he couldn't care less about her, that makes it better. But today he was so normal, and I never thought he could lie to me, I always thought he was an open book.

But I've been doing it for months. If it's in the open, will it be better? Will we be friends?

And what about her? Is it her fault? Perhaps we're just so similar. Perhaps he swept her away. I know that he can do that, he's done it to me.

But, fuck, Ella. It's Harrison. Realistically, how can we sit at a table all together again?

What the fuck am I going to do tomorrow? Should I ask Bea for the facts before I talk to him? What the fuck do I even say? Do I give him a chance to tell me?

I might knock Ella's door. I might ask her directly.

Oh my god, what if he's in there now?

Oh, fuck. No, I can't deal with that.

I'd ask why the damn hell this has happened to me, but I'm obviously paying a massive karmic debt. With interest. Maybe I'm even now.

Wiping the tears from his face, Harrison grabbed his hockey stick from across his room. His door slammed behind him.

Harrison stormed through the school, and rapped the stick on Hunter's office door. The door opened, and Harrison swung, narrowly missing Hunter's head. Hunter's consciousness at that moment was only thanks to his quick reflexes.

"What did you do to her?"

"For God's sake, Harrison," Hunter hissed in a sharp whisper, his eyes sweeping across the corridor. "Just come in and be quiet."

Hunter held the door open and wearily eyed Harrison as he sauntered into the room, his fury seeming to fill it. He exuded a sheer power, a force of nature that could smash everything in his arms' radius. Miss Jenkins came through from what Harrison assumed was the bedroom, wearing only Hunter's shirt.

"You slept with her! You had sex with her and then you…" Harrison began, his own loud voice ringing in his ears.

"Will you just be *quiet?*" Hunter cut him off, panicked.

"Let's not get hysterical," Miss Jenkins said, placing a hand on Harrison's arm, which he aggressively shrugged off, moving towards Hunter.

"Maria, please. I can deal with him," Hunter told her, taking a step back.

"She's dead! She's dead, and you've got something to do with it, you know what happened, you saw her that night…" Harrison continued, unaware of the words he was saying, only that he knew what Hunter was, and that he was the only person who could make this right.

Miss Jenkins turned quickly towards Hunter, so quickly, in fact, that he thought he heard her neck click.

"I didn't," Hunter said quietly.

"You did! You…"

"You need to calm down, Harrison. Let's get out of here. Let's go for a walk." Hunter was red in the face, running his fingers through his hair. He kissed Jenkins on the cheek and told her he'd be back in a bit. She only stared blankly, wide-eyed and rigid.

Harrison nodded, and waited for him to open the door. He walked a couple of paces behind Hunter for about twenty minutes, through the grounds, down towards the forest. His teacher looked skinnier, weedy even, feebler than he had seemed during his last lesson, not intimidating in the slightest. His new and pathetic little beard did nothing to strengthen his weak chin, and it just gave him the air of someone unkempt and unwashed. Harrison realised that he hated everything about him, that every molecule of his existence revolted him.

Hunter walked slowly, quietly, but Harrison could hear his breath quickening. They walked along the path, the sports field to their right, and to their left were the benches and sparse oak trees that they would sit at every lunch time in summer.

It was cold, and Harrison felt feverish. He was simultaneously chilled to his bone, yet his skin was hot to touch.

Hunter took him through the hole in the fence that the smokers used to escape and roll their cigarettes whenever possible. They crossed the cattle grid, and reached the edge of the forest, shrouded in almost complete darkness by the trees that created a blanket, shielding them from the stars.

Harrison stumbled a few times over tree roots, but in the darkness, he was anything but afraid. He was with Coco's killer, he knew it. Now he knew the truth, he wondered how he had been blind to it for all these years. He saw Hunter for what he was; the joker, pretending to be their friend, trying hard to fit in with them, begging them to take his class. He was pathetic, a pervert, and it was so clear to Harrison that he was just a sleazy bad guy.

But the anger masked any fear Harrison had. He revelled in the idea of ripping him apart, limb from limb. He was ready, his hands clenched, his heart pumping an ugly racket against his bones.

The forest was only a mile thick, and they had been

walking for a while. The trees led to the cliffs, and to the beach that was owned by the school. There wasn't much further to go until the hit the sea.

Harrison wondered how long Hunter would keep him walking, how far out he would take him, when they reached a clearing and Hunter turned towards him. "I have no idea what happened. I didn't see her that night."

"But you told her to see you- you were angry."

"She didn't turn up. I was seething, I admit that. I wanted to really tell her off for that stunt she pulled, but I didn't get the chance."

"She didn't put the knickers there."

"Of course she did. She texted me a couple of nights before, drunk I think. She wanted to ruin me," Hunter said and shrugged, anger flashing across his face as it must have done the night Coco text him.

"She had no idea about it! She was as confused as you were."

"No, she- how do you know all this, anyway?"

"She kept a diary."

Hunter paused for a moment, struck by this information that could put him deep in the shit. "Oh," he said.

"Yeah. You really fucked up," Harrison said, smirking at the way Hunter's face fell.

"It was a mistake, Harrison. she was upset."

"She was vulnerable! She was your *student*! She was upset and young, and you screwed her over and left her to pick up the pieces!"

"I know, and I know you loved her, but it was one time, it all happened so quickly. It was a mistake, a flash in the pan stupid thing that happened out of nowhere and ended as quickly as it started. It didn't mean anything. It was all over within a week, and then she just messages me out of the blue."

"It wasn't over in a week. Not for her. She was messed up."

"I'm sorry about that," Hunter said, with an attempt at earnestness that Harrison was not buying.

"All because of you."

"I can't undo it. I can't change how I treated her, can I? I can't change any of this, mate. I wish I could," Hunter said, too calmly, too friendly.

Harrison felt an angry red flush in his face. "That's not enough!" he yelled. Birds flew from a nearby tree. "You did this! You ruined her. You killed her too, didn't you?"

"No, I..." Hunter began, and then he blinked, stopping himself with a revelation, an Archimedes moment, a way out. He could barely hide his relief, his shrewd eyes widening. He had a new plan. "Are you sure she didn't do this to herself, if she was that messed up? It didn't get too much and, and..."

"I don't think you made her commit suicide, no," Harrison said acidly, a sharp voice unlike his own escaping him.

Hunter was put out, his relief gone as quickly as it came. He frowned, spluttered and tried to cling to straws. "She definitely didn't pull the knickers stunt?" he said.

"She says she didn't. Someone broke into her room a couple of weeks before. She didn't notice they were missing at the time."

Hunter looked surprised. He began pacing, his hands twitching, clenching, undoing his jacket zip, and zipping it up again. "Right," he said, "So someone wants to discredit her, or me. To do that is to want to warn us that they'll tell everyone about what we did, it has to be, to screw with us. But no one knew about us, only..."

They stared at each other for a moment, an understanding forming between them.

"Have you checked on your girlfriend lately?" Harrison asked, jerking his head towards the school.

"Maria's a friend. We spend a lot of time together, but it's usually just hanging out."

"Usually?"

"Well, alright, we sometimes sleep together. It's a casual thing."

"Was she jealous?"

Hunter shrugged. "She's the only person who knew about us." He sighed, as though faced with an unbearably cumbersome situation that he had not foreseen. It was as though Coco having the gall to die on him was a bit of a bother, a bit of admin he'd rather avoid.

Hunter looked at his phone like it was an alien object. "We should tell the police, right?" he asked. But he didn't look at Harrison's disbelieving face. He knew he needed to do this. His jaw tightened in displeasure, almost in frustration, and with a trembling hand he pressed the number.

"Jack, I know it's late. I want to talk with you about Coco. Can you meet me? Just off the path in the woods. I'll send you my location. It's a long story." He hung up.

Harrison could hear the blood pumping in his ears. "That was awfully informal," he said.

"Jack and I go back a bit."

"Covering your arse for when you fuck your students? This happens a lot, eh?"

Hunter was quiet for a while, before speaking too loudly for the situation. "You know, Harrison, she was capable of making her own decisions."

Harrison punched him in the face. He pinned Hunter to the tree by his hockey stick, pressing it against his neck so forcefully that he was choking, making gargling sounds as Harrison glowered over him.

"This isn't her fault," said Harrison. "You should have known better! You *grabbed* her. Before she knew what was going on, you were fucking her! Not to mention she was your *student*, in your care. You're a motherfucking *adult*, Hunter, you're the responsible one. Do you realise how fucked up that is? You're a sex offender!" He started to hit him and found it difficult to stop. Hunter's nose was misshapen and bleeding, his eye swollen. The man looked a mess.

"*Stop!*" Jenkins yelled, running into the clearing, now wearing jeans and a coat. "You'll kill him!"

"You... you hurt her." Harrison said it quietly, starting to sob as he took a step back and released Hunter, and Jenkins hurried over and fussed over the injuries.

Tearing his eyes from Harrison's desperate face, Hunter turned to Jenkins. "Maria, what did you do?" he asked.

221

She blinked at him. "What do you mean?"

"The underwear. Was that you?"

Suddenly, blue doused the clearing as the police car pulled up next to them. Hobbs slammed the door, clad in his full uniform.

"I was on duty. What's going on, Danny?"

Hunter winced at the nickname.

"What- what have you done?" Jenkins asked, her eyes darting wildly from Hunter to Hobbs. Her mouth was wide in horror.

"You know something about this, don't you?" Hunter asked shakily. Harrison understood his trepidation. He wasn't sure he was ready to hear the answer, either.

Jenkins spluttered, unable to answer, but eyeing Hobbs' gun.

"Answer him!" Harrison shouted, the words resounding in the clearing. Jenkins jumped in surprise.

"No, I don't. I barely had anything to do with her, I just walked in that day… I don't know anything."

"You're lying," Harrison said, his face a ghastly frown. "You're lying because you've got a lot of shit to hide. She came to you, she was a mess, she was confused and hurt, and you didn't help her. You tried to scare her, you tried to freak her out. She was just a…"

"She was a spoilt, privileged, little bitch!" Jenkins screamed, her face turning purple, contorting into a beastly snarl of rage. "She made a stupid decision, running off with him, not thinking about the consequences of her actions. None of you do! You all saunter around in your fancy cars and your fancy clothes, never sparing a thought for anyone else. I wanted to teach her a lesson."

"What did you do?" Hunter groaned, closing his eyes in either pain or frustration.

Jenkins answered immediately. She opened the can of worms that was this situation, and she couldn't stop. She was on a roll, ranting, and she could barely stop for air. Harrison doubted she even registered his voice. "I didn't mean to. I saw her in the corridor. I knew she was going to see him. I had to get her away from him. I thought she would be scared, and I thought he would be, too, after I did that with that *disgusting* thong of hers. I wanted them to be too afraid to even be in the same room as each other. It was for his own good, he'd lose his job, he'd lose everything. She was upset. I told her how angry Dan was, and she started getting hysterical. I asked if she wanted to get out of there, to go for a drive. She said she did, she wanted to be anywhere other than the school at that moment. So I took her to the cliffs. And I told her. I told her everything, that he was mine, that she had to stay away, or I'd ruin her, that she didn't want me as her enemy. She freaked out. She told me she had heard enough, that I was nuts. She told me she was sick of fucked up people, and she was going to tell someone about me, she was sick of keeping it to herself, she was trying to blame him. She was trying to pretend that it was all his fault. She ran, and I panicked. Dan would be ruined. He made a mistake, I didn't want him to suffer, too. I caught up with her in the woods, just over there."

She pointed vaguely into the trees behind Harrison, and she stopped talking for a second, too, her words drifting off, dreamily, as though this was the first time she thought about since that night. "She was on the floor, she must have fallen over and hit her head. She wasn't moving, she wasn't breathing. It was dark, but I knew it wouldn't be for long. It was nearly 2am. I panicked. We were only a few metres away from the cliff edge. We dragged her and…" She let out a rattling breath, her face puce, a purple vein pulsating on her forehead. She was manic.

"And I pushed her down. I didn't mean for her to die that night, but as she hit that last rock on the bottom, I was fucking glad."

Hunter blinked at Jenkins. He looked as though he had been hit forcefully across the head with a shovel.

Harrison was at a loss, numb in his disbelief that this had been how Coco left. It felt so inadequate, somehow. But he noticed Hobbs staring, open mouthed at the wild creature in front of them, frozen.

"Well, do something!" Harrison yelled. Hobbs blinked, and moved forwards slowly.

"Just do it, Jack," Miss Jenkins snapped, and Hobbs cautioned her, as he slipped handcuffs around her wrists. "Do you have nothing to say, Dan?" she asked.

Hunter stepped towards her, until he was inches from her face. "You mean nothing to me. You're sick, Maria."

Her face fell. "But this was all for you."

"I didn't ask for this!" Hunter yelled, his arms flailing around his head. He took several steps back, eying Jenkins as though she were a dangerous animal that had escaped the safety of its enclosure.

She grinned at him, a fake, ugly smile that hid her anger, her anguish, like a mask. "Fine," she said. "Then it's over for you, too. And Jack. I'll tell them everything, about the things you've hidden, protecting Dan. I've got nothing to lose, but you guys, you have a lot to burn to ashes."

Hobbs and Hunter stared at each other.

"Then it's over, right?" Hunter said.

"It doesn't have to be." Hobbs rubbed the back of his neck and started pacing.

"I think it does." Jenkins smiled, genuinely now, at his distress.

"Think, Danny. Think. I'm not going down for this."

Hobbs carried on pacing in circles around Miss Jenkins. He put his hands together to make a gun shape and pointed it at her. "I- I could shoot her. I could say she started attacking us and…" he said.

"What?" Harrison asked.

"No, Jack. We can't," Hunter gasped, seemingly as shocked as Harrison.

"We don't have a choice," Hobbs said, really pulling out his gun this time, and pointing it at Jenkins' head.

"No!" Harrison shouted.

"Dan…" Jenkins stared at him, wide-eyed and imploring. She fidgeted in her handcuffs as she watched him, biting her lips until they cracked.

When Harrison decided that Hunter was going to do

nothing, only stare into the trees, wide eyed, he stepped between Jenkins and Hobbs.

"She said 'we dragged her'." He turned to Hobbs. "You-you helped, didn't you? You've done this before, haven't you?"

Hunter shook his head, as though Harrison was losing his mind, but Hobbs shrugged.

"It was an accident. An accident innocent people would have suffered for. I'd do it again if I needed to."

"You knew?" Hunter asked, his eyes seeming to widen with every word Jenkins and Hobbs were saying.

"She called me." Hobbs cocked his head toward Jenkins. "It would have ruined you, Danny. All I had to do was grab her ankles, and…"

"You liars!" Harrison shouted, and in the night air the words were magnified.

Harrison ran towards Hobbs, who took the hit. They fell to the ground, and Hobbs pinned him down. On one knee, he pointed the gun towards him. Harrison lay, helpless, staring up at the barrel of a gun and the face of a man who had lost all sense.

"That was a stupid thing to do, kid."

"No!" Harrison heard from somewhere to his left, and they all turned. Ella was running into the clearing, and Conrad pulled her back, his other hand holding a phone that was pointed towards them.

"Oh, for Christ's sake, it's a fucking school outing," Hobbs spat, furious. As he clocked the phone in Conrad's hand, he pointed the gun at him. "Drop it, or I'll blow your head off."

Conrad threw the phone towards him, grinning broadly. Hobbs grabbed it and threw it towards Hunter, who caught it. Hunter stood immobile, overwhelmed.

"What's on there will screw with you, too, Danny. I did you a favour. You need to step up now," Hobbs said, watching him with an intense gaze. When Hunter continued to do nothing but stand still with a stupid gormless look on his face, Hobbs shouted again. "This is all for *you*, Danny!

Do something!"

Wincing, Hunter stomped on the phone hard. He was white in the face, his jaw tight.

"Now this is what's going to happen: you all saw her attack us with a knife, we'll get one from the kitchen. I had no choice, she was crazed, uncontrollable. What you heard stays here," Hobbs began, standing, skittishly looking between them all.

Conrad smirked. "And if we don't?" he asked.

"Either I'll splatter that pretty little head of yours against that tree, or I'll receive an anonymous tip off from the school about the use of class A drugs, and I'll send you all down for possession when I 'find' coke on you. And you've really pissed me off, so I think you'll be dealing it."

"What a pickle," Conrad said, grinning still. His arm was stuck out awkwardly in front of Ella. Hobbs glared at him, his nostrils flared.

Harrison started to stand.

"Get on the fucking floor!" Hobbs yelled, firing a warning shot.

"You don't want to do that," Conrad shouted.

"Oh, yeah? Why's that?" Hobbs asked through clenched teeth.

"Because your body count is getting a little high, don't you think? Oh, and because I already posted that video everywhere. Your age is showing, Hobbs. You forgot about live feeds."

Jenkins giggled quietly, an eery sound in the otherwise shocked silence that followed Conrad's news. "Oh, you are *fucked*," she whispered, barely containing her laugh.

"You little shit!" Hobbs yelled, firing the gun, losing all sense.

His hands were shaking so much that he missed Conrad's head, just, even at such short range.

"You... *fucking* .... Idiot!" Conrad yelled, charging him with a speed only the school's hockey star could muster, and punching him square in the jaw.

Harrison seized the moment and took the low road,

kicking Hobbs hard in the crotch as he was distracted. He watched as Conrad ducked under one of his punches. Harrison grabbed the gun from Hobbs' fingers, which had slackened in the confusion and potential concussion that Conrad was giving him, and threw it to Conrad.

Conrad stared at the gun for a second. He rolled it over in his hands, then smiled and pointed it at Hobbs, who was buckled on the floor, making a valiant effort to try and to stand.

"Stay where you are." Conrad said, glaring at Jenkins. "You too."

"You don't know how to use it," Hobbs said, narrowing his eyes in irritation despite the pain.

Conrad only shrugged. He casually placed his finger on the trigger and fired a warning shot to the sky, causing them all to jump. "Tell that to the pheasants I shoot every summer. Don't fucking move," he said.

They stopped as they all heard wailing sirens in the background, and it was only seconds before they were covered in flashes of blue once again. Six police officers rushed out of their cars, pausing for just a moment as they evaluated the scene. Conrad dropped the gun to the floor and explained what happened to the two officers that were coming towards him.

He was jostled towards a separate car to Ella and Harrison, and Hunter and Hobbs, but before they left, he rushed quickly towards Harrison and hugged him fiercely. "Don't worry, mate, we've got them," he said.

"How-" Harrison began, but Conrad patted his shoulder.

"Later," he said, straightening up and grinning at the two police officers. He climbed slowly into the car.

Chapter Sixteen

The funeral took place after a week of police stations, interviews, and of a whole lot of stress. Conrad and Harrison got away lightly when the story of Jenkins, Hunter and Hobbs, and their conspiring to escape any consequences for what they had done, paled the assault and bodily harm caused by the boys' fists. When it became obvious that the boys had been in danger, and that Hobbs, Jenkins and Hunter were unlikely to start a counterclaim, as they were busy defending themselves, Harrison and Conrad were sent back to normal life, if that was what they could call it now.

They managed to catch up, and Conrad told him how Ella heard someone in Coco's room, and had seen him leave. Scared, she messaged Conrad, who went into Harrison's room to tell him, and read Coco's diary, which he left behind. They guessed what happened: when he went to Hunter's office to find his door open, and no one inside, he knew he needed to find Harrison, and he saw Jenkins making her way to the forest. He told Ella, who insisted on not letting him go alone, and they followed the shouts into the clearing, staying for long enough to get enough evidence to fuck up Jenkins', Hunter's and Hobbs' lives in the process.

The school was in a state of mayhem, an absolute excitable hell in which Harrison and Conrad were expected to somehow exist through the gaggles of excited younger children, who had no real idea what was going on.

It wasn't the environment they all needed to be in, but they didn't have anywhere else to go. They wanted to be together, since they knew that that was the only way they would cope.

And, at any rate, Coco's funeral was to be held locally. Harriet wanted her friends from school to be able to attend.

Harrison didn't like that. He didn't like that Coco was laid to rest in the place where she spent so many months unhappy. But it was where he met her, where he loved her, where they could be together. It was also where he broke her heart.

They didn't go to lessons in that week. Harrison had a speech to write, and the four of them spent all the time they could away from the rest of the school, in one of their bedrooms, playing video games or watching movies, and talking a lot about Coco and the dumb stuff they used to do.

The day of the funeral came quickly, and Harrison was not prepared. He was nervous, about speaking, about being a bearer, about doing her justice as she was laid to rest right before her eyes, about having to deal with a whole lot of people in the village hall afterwards, at the wake.

Also, Harrison had not seen Harriet yet. She texted him, asking how he was doing, thanking him for everything. He found he couldn't put into words how sorry he was.

They stood outside the church, close to the door, as hundreds upon hundreds of people, mainly from school, were arriving in droves. There would only be enough room in the church for about a third of them. Even if they stood, most people would have to wait outside.

Flowers flooded the entrance to the church. The steps, the porch, the altar, were all covered in a sea of colour, all bright, beautiful flowers that Coco would have loved.

Harriet spotted them immediately, and swept over, hugging Harrison tight. "I've been worried about you, sweetheart. How are you?" she asked.

Harrison shrugged, and Harriet offered a sympathetic look that he hoped conveyed the absolute essay he would need to write to let Harriet know how he really felt, how the guilt would never leave him, how he failed her daughter.

But Harriet understood his inability to speak. She touched his face gently and said, "I know. I can't begin to process this either. But I'll be there for you if you need me, Harrison. You're a good boy, you were always so good to her, and I'm grateful."

He started sobbing and Harriet hugged him again.

"I- I just need a second, before we go in," Harrison said, and she nodded. He escaped around the corner, into a little garden in the church grounds, where a bench was surrounded by hedges and flowers, and he breathed deeply, his hands in his hair, as the rain began to fall. He felt like he was just finding out that Coco was gone again, and he knew he would. He was dreading this. After today, he could start the healing process.

"Harrison," Bea said quietly, as she sat down next to him and placed a hand on his shoulder.

"It's time to go, mate," Conrad said, eyeing him with concern.

He walked with Bea's arm around him until he arrived at the heavy wooden door. He, Conrad, Harvey, Coco's uncle and cousin, were bearers to the coffin, alongside Bea, who all but insisted that she do it. They walked down the church aisle and all Harrison could do was look ahead. He knew he wouldn't be able to digest the faces of the people crying.

When they placed Coco down softly, they walked along the edge of the pews, to a bench at the front that was saved for them by Ella, who sat alone, waiting for them to return, her head bowed as she sobbed into a tissue.

There was a lot of talk about religion and God, and there were hymns, and it all felt extremely un-Coco. There should have been funny stories and rude poems and upbeat songs from the musicals she was obsessed with. They should have all been sat by the side of an infinity pool on the Amalfi coast in their swimsuits sipping coconutty cocktails as hors d'oeuvres circulated around them. That would have been a very Coco event, but this was far too bland, far too muted.

It went by in a blur, until the priest finally called him to the lectern. "And now Coco's boyfriend, Harrison is going to say a few words about her," he said.

Harrison blinked. He found his legs did not want to move.

Conrad squeezed his shoulder. "You can do this. For her," he whispered.

Harrison stood, the paper containing his speech rustling in his shaking hands, and he made his way towards the lectern.

He cleared his throat, and breathed deeply, before speaking. "I was fortunate to love and be loved by Coco for three years," he said, "To know her was to know passion, to know loyalty, and to know true love. She was extraordinary, unlike anyone else I've ever known, and today..." He gulped and took a breath, willing himself to carry on, for her. He couldn't let her down. "Today we say goodbye." His voice broke as he gripped the lectern, and tears dripped onto the words he wrote. There was silence throughout the hall for what might have been seconds, or what might have been several long weeks.

Harrison jumped as he felt an arm around his shoulders. "Do you want me to carry on for you?" Conrad whispered. His face was red, wet from tears, but his jaw was set and his eyes serious, he looked determined. Harrison nodded and sat back down, balancing his elbows on his knees and holding his head in his hands, gripping his hair tightly in frustration and desperation at the situation he was somehow experiencing, that he had to come to terms with Coco not being around anymore.

Conrad cleared his throat as his eyes skimmed the following few sentences, trying to make out the words Harrison wrote in his shamefully untidy handwriting. "But let's not say goodbye in sadness. Coco lived her life with excitement and fun, and we should celebrate that we had the honour of knowing her, rather than mourning her loss.

"Today, myself and my friends will spend the time recalling the many, many days of fun that we had, knowing that Coco will remain with us forever, that we will remember her every day, in everything that we do.

"Coco was taken from us, and it has rocked us all. That is not something we change, and I suppose that nothing will really feel the same, but we should enjoy the fact that we are able to recall these memories, that she had such a profound effect on all of our lives. The empathy, gentleness, and support that she offered every one of us will leave a massive hole in our lives, but without it, many of us wouldn't be who we are today." Conrad spoke well, unfaltering, even with the tears that ran down his face.

"Harrison's right," he said, and a few people looked up in surprise at the deviation from the speech.

"Coco was brilliant. Far more brilliant than any of us, and we want to celebrate her brilliantness today. It's ironic that I can stand up here and speak today, because it is only due to Coco's support that I can do this. A little while ago, I lost my mum, and at that time, Coco would not rest until she made me talk, until she made me acknowledge my emotions, and stopped me from drawing into myself. It is because of the lessons that she taught me that I am stood here as I am right now, and for her, I'm going to pass that lesson on.

"I'm going to make sure that myself and my friends deal with this together, that they know that if they're not coping, they should talk about it. Because we are here today because Coco felt like she couldn't. She didn't follow her own fantastic advice, but we should.

"So that's the thing I'd like to say today. Coco gave us so many gifts, so many lessons. Pass them on."

Everyone in the church broke down at that moment, as *Isn't she lovely* played, and the coffin was lowered.

Afterwards, they headed to the village hall where there were so many people they could hardly move. They only really went in support of Harriet, who was overrun with people crying around her, and who were expressing their deep and genuine condolences. There was a separate memorial in the school for the students who weren't close to her, which, again, Harrison really didn't like the idea of, but he supposed his classmates had a right to say goodbye as well and there was nowhere big enough to hold everyone who wanted to mourn together. Coco's loss took over the school, the town, her thousands of followers. Her pages blew up online in that way that they tend to, hundreds, thousands of people claiming they knew her, that they knew what it was to lose her.

But even though they weren't feeling what he was feeling, or what Harriet and Harvey or Ella were feeling, Coco's loss was no less significant. He decided that he hated the grief circus a little less then, and he felt that the wailing masses were a testament to the powerful girl that was once his.

Harrison and the others found a table where they sat in silence for a couple of moments. Bea sat next to him, and Conrad sat the other side of him, his arm around Ella.

"What do you think she'd be saying right now?" Bea asked.

"She would probably be complaining about the lack of crab cakes at the buffet," Ella said, and they laughed.

"Nah, she wouldn't be saying anything, she'd be snogging Harrison," Conrad added.

"She would be saying how well you read, Con. Thanks for that."

No one was smiling anymore.

"I didn't know if you wanted me to go up or not, but I didn't want you to do it on your own," Conrad said, a worried frown crinkling his forehead.

"I couldn't do it. I wish I could. I have so much that I need to say to her, but I couldn't do it justice."

"Me too," Ella said, catching Harrison's eye for just a moment. It was the first time they had so much as glanced at each other in a couple of weeks. She was probably the only person at who understood what it was to not only feel this grief, but the mingled responsibility, the guilt that ate away at him at every waking moment, that seemed to slither and slide into his dreams at night.

"So say it, say everything you need to. Write a letter," Bea said simply. When they all turned towards her, she shrugged, blushing a little. "It's what Coco would have done about all of this. She would have holed herself up in her room, and wrote a letter, wrote down everything she felt, everything she needed to get out there. I'll write one too."

"And I will," Conrad said. "It's a great idea."

"But then what would we do with them?" Ella asked.

"We could keep them," Conrad began. "But I think I would just reread it over and over and I'd always feel the same way I did when I wrote it. I say we make a little campfire, in the grounds, by our rocks, and we set fire to them. We can always write her another one later on if we feel like we need to."

They all nodded.

"Tonight, then," Bea said.

"No." Harrison said it quietly. "I need longer than that. Tomorrow night?"

They stood to leave, to make their way through the crowd. Harriet found them before they could find her to say goodbye.

"I have something for you, Harrison." She smiled a little and handed him a big black handbag that was filled to the brim with notebooks.

"They're hers. I bought the first one for her for Christmas just before you started going out. There's a lot of stuff in here. The last one is hell, I know. The rest of them, well, as her mum, I didn't want to read all of it, but they're nice. She talks about you, all of you, about the fun you had together. I thought you'd like it. It's like she's here, almost. She didn't have many secrets, not in those days at least, so I don't think she'd mind. You were all so close. I thought you could read them together, today."

They stared at each other, at a loss for what to say.

"Thanks, Harriet." Bea said, when she realised that Harrison was unable to articulate himself.

"Can I talk to you for a moment?" He blurted out, and Harriet nodded. They left together and walked along the cobbled streets. Her high stiletto heels meant that she put her arm through his to keep her balance. She waited patiently, and he could feel his heart racing as he was about to divulge the worst of himself.

"I want to say how sorry I am."

"I can see that, darling."

"I treated her badly. She didn't deserve that. Me and Ella, we…"

"I know," she said quickly, cutting him off. "Harrison, you're only going to get more upset by saying this. I know what you did. And no, it wasn't a good thing to do. But times were hard for the pair of you. You're young, the fact that you

234

stuck with her through all of that is enough for me, even though you didn't know what was going on, you knew she was going through something. You couldn't make her act any differently. She knew you were there, wanting to help her. But she was stuck, and it's not your fault that it all festered and blew up in an ugly way between you and her and Ella. You're so young, sweetheart. I understand what it's like. I don't blame you. I wish it hadn't come to that, and I wish Ella had acted differently too, but you both loved her so much. That one mistake doesn't define you."

Harriet smiled up at him, the same smile as Coco's. "You have so much love to give, more than any teenage boy I've ever known of," she said. "You're a good boy, a bit of an idiot sometimes, but a good person. Don't dwell on it, sweetheart. She wouldn't want that."

He pulled her into a fierce hug. "I loved her so much," he said into her shoulder, and she nodded, tears rolling down her cheeks.

"I know you did. I'm sorry it came to this," she said.

They broke apart, and she reached into her pocket, and pulled out a little white box. "I'm glad we got to do this, I wanted to give this to you, away from the others."

Harrison opened the box to see the 'H' necklace he bought for her.

"She took it off. That night, it was the first time she had even taken it off," he said.

"Which says a lot. You were with her everywhere with this around her neck," Harriet offered a small, fond smile that seemed to warm him from the inside out on the cold November day.

They strolled back up the street towards the town hall together, meeting the others at the entrance.

"Read them, and have fun doing it. You were all good friends to her, and I'm so grateful to you all." Harriet emphasised the last word, her eyes meeting Ella's, who gave a small smile in response.

They went back to the school, and sat on the floor in Conrad's room, reading her notebooks. Together they shared memories, laughing at the pretentious way she wrote things, at the silly things they used to do, groaning at the embarrassing things one of them had done, or at the reminder of difficult tests they had failed, or times that had gotten into trouble. It was a strange night, a rollercoaster of laughter and tears. They wrote their letters, silently, in separate corners of the room, in their best handwriting, on Ella's unnecessarily fancy paper that she had as a gift one birthday from her weird aunt, and they felt as though, somehow, she would know.

Coco was sat beside all of them, rolling her eyes at their spelling errors and bad grammar, grinning at the compliments, and their insistence that she was one of the best things that had happened to them. They could feel her. Every word they wrote breathed life into what was now her memory.

They knew that to say she wasn't with them anymore, was not exactly true. She was. Because, for every conversation they would have, they would hear Coco's response, in her words, in her voice. They would see her vividly, in the expensive clothes she would wear, or in her school uniform. They would smell her coconutty scent. They would feel her hair tickling their face, as it did when she would hug them. Coco might have died, but she was by no means gone.

The next day, they woke up early, and as the sun rose over the hill in the distance, they burned their letters in the fire they created using nearby twigs. It was only small, but big enough for them to do everything they needed. It was big enough for them to watch the paper curl and burn, to watch the ink disappear, and see the smoke rise and get lost in the increasingly pink and brilliant sky.

"This was a good idea, Bea," Conrad said, encouragingly.

"I feel like a bit of weight has been lifted. I feel like she knows now, somehow. Is that weird?" Ella asked, crossing her legs, and poking the fire with a stick.

"No, I feel that, too." They were the first words Harrison

spoke all morning. He was focused, and he was taking this seriously, because he had no other choice than to use today as his day to speak with Coco, and apologise for everything. He needed to have that unsaid conversation with her, or it would forever eat him from within. He knew he could not live with torturing himself for the rest of his life, so he wrote the letter. His room was filled with discarded pieces of paper, because he wrote and rewrote everything he needed to say in the best way he could.

He panicked as he ran out of time. He knew he overused the word 'sorry.' But he really felt that there was nothing more important to say, than sorry, although he knew that he could never adequately convey how sorry he was.

Harrison's was the longest letter: ten pages of tear-stained, badly worded, untidy, clumsy attempts of conveying his feelings. He watched it burn. He watched as he put his in the fire, before all the others, and watched it turn to white ash.

He liked that they made a fire, because that was what he still felt inside, still: a fire that seemed to scorch his insides, his organs, his entire being. He wondered whether, maybe, that feeling had always been there. He knew that he had always harboured a fire, a passion, for Coco. It was there when he had fallen in love with her, and it was there when he had fought with her. It was there when he had felt protective over her, and it had glowed on hot coals even at his most apathetic. It was there when he had laid in bed the day he found out that she was dead, as the force of his loss hit him.

Love is devastating when it's both lost and found. Harrison knew that it would never be more devastating than at this moment.

PART FIVE
GENEVIEVE

Chapter Seventeen

The boys sat at their usual table for dinner as the burning sun set over the beautiful grounds of Lainsbury Hall School. Conrad talked non-stop, over chicken pie and mash, about his most recent spectacular hockey goal. Harrison was half listening, scrolling through his phone.

"I just can't believe it bounced off his head. Bloody beautiful!"

Harrison rolled his eyes. "It was great," he said.

Conrad hesitated a moment before speaking. Harrison fidgeted with his blazer buttons under his gaze, feeling scrutinised.

"I wish you'd played, Fletch,"

"I will, I promise. I just need to get in the swing of it again."

"Just come to training tonight. Do whatever you like. Leave ten minutes in if you want," Conrad said, in an overly hearty, bracing voice.

"Yeah, I'll come by. I'll be rubbish, though. It's been over a month."

"You'll be fine."

The two girls placed their trays on the table. Ella kissed Conrad briefly before turning to her Quorn sausages.

"Is he still on about that goal?" Ella asked, rolling her eyes in mock exasperation.

"Hey, you were cheering like mad! I saw you." Conrad nudged her gently, grinning.

"Probably because the game was over," Bea added, smiling slyly.

When Conrad looked wounded, Ella gave in. "Okay, it was exciting," she said. "But I was there. I don't need it described in great detail any more."

Bea coughed awkwardly, and turned her body towards the wall as Genevieve walked past.

"What's going on there?" Conrad narrowed his eyes.

"Nothing," Bea said instinctively. Conrad and Ella offered her a disbelieving stare. "Alright, I haven't messaged her back."

"Why not?" Harrison asked, making an all too obvious show of staring at Genevieve's table.

"I'm not entirely sure she's everything I thought she was. I think she's a pretty bad person actually… bitter. It was as if I wasn't with her, as if I wasn't allowed to be happy. I don't need that right now." Bea took a deep breath. "And I finally bit the bullet and told India it was over last night."

Ella raised her eyebrows, and Conrad gasped dramatically.

"Probably a good decision," Harrison said, putting an arm around her and supportively stroking her arm. "Are you okay?" he asked, as she pushed him off.

"Yeah, I'm fine. As you said, it was a good decision, right?"

"Absolutely," Ella said quickly.

"Well…" Conrad teased.

"Alright, she was fit, Con. We get it," Bea said, and rolled her eyes. She offered him a reluctant smile. "But that's not a good enough reason to stay with someone."

"Maybe *you* should go out with her if she's so hot," Ella joked, stealing Conrad's chip.

"Never. India? Bleugh, disgusting," he said, and Ella giggled as he kissed her. Harrison and Bea averted their eyes, offering wary glances at each other.

"Was it this annoying when me and Coco did it?"

"Yes. You were ten times as bad," Bea said and laughed, and Harrison joined in.

"I'm sorry." Harrison smiled a smile which shrunk as they all turned to him. "I miss it."

Bea rubbed his back. "You're doing a lot better," she said.

"I'm doing okay."

"Better than not okay at all." Conrad shrugged.

"More than anything, it still feels weird, you know?"

"It will do, for a long time, I think," Ella said, frowning. "It'll be a long time before I stop expecting her to giggle her way over to our table and complain about how she looked into it and it's actually completely against our human rights to make us do PE."

They ate and chatted for a long time, unaware that Gen was listening to their conversation, as she always did. Her sharp hearing, their loud voices and her general paranoia meant that she spent most mealtimes festering in a hot, burning rage and embarrassment, listening to them regularly psych Bea up, cruelly at her expense.

Bea was always okay, of course, although she laughed more than she should, but she was always still completely in love with her. Or, at least until now, apparently.

It was the others Gen hated, like that fucking Conrad, the cocky arsehole who cared for no one other than himself, his hockey stick, and the reams of girls he'd slept with. Gen thought perhaps she hated him the most, scowling behind her fringe and glasses as she stabbed hard at her sausages with her fork, as though the pig itself was doing her a great injustice.

But, she realised, *the others aren't much better; Ella and Harrison, probably never an independent thought between them, although of course they're the 'smartest' in the school. All they're good at is saying what people want them to hear.* They were sometimes the meanest, bitching loudly, so the whole hall could hear them put her down.

And Coco. Although, obviously, not a problem anymore, or at least for the time being. Fuck knows what the investigation would bring to light.

Although Gen did throw the rock that she hit her with down the cliffs with her body.

She was fortunate. All Gen wanted was some ammunition, something to use against her, to really tweet something that would ruin her. She could have stopped as she followed her to Hunter's room. She was sleeping with him, that was obvious. *He was so the type. Pathetic, desperate to fit in with the popular kids, of course they were sleeping together, and of course airy fairy Coco went along with it, wide-eyed and slack mouthed.*

And then it became interesting. From around the corner, she saw Jenkins stop her, she saw Coco break down, crumbling before her.

Coco had started rambling about Harrison and Ella - a piece of juicy gossip that Gen was surprised by. It wasn't like them, or maybe it was, as there was no ounce of loyalty between them, that was evidently why Bea fit in so much.

And then Jenkins took her away. She said that they could go for a walk on the cliffs. Gen wasn't really sure why, but she went, too. She ran through the forest until it started to become more and more sparse, and the sky was revealed before her, inky at that time, along the horizon.

She heard their voices and hid behind a tree. She could see them, as Coco stepped away from Jenkins, her hair wild, and her eyes wide with horror.

"You're unhinged. You're fucking nuts. You're all fucking nuts, you're all fucked up! Stay away from me, I'll…" Coco yelled.

"Of course you just want this problem to go away. It's what you always want, isn't it, for everything just to go your way as it always does?" Jenkins's voice was poisonous and bitter as it was carried through the trees in the wind. Gen couldn't argue with that, it was pretty accurate. Coco slapped her, and Jenkins only smiled. Gen wondered if she should intervene, but it was interesting, and she couldn't honestly say she was wholly on Coco's side. *When you're stupid enough to sleep with a teacher, what do you expect to happen?* Although it was evident that Jenkins was unbalanced. *Shame*, Gen thought. She had always liked her.

And in that moment, Gen thought about how Coco was the girl who had everything, and how she had nothing now. Coco had seen to that. She took Bea in, and took her away from her. All Gen wanted was for Bea to commit to her, but Coco's meddling meant that she was with bloody India. And the minute Gen had seen them together, she knew that was it, she

244

was done for. How could she compete? India was a beauty of supermodel proportions, and she fit well into Bea's new extravagant life, of sunsets on a beach in Miami, of expensive clothes, of cruel inside jokes.

Bea was so different before Coco changed her. She was smart, and she was so unafraid to go against the fray. But now she begged for the spotlight, desperately doing all she could to draw stares from across a crowded room. Since they broke up, her Instagram followers count had risen by thousands. Hell, she was even sponsored by beauty brands and piercing shops.

But when they were together, they had been happy. Gen wondered if it was enough, if she was enough. Bea used the excuse of being unable to come out, but she had done that only months after they broke up. Another thing she suspected Coco of engineering.

They used to have fun, in their little bubble of wine sodden nights together and Disney movies. It was a dream, although apparently not for Bea.

Bea was still in love with her, she was sure of that. But she would never call her again. A heavy, guilty feeling sank down into Gen's stomach. She did perhaps treat her badly, she took away Bea's friends, she took away everything from her, in the hopes that it would bring her back. But the resilience that she admired so much in her, meant she had risen from the ashes and started again. It wasn't something Gen could have predicted.

And it was all Coco's fault.

How could I not hate her? Gen thought. How could she stay neutral when Coco and her friends sauntered around the school as if they owned the place? When they dictated lessons with their stupid questions that lead them on tangents, when they all hated her anyway.

And then Coco started running away from Jenkins, right past where Gen was stood. She didn't know why she did it, but in that split second that she had to think, she grabbed a rock that rolled under her foot. She struck Coco's temple as she ran fast past her. When she fell, Gen hit her again, in the same place, but harder this time. And then Coco wasn't moving, and Gen had a weapon in her hand. She backed away, slowly, into the trees, and watched as Jenkins found Coco and freaked out. She called someone, oddly, a policeman by his uniform, who came by and helped. She gasped into the howling wind, as Coco flew through the air, and hit the rock bed at the bottom of the cliff. Even dead, or maybe unconscious, she fell with a certain grace, her white nightshirt and dressing gown billowing around her. Although she did land with a sickening crack.

They left quickly, as the man told Jenkins off, telling her how stupid she had been. But Jenkins was ranting, about how Coco would have ruined Hunter's life, and her friend was placated.

When they left, Gen stared over the cliff as Coco's body washed away. She threw the rock and got the hell out of there, showering and getting to lessons first that day. She spent so much time thinking about how to appear that she had nothing to do with Coco's disappearance, that st he was sure she looked guilty as sin. But no one knew, no one had any reason to think she was there that night. And now everyone had been arrested. *Three more lives ruined by Coco*, she thought, and her name hadn't come up. Not yet, anyway.

Gen was sorry. Coco didn't have to die. But as the rage filled her that night, when all she could see was a red mist and a bush of messy hair, it was instinctive.

Bea, Ella, Harrison and Conrad walked from the hall, whispering and giggling together.

"I could have sworn she was staring," Bea said.

"I think she was, too," Ella said, grinning. "Treat them mean, keep them keen, right?"

They walked to the common room, through the labyrinth of dimly lit corridors that for so long had held so many secrets, still blissfully unaware of the biggest of all.

Fantastic Books
Great Authors

darkstroke is
an imprint of
Crooked Cat Books

- Gripping Thrillers
- Cosy Mysteries
- Romantic Chick-Lit
- Fascinating Historicals
- Exciting Fantasy
- Young Adult Adventures
- Non-Fiction

Discover us online
www.darkstroke.com

Find us on instagram:
www.instagram.com/darkstrokebooks

Printed in Great Britain
by Amazon